THE LOST SAGA

RENOIR

MEREDIAN

❀ Created with Vellum

It's said that history is written by the survivors -
what if there are none?

CONTENTS

1

THE BEGINNING OF THE END

The passing of time, in chunks that later generations would call weeks, months and years, was seen in the rise and fall of the sun and measured only by the phases of the moon. They had sailed for so long and so far that seasons had become meaningless. The cold of Hofn was a distant memory.

Before them lay another beach. Another group of men burned black by the remorseless sun would be waiting on the shore. Could they at last somehow provide the means of returning home in wealth and comfort? It seemed unlikely. They barely had the wherewithal to clothe themselves, according to what they'd been told. Not that the burden of clothes was a welcome one in this heat.

The ragged sail bore them along in the wake of the small narrow boats of the small brown men they'd encountered at sea, days earlier. A groan came from the gaunt sunburned figure who clung to the tiller, it holding him upright as much as he steered the longship.

This would be their last landfall. In his heart, Sigurd knew that.

.ooo.

ICELAND – SETTING SAIL

I t had been part accident, part the spirit of bold adventure. They were viking. Not the race, the occupation. To go viking – to go to sea seeking new property, goods or land, whether by trade, conquest or pillage. Whichever was most convenient at the time.

As a group, they were Norse – people of the north. At the outset Icelanders, Norwegians, a few Danes and a smattering of others from the fringes of the North Sea.

Sigurd Saemundsson had led a small company of ships south from Hofn in Iceland. There was his own longship: *Serpentfang*, with eighty crew on board, fifteen tons of supplies and bristling with weaponry. With her were the two knarrs, *Red Whale* and *Stormbearer*, tubbier than his proud vessel but eminently practical, each able to take more than forty tons of cargo.

Had he been forced on the question, Sigurd would probably have dismissed the notion of 'bold adventure' from his motives for the journey. He saw himself first and foremost as a trader. Hardly the most successful trader in Iceland, but he did well enough to provide for his wife Thordja and be a respected voice at the Althing when that body gathered to administer the settlements.

Sigurd was technically a chieftain, although the family group over which he presided was neither large nor politically influential. Marrying Thordja Olafsdottir ought to have substantially improved his holdings, but his father-in-law proved all too worthy of his nickname of Olaf the Sly.

Olaf's nefarious dealings were revealed at an assembly of the Althing in Thingvellir soon after Sigurd's marriage. The older man was banished and his property distributed amongst those he'd been found to have cheated and robbed. There was sympathy for Sigurd of course. The new matrimonial bond meant he could hardly vote down his new bride's father, but neither could he ignore the clear evidence of Olaf's misdeeds.

Thus his marriage had, from early days, a shadow over it. But neither Sigurd nor Thordja were particularly romantic in any case, and their relationship soon settled into a business partnership, with occasional benefits on particularly cold nights.

It had proved an effective partnership though. Thordja was an excellent manager. She had a natural talent for organisation (which her father would have done well to recognise and make use of himself) and kept a firm, fair discipline on both herself and their workers. Some Icelandic wives in her position gained reputations as harridans or bullies, but Thordja gained only respect.

Her husband's forte as a businessman was a keen eye for seeing potential value. He could spot damaged goods that might readily be repaired and resold, or a product that while, not yet fashionable, might soon be. He was also a shrewd bargainer, and seldom was the worst off in a trade deal.

Hofn was among the less salubrious points on the sea roads criss-crossing the North Sea. The local fish were plentiful and of good quality, with the lobster being especially prized. But while the harbour itself was sound, the entrance to it was often challenging. Shoals and sandbars shifted with the currents and captains arriving and leaving had to sail warily at all times.

In years to come the harbour would silt up badly and become treacherously shallow. After a series of severe winters when the waters froze over, the settlement would almost fail completely. It was only when the practice of dredging became established that the hardy souls who'd hung on saw a revived town grow there.

During Sigurd's days though, those difficult conditions also meant that the sailors of Hofn were among the best that Iceland produced. Certainly they were among the most watchful and naturally cautious!

It was Sigurd's interest in trade goods out of the ordinary that was ostensibly the primary reason for his latest voyage. Regular trips around the North Sea bearing salted or fresh fish, lobster, wool, a little gold and the ivory of the red land whales (as the walrus was then known) were modestly lucrative, but it was more exotic items that drew Sigurd's attention.

Jewellery and carvings of strange attractive form. Timbers of unusual colour and hardness. Furs and fabrics of surprising texture and colour. All of these were to be found in the market places of Iceland, Greenland, Shetland, and Norway's own Kaupang and even the fledgling trading centre of Bergen. It was the source of these items that fascinated Sigurd.

He knew other Norsemen were trading to the south – east and west. He knew, by name at least, of Baghdad and Constantinople. There were strange and marvellous things that made their way to those metropolitan centres and thence onto the longboats. If merchants there were prepared to trade for the products of the north like sea ivory and white furs, he would willingly accommodate them.

A voyage south beckoned, along the western coast of the continent later called Europe, and beyond to the mysterious fabled lands beyond with their strange cultures and stranger beasts. Sigurd may find himself a little ahead of the wave of fashion in trade goods that he really hoped to lead, but if there wasn't a fortune to be made, there was certainly a real prospect of profit.

There was another impetus to Sigurd's desire for travel, although not one he admitted openly, or perhaps even to himself.

Like many in Iceland at that time, Thordja (despite her being named for one of the mightiest of old deities) had recently adopted the New Religion. It seemed strange to him to call it that – there were monks of that faith on the island before the Norsemen themselves had arrived. But the rise in power of the bishops who sat beside, or even on thrones around the region had seen adherence to the Church of the One True God creep closer to becoming compulsory.

The boatmaster was not one of the stubborn ones who rigidly held to the traditional gods and their trappings. Indeed, he had no problem with the concept of a single Supreme Being as creator of all things – that seemed quite sensible and far more efficient than a messy, complex pantheon of squabbling gods.

Some of the individual representatives of the New Religion seemed to be good men. He'd encountered one Liljeblad, a man from Oulo in the far east, in a country later to be called Finland. Liljeblad lived by a rigid set of rules to honour his One God, but while he preached those rules, and exhorted others to follow them, he spoke more of a God of grace than a God of vengeance – a distinction that Sigurd considered important. A man like Liljeblad was a good advertisement for his God, the trader thought.

Sigurd was, however, deeply distrustful of the organisation called The Church. He suspected that it was a means by which ambitious men were grasping power and influence themselves in the name of divine authority. Much of what the bishops sought and commanded seemed at sharp variance with what he understood of the teachings of this Christ fellow a thousand years earlier.

Thordja did not share her husband's cynicism and, while they rarely went so far as to argue about it, the trader could see that the gulf between them was only widening. As yet, her contributions to the Church did not go far beyond those now required by law, but he could foresee a future where his wife would be more than eager to increase her generosity.

A successful trade journey would provide wealth to accommodate her wishes without sacrificing his own modest desires for earthly comfort, as well as taking him away from the developing tension.

Sigurd's father, Saemund Ragnarson had spent much of his life ploughing the waters between Greenland and Norway before settling in Iceland and establishing the business that his only son now owned. The inheritance had come sooner than anticipated, as it turned out that 'settling down' was so alien to the old sailor's nature that he'd died within a year.

One of the most important things that Sigurd Saemundsson had learned at his father's side, and in the years since, was how vital it was to have a crew who got on. Especially for the duration of the long voyage in prospect, it was essential that the men and women on each of the boats were able to work harmoniously.

An individual's strength and skill were important, but the captain knew that there were plenty of strong and skilful people to choose from, even in a modestly sized community such as Hofn. It was far more important to him to identify those who could routinely take orders, work hard and co-operate with each other.

Being fierce in battle was useful, but fighting occupied only a small proportion of their time. As little as possible was Sigurd's preference. He preferred to be a hard but fair bargainer, rather than a raider like some of his competitors. It made plain business sense to allow more goods to be grown or produced for future commerce from a position of respect, than to devastate a community for a once-only gain.

This clear-eyed view was shared by Hrolf Maddadarson (more usually called Hrolf the Dark for his unusually black bushy hair), who served as Sigurd's right hand man.

He was a less adept negotiator than his employer but he was shrewd and alert. Any merchant who tried to cheat Sigurd Saemundsson was likely to come to grief under Hrolf's watchful eye. Short measures and the disguising of inferior goods were occupational hazards for many Norse traders, but rare occurrences for the *Serpentfang* enterprise. Hrolf the Dark carried a shield with a hollow boss, in which he kept a tough leather purse. The purse contained a small set of very precise lead weights that he used for measuring the amounts of spices and the like. Cunningly wrought pieces seemingly adorning his leather belt as decoration actually served the same purpose for measuring larger goods – Hrolf knew the weight of each one and would trust no other man's scales.

Command of the cargo-bearing knarrs fell to Sigurd's cousin Corri and old Sverrir Bent-Knee. Both men were highly capable, and absolutely loyal to the captain of *Serpentfang*.

Sverrir had sustained the injury that gave him his name while sailing alongside Saemund Ragnarson. He'd watched his former captain's rapid demise in Iceland and had vowed not to meet the same fate. Any opportunity to sail was seized enthusiastically.

"I'll sail 'til I die, and damn the man as says I can't!" he'd declare angrily at any suggestion he might do otherwise.

Sigurd was happy to accommodate this stubbornness. Sverrir was wiry but still strong. More importantly he was an intuitive sailor. Reading the stars and the winds was second nature to most experienced Norse seamen, but Bent-Knee could read currents and movement in the water better than anyone Saemundsson had met.

On *Stormbearer* Corri was a less accomplished sailor – no disgrace as few were the old fellow's equals – but a good leader of his crew. Creative, he might have been a good craftsman had it not been for what he self-deprecatingly described as "two hands full of thumbs". Instead he turned his imagination to storytelling.

When his glib tongue was not winning the best efforts of his knarr's crew, or winning over a suspicious trader on his cousin's behalf, he was spinning tales of fantastic locales or far-off times. Sigurd delighted in those tales. They'd made Corri his favourite kinsman, although that would have counted for nothing as a commander had the cousin not proved himself a good navigator and reliable tactician.

Although he never said as much openly, Sigurd nursed the hope that the expedition he planned might take them to locales that would prove grist to his cousin's creative mill. A saga might be too much to hope for, but perhaps a tale, or tales told over roaring fires and foaming ales, even at the great Althing of Thingvellir.

When Sigurd had assembled his regular crew to announce his plans for the voyage there was only a handful that showed any reluctance. Saemundsson was content to let them seek service elsewhere. Some went to work for Thordja, believing they might return to

Serpentfang after the long journey, happy to undertake the more familiar sailings. Others joined other boats with more settled, dependable itineraries.

Serpentfang's captain knew they could all be replaced. He didn't want to sail with anyone who didn't want to be there. Nor with hotheads, braggarts, habitual drunks, or idlers. Such personality traits might show up in anyone from time to time – Sigurd knew he was sometimes overly fond of good ale – but when they were the dominant part of a personality it was a problem for the discipline of the whole crew.

Each boat had one person responsible for enforcing their captain's authority when required. Corri had the hulking Odd Arisson, who wasn't always as gentle as he seemed. On *Red Whale* discipline fell to Bjorn Breakneck, in whom Sverrir fancied he saw himself as a younger man.

Aboard his own boat Sigurd relied on the unlikely figure of Hervor Elsdottir. At first glance she seemed a slight woman, more distinctive for her habit of leaving her long wavy locks unfashionably untied than any imposing physical presence. Perhaps it was having been named for a legendary Valkyrie, but Hervor was tougher than many men and women in the crew who were much larger than her.

She'd originally come on board as a walrus hunter. She didn't need shoulders like an oxen yoke when she could lodge a spear with brutal accuracy in a tender spot of her quarry. Hervor's singular talent seemed to be to find a weak point and target it.

Usually pleasant in demeanour, occasionally passionate and other times aggressive, she'd quickly become respected among the crew, if not universally popular. Sigurd appreciated the hunter's obvious efforts to mostly contain the sharper side of her nature while recognising that she did so for his benefit as captain. The woman seemingly didn't really care about being liked, making her an ideal choice as his 'enforcer'. She wasn't averse to landing a sharp blow with hand or knee to emphasise a point, but the short spear and shorter sharp knife both worn at her waist were rightly feared.

Winter had barely lifted her veil from Hofn when Sigurd was

nigh finished preparing for his expedition. Over the cold months all three boats and all their fittings had been thoroughly checked, repaired and refurbished. Supplies had been gathered and were in the final stages of being loaded. There were sufficient provisions to see them to at least the third of the anticipated landfalls, and even if they weren't able to restock as planned there were adequate reserves of dried and salted foodstuffs.

The choice and assembly of trading goods required greater exercise of the captain's mind. The majority of his mercantile experience was local – he knew what the customers around the North Sea wanted. But what about those further afield?

Sigurd spent time talking to those who'd sailed far south. Gudmund Thorbaldson claimed to have been as far as a land peopled only by black-skinned men, but Gudmund was known as a stranger to the truth. It was conceivable though that he'd traded with others who had made such a trip. Such traders were really Saemundsson's best source of information. What had those merchants from afar been seeking? What had caught their acquisitive eyes? What was known of their homelands, and the goods that could be useful or desirable there?

Any and all information that he could gather went into compiling an inventory. Some of the goods characteristic of Iceland seemed obvious, but would furs, whatever their colour, be valued in the warmer climates he knew lay to the south? He'd seen a solitary piece of ivory from somewhere called Ethiopia that was far larger and probably finer than the sea ivory that was his regular stock.

Best to leave much of what he held of such things with Thordja. She would maintain a profitable local trade until his return, especially if she could resist the urge to endow the Church with too much of the money earned.

The wily trader sought goods that had been acquired from lands to the east. Things like spices, fabrics, gems and jewellery that, he reasoned, would be rarities and thus valuable in the markets along the western coast.

So the copious spaces below the decks of *Red Whale* and *Storm-*

bearer were well stocked with a diverse range of goods and chattels. The scents of the spices and woods were potent accompaniments to the feast for the eyes provided by the colourful bolts of fabric. A modest quantity of sea ivory was packed. Securely locked boxes stacked in the centre of the ships' holds hid the glitter of jewellery and ornaments. Furs and walrus hides buffered the boxes. Provisions nestled beside the stock.

Unlike some of his fellow traders who went viking, Sigurd chose to split both goods and supplies between all of his vessels including his own. Thus *Serpentfang*, although more predominantly equipped with food and drink, held her own stock of valuable trade goods.

Thordja had come down to the harbour with a small retinue to see off her husband's expedition. She and Sigurd shared a fond, if not especially passionate embrace before the captain stepped away, ready to board his ship. Just before he turned a short young man detached himself from Thordja's group and approached the trader. This was Erp, the priest who had inveigled his way into her favour.

"I trust that your travels shall be blessed by the King of the House of the Wind, good captain, and that upon your return you shall show proper regard for His generosity by giving richly to the Church," said Erp.

Sigurd stopped. He looked at the young man appraisingly. Soft hands, soft features and already showing signs of running to fat, the priest appeared to have been living comfortably. Perhaps the Saemundsson estate was already providing more generously than he had realised during his regular absences, the chieftain wondered. He folded his arms and kept his expression carefully neutral.

"Whatever wealth is earned by my efforts and those of my crew will come to my estate – my family and the families of those who sail with me. This is as it should be. Should any of them choose to share their fortune with you - excuse me, your Church, then that is their right. For myself, I have no wish to add my own name to the growing list of benefactors, especially when your Church seems more concerned with finance than faith. My beliefs are my own business, as indeed is my business."

As the trader turned and walked away Erp's face coloured. His mouth worked soundlessly for a moment while he assembled the words for his outrage.

Just as the captain set his foot aboard *Serpentfang* the vitriol burst from the priest. "Pig! You defy He who fashioned the earth, the sky and the faithful people! By my voice, you shall *not* receive the blessing of the sole King of the Sun. This land, this Church, is His house. I abhor your attitude. Do not think to return - you are henceforth not welcome here!"

Thordja paled. She had never seen this side of the young man, and she wasn't impressed.

She strode forward and in a clear voice called. "Erp! I have come to much admire this Christ whose teachings you have claimed to espouse. This outburst, this curse upon my husband, does not sit well with those teachings!"

The priest dropped his head. He could not afford to lose the favour of the patroness he'd been so carefully grooming.

"I apologise for my intemperate language, gentle lady. When I feel the true faith is challenged I fear my blood rises..."

From his deck, Sigurd laughed. "You are entitled to your faith, boy, as I am to mine. My issue is with your Church which, not content with the treasury of the throne, seeks to obtain as much as it can of the wealth of the rest of us!"

His wife raised an admonishing hand. "You would do well to curb your tongue too, husband. Concentrate on your objectives and your departure. I shall deal with this young man."

Saemundsson grinned. He knew by that tone of voice that Erp's welcome at their estate was gone. Some new mouthpiece of the Church may come along, but for the immediate future at least, he was confident that the worth of his holding was secure.

From the corner of his eye the captain noticed a look of concern on the face of his brawny steersman Fafhrd. The burly man took one large hand from the tiller and with his thumb, pressed into his palm the pendant he wore around his neck.

The talisman was a skilfully carved representation of Yggdrasil, the world tree. Fafhrd was one who still held to the old beliefs. He was not an evangelical believer, but neither had he felt cause to reject the religion he'd been raised under. Much as he loved roistering and brawling, in his quieter moments the farmer-turned-tillerman was a deep thinker. The notion of sailing under any sort of curse, even one uttered by an officer of a church he held no regard for, made him uneasy.

Sigurd felt no such qualms. With a last wave to shore he gave the call for his little fleet to cast off and set sail. His hopes were high. An unknown future beckoned but he held his ships and his crews in much higher regard than the words of an angry priest.

.ooo.

SHETLAND – THE WELL TRAVELLED MAN

From a purely commercial perspective, there was little to commend stopping in Shetland. Saemundsson's ships were already well provisioned and well stocked with trade goods. There was little different to be obtained from the trading town of Framgord that the captain had visited many times in the past. The soapstone bowls, carved straight from the islands' bare rock, were far more durable than the pottery favoured elsewhere, but they were hardly decorative and the market for them was limited.

But those past visits held the key to Sigurd's real reason for coming to Framgord, despite having to sail against the prevailing winds – a task that added days to a journey that in opposite circumstances would have seen no more than ten sunsets. One or two new recruits may have scratched their heads in puzzlement. Others muttered at the extra effort on the oars, earning sharp rebukes or more from Odd Arisson or Hervor Elsdottir.

Like the rest of Sigurd's regular crew, Hervor and Odd were experienced enough to know that their captain did nothing on a whim. They may not completely understand his reasoning, and may quietly ask him questions in private, but they followed and enforced his orders.

In this instance, that reasoning was to make contact with one particular veteran merchant.

Before settling in the northern reaches of the Shetlands, Jon Sveinbjornsson had commanded his own longboat on voyages along coastlines far to the south and east. He'd earned the sobriquet Jon the Far-strider.

Most importantly to Sigurd Saemundsson, old Jon had built up a wealth of knowledge from his travels, and especially from the men and women he'd dealt with on those travels. The Far-strider was famously garrulous ("Could talk the hilt off a sword," was one thing said of him) and blessed with a prodigious memory.

He was also neither foolishly gullible nor blinkered by excessive cynicism. Over the years Jon had been told many tales that seemed too wild to be believed. When he couldn't support them with the evidence of his own experience he would ask apparently unrelated questions of the taleteller (often about subjects he quietly *did* know). Thus he'd make an assessment of the character of the man or woman he conversed with. That would be the basis on which he'd accept or reject what he'd been told.

The Icelandic captain found the man he sought in the longhouse that sat on the slope overlooking the bay. The tables were quite full of men and women drinking and talking, so it took some time, and several ales, before Sigurd could engage Jon in anything like a private conversation.

It wasn't that he was being secretive about his voyage, but it was the thoughts of Jon the Far-strider he sought, not any of the other ale-fuelled would-be experts who frequented Framgord.

Old Jon nodded thoughtfully while Saemundsson explained the types of wares he had in mind to trade for. Occasionally he'd question why a particular item had caught the younger man's attention, and offer his thoughts on whether it was really a sound commercial judgement. He listened with a patience that would have surprised some who knew his reputation as a talker.

When Sigurd eventually had detailed his plans and ambitions as thoroughly as he could, the veteran trader laid a hand on his companion's shoulder.

"Walk with me," he said, and led the way out of the longhouse.

The pair walked in silence along the green slope for some time. Both walked with the rolling gait that signified lives spent shipboard. Sigurd, though puzzled, held his peace while the older man was evidently deep in thought.

At last Jon spoke, without breaking stride. "You do well to set your sights south. There's much to be found there that will lift the spirits far beyond the daily bleakness of your icebound land."

"Not always icebound," corrected Sigurd with a smile. "The place is green and fertile for a good part of the year. Well, some of it! I think you've yet to cast off the cape of this past winter."

"I fear you're right. Each year the cold grips my bones tighter, and takes longer to release its hold. Don't grow old, Sigurd. Or if you must, do it somewhere warm. And I mean truly warm. I set down here thinking it far milder than my old home in Tromso. So it is, but not enough for my battered body, it seems."

He stretched and arched his back, an audible crack lending support to his complaints. Then he continued, "Yes, to the south. If you've the courage and the crew there's a fortune to be made that way."

"I've got both in full measure, Jon. They're good sailors, loyal and tough."

That won an approving nod. "Well said. That's what you'll need. Much of the coastline offers smooth sailing, but there are parts where the weather is wild. And on shore the women wilder. The trading can be fierce, too. Keep one hand on your purse and the other on your axe."

"I'm happier with my sword," replied the smiling Sigurd. "And happier still if I can get what I want without needing either."

Jon Far-strider stopped, and turned Saemundsson at the shoulder to look at him squarely. "I know that," he said. "I remember you well as a hard dealer, but always a fair one. That will go well with you, wherever you find yourself. Do you know of al-Andalus?"

"By reputation, at least, yes. A little."

"A huge peninsula, the whole of which is greater in size than Iceland. It's ruled by dark-skinned men whose own rulers are of a religion they call Islam," Jon explained.

"The rulers you say? Not necessarily their subjects? That sounds... familiar," said the Icelander wryly.

"Hmm. Perhaps, but don't take too light a tone talking to a believer there. They're for the most part a tolerant lot – the country has many Christians and Jews as well as Muslims who all seem to accept each others' presence, but there are some hard heads too. Those who think that their way should be the only way."

"Oh yes, I know the type," Saemundsson replied.

Far-strider continued. "It's a long journey. The direct passage from Iceland to Norway is a little shorter than the way from west coast of Ireland to the south of al-Andalus."

"The west of Ireland? I'd not particularly thought to stop there..."

The shrewd old merchant gave a knowing smile. "Cahercommaun can provide you with two commodities that will serve you well in the markets you seek to the south. Wool as fine as any I've ever seen, and labour."

"Slaves aren't a cargo I've done much business in," said Sigurd, his voice carefully neutral.

"Then don't use the term. The elite of al-Andalus value white men and women as workers, and the men as fighters and guards. I was told they're treated well, fed, housed and sometimes even paid. Believe me, my young friend, such a life is a great improvement for many on that blighted shore. You'll see."

"I'll consider it. You do make a fair point about the comparative harshness of different types of life." The trader was considering some of the impoverished smallholders he'd met in Norway, and even some of the fisher folk around his home port of Hofn in a bad season. "Tell me more of this al-Andalus."

"Near the south-eastern tip of the peninsula, at the mouth of a river, is a port called Zawaia. It's not big, but important. Zawaia holds privileged access to Silves, the capital of al-Gharb. That's a major province of the peninsula – the name just means 'the West'. A community of Jewish merchants conducts most of the trade. There is a small enclave of Norse and Danish merchants who've settled there. I think it's the most southerly recognisable trading post we have – certainly it was in my time. Individual sailors will have gone further of course. I considered it."

"You don't recommend it?" Sigurd asked.

"Oh, I wouldn't necessarily say that. If you're well prepared, and you find the climate to your liking – it's far far hotter than anything you've ever experienced – and you can assemble a trustworthy crew who are similarly inclined... That was my problem, together with a boat that was nearing the end of her days. I heard plenty of stories about rough conditions off the great continent that lies south of Zawaia. Getting home intact was my main concern."

Saemundsson stroked his curling moustache, an unconscious habit when he was deep in thought.

As the two men resumed walking, Sigurd said, "This continent to the south is the origin of many of the exotic items I seek. I've heard of a land called Ethiopia, and what is reputed to be the world's greatest marketplace in Baghdad."

Jon's eyes gazed wistfully out over the water. "Ah, Baghdad. A legend among merchants indeed. I've seen some of its wares and they're truly spectacular. A smattering of them have made their way to places I've visited, including Zawaia. It lies far to the east of al-Andalus I gather."

"On the east of this great continent?"

"Perhaps. Presumably. I know nobody who's been there, in my time or in story."

If Jon Far-strider had been looking at his companion's face at that moment he would have seen the younger man's eyes involuntarily light up. To be the first man to go viking to Baghdad, now *there* was a story for Corri to tell.

Plus the wealth to be garnered there, of course. That would set up his estate for life. And the lives of generations to come. Not that he and Thordja had sons or daughters yet. But with the comfort of great wealth, well, a family would surely follow.

"You're quiet, Sigurd Saemundsson. Does the idea appeal, or have I deterred you already?"

Sigurd laughed and answered, "Deterred? Not at all, my friend. You've added steel to my resolve. I've already warned my crew of what perils may lie ahead, and shed those who were unwilling to boldly go. If others' spirits weaken, well, I'll find replacements as I travel."

"Well said, my friend! I'll give you the names of men I met in Zawaia who I believe can be trusted. No women traders there, not that I ever encountered – with one or two notable exceptions, the Muslims hold a less generous view of female prowess than we do."

"Again I see a parallel with an ominous future for our people. These bishops who sit beside our thrones seem to have a similar attitude. Still, I'm sure there are plenty of women like Hervor in my crew who'll deal bluntly with any Church man who tries to tell her her place!" His voice softened as he turned to Jon. "You spoke of wanting a warmer home. There is a place on *Serpentfang* for you, if you would join me."

The old trader put a hand on his arm but didn't meet his eyes. "That's a generous offer, my friend, and one I appreciate. But I'd add no value to your crew. My strength deserts me, my eyes dim, and all too often now I wake to find my wits addled."

"I think your mind is still quite strong, Jon Far-strider, and you've knowledge and experience I'd value."

There was a shake of the grizzled head, and a reply in a softer voice. "The truth is, I'm dying, Sigurd. I feel it inside. When I cough, and the back of my hand is spattered with my blood. It would call down the worst of luck on a boat to die aboard, not in battle. I wouldn't risk that curse on you."

Erp's blandishments hadn't bothered Sigurd, but this was an ancient tradition he knew and understood. Furthermore he knew that many among his crew would hold a similar view and hold it strongly. He had to respect Jon's argument.

"I'm sorry," was the best he could find to say.

"Ah, don't be. Proud to have been asked, but I'm content to close my eyes for the final time looking out over this view."

For some moments the two stood gazing out over the sea stretching westwards. A few boats were visible, beating their way to and from Norway.

"I know someone who might be of service to you in my stead," Jon said suddenly.

Sigurd regarded him, curiosity vying with anticipation.

"Sailed with me for my last few voyages, including that final trip to Zawaia. Willing enough but less use in a fight than I'd have liked, except perhaps for causing them. Better now, I believe. However an excellent mind with a real talent for languages – reading, writing and speaking," Jon enthused.

"Sounds promising, except for the bit about causing fights," was the dubious reply.

The old man shrugged. "Not her fault that she was especially beautiful in her youth. I didn't see her ever set out to incite trouble. She's quite a bit older now of course. I'm sure that'll diminish her appeal for the hot-blooded young bucks that were usually the real source of problems."

"Well... they're not the sorts I look to have in my crew anyway. You don't need youth to be strong – I prefer quiet, self-disciplined men when I can find them. And women."

"Then this one's just what you want. A good Icelandic lass too, come to think of it. Come – she's usually to be found in the chapel poring over some text or other."

The walk from the longhouse to the chapel wasn't a long one. The two traders spent it in amiable, if animated, conversation about the strangest things they'd ever seen offered in a market. Jon's long experience and wider travels gave him an obviously greater catalogue from which to draw. But Sigurd too had a perceptive eye and a good memory.

"Who would think that any self-respecting Norwegian would buy the shrivelled head of some poor black fellow they'd never met?"

chuckled Saemundsson. "And yet there they were, hanging like a bunch of fruit from a pole in the market at Kaupang."

"Never over-estimate the decency of seemingly ordinary people," said Jon, abruptly serious. "I've seen respectable Reykjavik matrons come to blows over haggling for a piece of rope used to hang a man. I knew of a quiet and sombre Danish farmer who gutted his neighbour because he thought the man's entrails could be used to grow a better crop. People can be less than you'd hope."

"And more. Yes?"

"Yes, trust the gods!" the old man said as they reached the door of the chapel.

He led the way to a chamber at the rear of the stone building. Sigurd's first impression was of a mass of wavy brown hair bent low over a small piece of parchment, lit by the low sun streaming through the window slit.

"Sigurd Saemundsson, meet Katrine av Ord. Katrine, my old ship-mate, Sigurd was among the best of my competition in the markets of the north. A good man, I'd vouch, and he has a proposal for you."

The woman stood and brushed the hair from her face. Eyes the colour of midsummer sky looked across the small room at the two traders. There was no smile, but an expression of curiosity.

"What are you working on?" asked the captain from Hofn.

Not the question she expected.

"This manuscript – it's only a fragment really – it's in an old version of Aramaic. I think it may be a piece of a Gospel written by a woman named Mary Magdalene. I'm sorry, do you know much of Christian scripture?"

Saemundsson smiled. "Less than my wife's priest would like, but more than he realises. You read this Aramaic?"

"I read Arabic. There are similarities." She waved a hand toward the table where she'd been working. "This text is over four hundred years old. I found it in the pages of a book Jon got hold of in our travels."

"A stroke of luck for you that it found its way there," said Sigurd, carefully not looking sideways at the Far-strider. "I wonder what other marvels are out there in the markets of the world?" He paused. "Do you want to find out?"

The scribe took another few paces forward. The captain studied her. As Jon had said, she was no longer young, any more than he was. Still striking, though. He was surprised she'd been described as underwhelming in a fight – her shoulders were broad and her arms still quite well muscled. Backlit by the sun through the window, her threadbare skirt revealed long, toned legs. There were lines on her face, the results of sun exposure and a brow creased for long hours over pages and scrolls of writing. It was her eyes that were remarkable. Even in a land full of blue eyes, Katrine's were instantly memorable for their shade and their brightness.

For her part, Katrine saw a man of a little more than average height and a build that was solid rather than muscular. His shoulders weren't much broader than her own, but his chest was deep. Long straight hair was left untied, too brown to be red, too red to be brown. The red was more obvious in the generous moustache, and would presumably show in the beard that was presently no more than a shadow. A man who shaved when ashore but not at sea, it seemed. His grey eyes were alert and suggested inquisitiveness. Interested, and interesting.

Each held out a hand, and grasped the other's wrist.

"Tell me more," the woman said.

Jon Far-strider smiled, perhaps a little wistfully.

.ooo.

4

IRELAND – A LOOMING DESOLATION

The short sojourn in the west of Ireland was in many ways unsatisfying. The trade was poor. The place called 'Burren' was said to have once been fertile farmland, but that must have been a long time ago. Or else their farming methods were all wrong.

The soil was thin. Pastures and crops were failing. The sheep that tugged at the stubble were the only creatures that looked to eat regularly, and even they were leaner than a good shepherd would like. Already, rocks were showing through the fields like bones through the fraying skin of a carcass.

Pall Jansson, who had come from a farm in the old country before arriving in Iceland, had cast his experienced eye over the land.

"In a few years there'll be nothing here but rock," he announced gloomily. But then, Pall was gloomy about most things. He'd lost his share of the family holding after a blazing row with his brother's wife.

Still, Sigurd mused, it was hard to disagree as he looked around the bleak landscape. Even the locals seemed dispirited with it.

Cahercommaun was as Jon Far-strider had described it. The wool was certainly of excellent quality. Perversely that was the problem. The success of the wool industry, the health of the sheep, had taken priority over the welfare of the people and the condition of the land.

Some animals graze by nibbling the tops of whatever foliage they find – stems, leaves, the blades of grasses. Sheep are more destructive, grasping plants in their teeth, pulling and devouring whatever they tear up, roots and dirt included. Their dung returns some of that to the earth, but there is an inexorable slow loss in the equation.

Across the generations, as the pastures had deteriorated, trees had been stripped to allow more room for grass. The shallow roots of that grass were far less able to bind the earth against the wind and rain that blew in from the ocean than those of the trees. Gradually the topsoil was slipping into the sea and washing away.

Finally, as it became harder to adequately feed the sheep, the graziers who'd made the most money from the fleeces had bought out their poorer neighbours. People were driven off their land, some more willingly than others. Their homes, or hovels, were cleared to allow yet more room for grass to grow and sheep to feed.

Those displaced had limited options. Many took their scant belongings and headed east towards Limerick and Dublin, hoping to find work or a home somewhere along the way. A few stayed around the bay at Cahercommaun, eking whatever living they could from the sea, or those who sailed upon it.

It was amongst that sad and desperate population that Sigurd found the men and women that Jon had described. Those whose lot in life was so wretched that they'd accept any form of servitude if it meant regular food. A bed, however rough, would be a bonus. A roof over that bed, a blessing.

The trader found himself at a table in the chief's hall conducting interviews to determine who might be considered to be of enough potential value to feed on the journey south to a market where their labour, or more honestly their bodies, could be bartered. It felt slightly surreal to a man who prized his own dignity as highly as Sigurd did.

Hrolf the Dark, Corri and Sverrir Bent-Knee were also at the table. Sigurd and Corri did most of the talking, but all four looked and listened critically as a succession of men and women presented themselves to be taken on the voyage.

Did they seem strong and healthy? None were in good condition, of course, but they looked for sturdy frames (good) and any indications of disease (bad). What was their demeanour? Surly or argumentative – only a few but immediate grounds for rejection. Completely abject wasn't good either. A broken spirit may or may not deter a buyer, but made poor company in the close environment of a ship at sea.

Hrolf sat immediately alongside his captain, scratching notes in charcoal on the back of a rough square of cowhide as each ragged local attempted to sell him- or herself into slavery.

At the doorway, Odd and Hervor managed the passage in and out of the substantial queue. It hadn't been a queue until Hervor had hectored the rabble into a semblance of order. In doing so she'd been unexpectedly assisted by a large woman who barked the walrus hunter's orders into the local dialect for those who evidently didn't understand the Norse tongue. When necessary, she'd smack a head to hasten compliance, which Elsdottir approved of.

Having provided this assistance, the woman assumed a place in the latter part of the queue, continuing to organise late arrivals who duly lined up behind her. Hervor invited her to move to the front of the line but was answered by a shake of the head.

"They were here before me," was the simple explanation.

Hervor shrugged and didn't argue, but when it was time for the woman to be ushered in she caught Sigurd's eye and gave a clear gesture of approval. Behind the woman's back of course – it wouldn't do to make her favour obvious.

Carefully not reacting to the signal, the captain beckoned the large woman to approach.

She was large in both height and physique. A little taller than Sigurd, she'd outweigh him by a good margin. There was nothing soft about her though. Buxom, yes, but the weight was mostly a matter of muscle on a big-boned frame. Her clothes indicated poverty, but her build indicated that wasn't from a lack of hard work.

"Cailin Ruiteach," the woman replied, when asked her name. "Since my Da and I were thrown off our little piece of dirt, such as it was, I've made my way helping out with such boats as come into harbour here. Loading and unloading, writing up inventories for those as need them. Now Da has passed on, I'd like to get myself onto one of the boats and get away from here. As far away as I can," she said, her otherwise carefully controlled voice slipping into a betrayal of some bitterness.

"Writing inventories, you say?" said Hrolf the Dark, curious. "A good way to numb the hand and the brain, I find."

Cailin shrugged. "I've never minded. I kept Da's things in order when we had workings of our own, ever since I was a girl. No trial if you work to a regular system. I like grids. See those notes you're making..." She pointed to the dark haired man's cowhide. "Lay them out neatly, in rows and columns. Much easier to find and compare things when you need to."

"I can usually find what I've written," said Hrolf, more intrigued than defensive.

His captain chuckled. "But I can't always, old friend. Tell me, Cailin, have you been to sea before?"

"A small boat up and down the shore hereabouts, sir. A couple of short trips out on a fishing boat." Her voice suggested some discomfort.

Sverrir caught the tone. "Stomach not so good on the water, eh?" he suggested.

"Oh, my stomach's fine. The motion of the waves doesn't worry me, even when the sea's been rough. It's... er... well, it's my eyes. I can see all of you clearly. I can see the length of a boat, or the dock, well enough. Beyond that things get, well, blurry."

The embarrassment in her voice made it clear the big woman thought she'd just dealt a blow to her chances of departing Cahercommaun.

"Glad you're honest," said Sigurd. "We know you won't make a navigator, at least."

The lightness of his tone caught Cailin off guard. She looked at him in surprise, unsure of what to say.

The trader continued. "You'd be surprised at how many sailors can't make out a horizon on a clear day. A crew works as a team. Each person has strengths and weaknesses, and it's up to a captain to put the right job in the right hands. We've yet to discuss most of your compatriots, but in your case I'm happy to follow my instinct. If al-Andalus or other ports prove to be more to your taste so be it, but you're invited to join my *Serpentfang*, Cailin Ruiteach."

His pronunciation mangled her Gaelic name, but Cailin didn't care. Although she fought down the urge to pick the man up and hug him, her broad smile was ample evidence of her delighted acceptance of the invitation.

Stroking his moustache, Sigurd turned to Hrolf. "You've another of those hides, old friend? Good. Cailin, sit by Hrolf there. Note down such observations as any of us make as we meet the rest still lined up out there. Tabulate them as you suggested, then with Hrolf pull together the notes he's already made. My captains and I will mull over them this evening, and announce decisions tomorrow."

The Irishwoman nodded briskly and drew up a chair as indicated, ready to get to work immediately.

"Your command of our tongue does you credit, lass," observed Corri as she sat down. "Cousin, it occurs to me that some of those we dismissed earlier because of an inability to communicate might be worth further consideration now you've determined there'll be at least one translator among the crew."

A finger still laid along his upper lip, Sigurd nodded. "Perhaps. I've no mind to re-interview anyone though. This is a long enough process as is. Hrolf, when you and Cailin are reviewing the work thus far, you should discuss those we rejected as Corri said. You know what – who we're looking for. Those that the two of you deem worthy can be entered on your new grid and we'll consider them further."

"Right, captain," said the dark haired man.

Cailin wondered at the manner in which this trader handed out responsibility, and his readiness to trust the judgement of others as readily as he trusted his own. It dawned on her that one was the product of the other. He simply had confidence in his own appraisal of character.

That assessment was accurate. If Sigurd's confidence in someone proved misplaced, he'd accept responsibility. Mistakes could be tolerated if they were learned from. Incompetence or abuse of position would not be. If either were proven the guilty party would lose their position of trust immediately – and possibly a lot more at the hands of one of the three 'enforcers'.

Saemundsson called to Hervor and indicated the next person was to be summoned in. The walrus hunter noted the Irishwoman's placement beside Hrolf and gave a small, satisfied nod. In turn she received the slightest of winks from the captain, barely a twitch but enough to indicate her own input had been noted and was acknowledged.

A few more hours had passed. Tallow candles lit the interior of the stone and daub building – little more than an oversized hut – that did service as Cahercommaun's tavern.

The three captains and their two clerks (a role Hrolf was keen to hand on to his new assistant) had a corner to themselves. Had they wanted to stay on in the hall they would have had no argument from the chieftain. He had high hopes they'd take all the landless away with them. Less hungry mouths would mean less trouble in the settlement. But it had been a long day for the *Serpentfang* personnel and they were keen for a change of location.

A perimeter of sailors from the three Norse vessels, sitting drinking at their own tables, kept the locals at a discreet distance. Anyone looking to approach the captain to press their case or otherwise be a nuisance found their way blocked by a firm grip, or a menacing hint of steel.

On the fringe of that group sat Katrine av Ord, practicing her Gaelic on a local shepherd who was surprised and delighted by the attention. If he had any hopes there might be attention of a more tactile nature in his immediate future, he was doomed to disappointment. Her new crewmates had already worked that out. Several weren't able to hide their amusement at the shepherd's wide-eyed expression.

The group in the corner was heedless of the little sideshow, deep in their own discussion.

"I don't know why, but the business of business is always a damn sight more tiring than actually doing the business," grumbled Sverrir.

It took Cailin some moments to follow what *Red Whale's* old commander meant by that. It became clearer to her when Hrolf responded.

"It's simple, Bent-Knee. The sailing's what you love, and no one ever tires of doing the thing they love. But without doing some administrative stuff, bloody tiresome as it is, we'd soon be sailing without point or purpose," the dark-haired fellow explained.

"And ultimately, without the income we need to be able to *keep* sailing. Alas, I'm sorry, old man," Sigurd added with a sympathetic smile.

He truly felt for his father's old comrade. He knew this part of the burden of command did not sit very well with the veteran. But his experience demanded a position of some leadership and on a voyage of trade, the irksome tasks on shore were as much a captain's responsibility as the running of the boat at sea.

Saemundsson raised his tankard. The Irish beer was darker and thicker than the ale he usually preferred, but it was strong and he was enjoying it.

"Men – and Cailin – I'm satisfied our decisions are made. Not a great number to set sail with us. Less than I might have hoped after talking with Jon Far-strider. More than I might have thought before we had the means of the local dialect that jammed like pebbles in my ear. Grateful for that, young lady."

The big woman blushed. She couldn't recall ever being called that except in jest by a few locals, or in scolding by her Da.

"Everyone was told to gather back at the hall tomorrow morning. I'll make my announcements then," Sigurd said, one finger tapping at the charcoaled gridded cowhide on the table. "With appropriate translation as required."

"Casks of water and beer already aboard. The wool's all bundled and almost all loaded," Corri confirmed.

"Same on my boat," agreed Sverrir. "How long d'you reckon to ready the... er... new folks?"

He'd stopped short of saying the word 'slaves'. He knew Sigurd didn't want to think of himself as a slave trader. Couldn't see the dishonour in it himself, trade was trade, but that was young people today for you. And the new lass had proved useful already. If she could reduce the amount of time he had to spend on damned record keeping it'd be worth not upsetting her.

Ruiteach twisted her lip and replied, "Not much. There's none of them – none of us – have reason to linger. If Cahercommaun had anything to offer them they'd not have been so quick to want to sail with you."

"Right. First full tide, next sunrise after tomorrow," declared the captain.

Tankards were raised around the table. Depending on winds and conditions, they may see ten or fifteen sunsets before reaching Jon's great peninsula of dark-skinned men. That didn't seem too long a wait for a rich new future.

When they did depart there was no looking back by any man or woman on any of the three boats. Especially not by the Irish newly boarded. They'd come willingly enough, and would serve as crew, or companions perhaps, until their attraction waned. At that point there were markets to the south where Saemundsson would fetch a return on the investment of feeding those not wanted, or not wanting to stay on.

In truth there was little to be taken from the Burren, even pity.

.ooo.

5

SPAIN – OF SWORDS, AND TRUST

The journey south along the coasts of first Ireland and then the main continent was an unusual one for the crews of Saemundsson's three boats.

It wasn't because of the weather, which was mostly fair. The occasional squalls didn't bother the experienced crews. One or two of the newly recruited Irish folk struggled with the first rough weather, but they adapted quickly. A rough sea was still preferred to the misery of Cahercommaun.

No, the peculiarity was in the rowing. Ordinarily the oarsmen would work to the rhythm beaten out by a drummer stationed at the prow of their boat, usually singing any of the old songs as they worked. New verses often were created spontaneously and just as quickly forgotten unless they happened to be especially appealing.

On this occasion though Sigurd introduced something new. To the metre of their strokes the rowers were directed in chanting words. Katrine av Ord would stand beside the drummer, and in a clear carrying voice shout a word or phrase in Norse, followed by its equivalent in Arabic then Berber. The sailors would repeat the words, cunningly fashioned to suit the timing of their movements.

Katrine kept the vocabulary short and simple. At Sigurd's instruction she'd quickly developed a list of 'essentials' that he hoped would be enough to keep them out of trouble in the new environment they were aiming for. Whenever possible Katrine would be transferred from boat to boat so everyone got some exposure to the unorthodox teaching technique.

The linguist was kept busy on the voyage. When she was not training the rowers Sigurd had her working with the captains, the clerks and the enforcers. He figured that they would require a greater vocabulary to be effective in their duties ashore in al-Andalus. And whenever he could manage it he would spend time with her himself, testing his new language skills and extending his 'word list' to be able to negotiate and haggle as effectively as possible.

The teaching was unorthodox but effective. By the time they were in sight of the Roman-built walls of Zawaia all but the most slow-witted of the crew had at least a handful of local words committed to memory. Saemundsson himself had a modest degree of confidence that he could hold a reasonable conversation, although he planned to keep Katrine close by for business dealings.

Serpentfang was the first of the three to dock. As was their usual practice whenever possible, the two cargo vessels held a position a little way to sea awaiting a plume of smoke from Sigurd advising all was good.

He'd barely set foot ashore when Sigurd got a sense of tension in the air. The harbourmaster was a taciturn fellow. There was nothing unusual in that. It could be a demanding job and often tried the spirit of the most amiable souls. The captain was privately disappointed when the man showed no particular surprise or appreciation at being addressed in his own tongue. But then, he thought, do we not naturally expect to be addressed in Norse in our own ports?

There was more, though. A certain suspicion showed in the man's eyes. There were guarded looks from others on the dock. One or two glared openly while some discreetly kept their distance or changed direction to be clear of the newcomers. There was no obvious threat, but neither was there a welcome.

Before the harbourmaster could scuttle away Sigurd dropped a hand on his shoulder. That drew a discernible flinch that the Norseman ignored.

"I'm told there's a place here where I might find some of my countrymen trading. Could you direct me to it? Please," he asked formally.

Perhaps the politeness was more unexpected than the language, because the dockman looked up sharply. He didn't smile, but tilted his head in some measure of respect.

"Yes captain, there is such a place. I can explain where it is, but cannot be sure of who or what you'll find there."

With that cryptic introduction, the harbourmaster proceeded to give a succinct explanation of where the new arrival should seek his Norse fellows. As soon as he'd finished he squirmed from Sigurd's grasp and hurried away.

"Odd," said Hrolf the Dark.

"Mm," agreed the trader. "There seems no obvious danger, though. We've not been warned off by word or deed. I see no bare steel threatening us."

"The greatest threats are often those hidden, captain," Hervor reminded him, her hand resting on the axe at her belt.

"True. This dock doesn't seem badly laid out for fight or flight, though. Have the fire lit to call the others in, but for now we'll keep everyone close to the boats. Guards on board at all times. Hrolf, Hervor, stay here for now and attend to things as required. Katrine, I'll take you with me. You've been here before, and if that fellow's instructions mislead me then I'll either need you or have to seek directions. I thought I had some comfort with the language but the speed that man gabbled at threw me."

"Don't be disappointed in yourself captain," said the linguist. "Hearing a new tongue spoken by a native for the first time, well, it often seems ridiculously fast. It's a matter of practice, for the ear and the brain. You made yourself plainly understood, and seemed to understand him."

"An illusion on my part at times, perhaps," Sigurd said with a smile. "Thank you for the encouragement. Now, I'll take Lars Longshanks and Lars Magnusson with me. Anna Sjelsdottir too – she's fast on her feet and fast with a long knife."

In minutes Saemundsson and his little party were on their way through the gates of the fortified wall and into mazy streets of Zawaia. The women flanked their captain, the two Lars' a couple of paces behind with their eyes and ears on high alert. Behind them at the dock, the orders were being followed with the efficiency that was expected.

Sigurd had chosen his personal guard well. All three were as loyal and capable as any on his crew, but they weren't imaginative. More creative minds would likely have been distracted by the sounds, smells and sights around them – strange music and voices, unfamiliar spices, and fabulous bright geometric tiles decorating walls all about. Anna and the men noticed all those, but took no interest in them other than as background to their task of being on the watch for danger.

As on the docks, their passing attracted a range of looks, from fear to hostility, scarcely masked but not acted upon. The Norse kept wary hands near their weapons.

"Is it us, do you think? Or is there something broader going on?" Katrine wondered aloud.

"Something broader, I reckon. I smell politics in the air," was the captain's quiet reply.

They turned down the passage they'd been directed to. Slowing their pace, they walked past a series of closed and barred doors. There were a few clues they were in the right place – faint but familiar aromas, some words of Norse scribbled on walls or signs. No sign of activity though, unlike the other streets they'd travelled.

With only a few buildings left they spotted an open door on their right. The window shutters were still closed but it was better than they'd found so far. Approaching cautiously – the whole situation was making him uneasy – Sigurd called a greeting in Norse. To some relief he received a reply in the same tongue.

Nonetheless, he approached the threshold with a hand on his sword's hilt.

"Come in, come in!" ordered a raspy voice.

The rectangle of sunlight from the doorway didn't extend far into the room. It was as if the walls swallowed up light. The dismally dim glow from a brazier on the far side of the chamber only seemed to emphasise the darkness.

As their eyes adjusted to the gloom the sailors were able to make out that there was a table over to their left. Someone was sitting at it, the owner of the raspy voice presumably.

A small flame suddenly erupted from the brazier. It illuminated a small hand that carried the flame to the table and applied it to a candle. The wick flared and the light improved a little.

The flame had been carried by a girl of perhaps eight years age. Dark-skinned and blue eyed, she stared wordlessly towards the new arrivals. A wrinkled hand reached out and stroked the child's long black hair.

"Thank you, Cara," croaked the rough voice. "Welcome, guests. There are stools under the table if you want to sit."

Cautiously the folk from *Serpentfang* made their way inside. It was an old woman seated at the table - that was all they could make out.

"Could we, er, open a shutter, do you think?" ventured Sigurd.

"Eh? Oh, yes, of course. Forgive my manners. Never think of them, myself."

Lars Magnusson managed to force open the bolt securing the solid timber panels and pushed them open before stationing himself outside the entranceway. The daylight revealed their hostess, and the reason why the windows were of no consequence to her.

The old woman's eyes were clouded, as if they floated in thin milk. An old scar was across her throat, providing a likely explanation for the voice. Her grey hair was still thick, inexpertly tied in two bunches on either side of her head.

"Seems a long time since I heard this language from any mouth but my own, or Cara's. Sit down, sit down! I can tell if you're near. I won't bite. Unless asked to," she added with a cackle.

Sigurd pulled out a stool and sat. The incongruous moment of flirting had done much to set his mind at ease, about the old woman at least. He directed Katrine to take the other stool. Anna and Longshanks took up positions where they judged they could move quickly and decisively if required.

The captain introduced himself courteously, explaining who they were, where they'd come from, and that they were looking to trade. He managed to not ask questions, hoping that the old woman would provide explanations unbidden.

To some extent, she did. Her name was Gerda. She had come to al-Andalus years before with her son Thorir Eirikson. Like Sigurd, Thorir had thought to make his fortune in the distant outpost. But Thorir, she lamented, was like Eirik had been, more raider than trader. He'd made his living by renting himself and some of his followers out as a sort of small, hired army.

He'd fathered a daughter by a local woman who'd then been foolish enough to accompany him on an exploit, getting herself killed in short order. The baby, Cara, had been left to be raised by her Norse grandmother. As the girl grew up she'd proved invaluable to the old woman whose eyes were rapidly failing her.

Now, alas, some unknown affliction was robbing Cara of her own vision. Not yet quite blind, she was scarcely less disadvantaged than her grandmother by darkness. Thorir had expressed some disappointment and sympathy at this turn of events, but not enough to curtail his activities as a mercenary fighter.

For a long time this business had been quite successful, although it was not to the liking of all the other Norsemen in the little community. Some had joined up with Thorir but others preferred to ply quieter trade amongst the marketplace.

Mercenaries made enemies, Gerda said ruefully, a finger tracing the scar on her throat. She'd been lucky to escape death when one of Almanzor's Berbers had sought to warn her son off siding with those loyal to the Caliph Hisham.

The names were meaningless to Sigurd, but it was enough to confirm his suspicions that there was a power struggle in progress.

"So where are these other Norsemen to be found?" asked the captain. "The ones who'd rather cross palms than cross swords." He stopped short of openly admitting that he favoured their view – no telling where the old woman's loyalties might lie.

Sighing sadly, Gerda explained that some time ago – she wasn't sure how long, without sight the passing of days was less easy to keep track of – things had "escalated". Thorir had raised his profile too high. He was a bloody fool according to his mother, to Sigurd's reassurance. Not taking sides was no longer an option. Those Norsemen who could hold a weapon were regarded as soldiers, either openly or covertly.

Some took to their boats and abandoned Zawaia. Most of the rest grudgingly joined her son's force. As far as she knew, they were headed for the provincial capital Silves. Those who had families had taken them with them. The handful who'd remained had gradually disappeared, slipping away quietly or, she feared, vanishing under darker circumstances.

The captain's moustache was receiving its usual treatment as he considered his options.

"A fight is one thing, but I've no desire to blunder into a war and this has all the trappings of one. I came here seeking trade. Goods that would be unique enough to fetch high prices in the markets of home..."

He paused and looked at the candle, then at Cara. "Gerda, when we arrived, Cara appeared to carry a flame in her fingers. How is that possible?"

"Magic!" cried the old woman, and gave a happy cackle. "Ah, no, lad. Something cleverer than that."

She waved a creased hand in the direction she knew her grandchild to be standing. "Bring me the little tapers, child," she commanded.

Cara produced a black lacquer box from the back of a gloomy cupboard. Coated with dust, it could have been found by someone who knew it was there. Certainly Anna, standing nearby, hadn't seen it, and she was a very clear-eyed observer. The girl placed the box on the table in front of the trader, and then opened it for him.

Scattered across the bottom of the small container were a dozen or so thin sticks. They were about half the length of Sigurd's thumb. A pungent aroma came from the box, which evidently sealed tightly enough to prevent the sharp smell from escaping.

"Pinewood, steeped in sulphur," explained Gerda. "Brought from somewhere far to the east. One of the Jews down by the harbour traded for them from a man who'd got them from a man who'd... well, you're a trader. You know how it works. The Jew traded them on to one of our neighbours. His wife left them with me when departing for Silves. Stupid superstitious woman – she thought they were some kind of demon's work. Touch one to a fire, even an ember, and it'll blaze straight away, not like the limp soggy tapers of Norway, eh? The traders called them 'fire inch-sticks' as I remember."

Sigurd shook the box gently. There were so few left. He'd seen nothing like them, and would have bet that neither had anyone else around the North Sea. This was exactly the sort of thing he'd wanted to find, and obtain in good commercial quantity.

"This Jew – do you know his name, and where I might find him?" he asked optimistically.

Another cackle came from Gerda before she answered. "Look for two brothers named ben Moshe. They were the ones most often did business with the Norse. I think we frighten a lot of them."

Katrine touched her captain's sleeve. "The name is familiar from my days with Jon Sveinbjornsson," she said.

"Jon Far-strider? He still lives? He'd be not much younger than me," Gerda cackled. Then her voice softened, as much as the damaged tissue would allow. "I hope the years have been kinder to him than to me. I remember him as a handsome fellow. Ah well, back to business. What'll you trade for these fire sticks?"

"Nothing," Sigurd replied, surprising the old woman, and his crew. "There aren't enough here to be of real value to me. Besides, there's little enough light in the lives of you and Cara as it is."

Gerda reached in the direction of his voice and found his arm. Bony fingers squeezed as she said, "There's some around here who say the folk of Iceland have hearts as cold as where they hail from. I know fine that's not true. Freya keep you, lad."

Patting the withered hand, the trader replied, "Thank you, lady. May she keep you and Cara too. We'll take our leave. I want to talk to my people, and look for these brothers."

"If you're determined to trade, they're your men. Don't trust them too far, mind. Don't trust anyone too far. This is a town divided, and the line of that divide can shift like a snowdrift."

Each of the *Serpentfang* sailors turned those words over in their heads as they retraced their steps back to the boat's mooring. Lars Longshanks pondered whether his fighting skills might earn great reward here. It was no lack of loyalty to his captain, but Lars was young and tempted by the prospect of wealth accruing faster than his share of the profits of trade.

As they walked, a man in silk breeches and shirt fell into step beside them. He said nothing at first, but watched Sigurd, giving the captain a smile and a tilt of the head when his gaze was returned. Anna's hand went to her knife. The stranger's hand made a corresponding movement to the hilt of the sword he wore.

Sigurd stopped suddenly, the two Lars' almost colliding with his back.

"Who are you?" he snapped in Arabic.

Grinning, the man replied in a torrent of words that were faintly familiar to the captain, but not enough to be understood. Katrine softly explained that it was the old language of this country, from before the Arabs' conquest long ago.

Before she could attempt a translation the newcomer spoke again, this time in strangely accented but passable Norse.

"My apologies. My name is Andres Diego Almendarez dos Mandujano." Seeing Saemundsson's blank look he continued, "I am more usually called Andres el Espada."

He held out his hand. Cautiously Sigurd returned the gesture, and found his arm gripped in the familiar northern greeting. The captain relaxed very slightly.

"I have, or at least had, friends in the street you just left. I had not thought to see their like again, and am glad to have been wrong. Welcome to Zawaia, captain. What is your business here?"

The old woman's warning about not trusting anyone was clear in the captain's mind. This silk-garbed man's command of the language certainly indicated familiarity with the people of the northern enclave, but where did he stand in relation to the messy situation Gerda had described? The question raced through his head as he still grasped Andres' arm. A measured level of honesty seemed the safest response.

Introducing himself but not his compatriots, Sigurd explained briefly that he had come seeking trade goods that would be novel and appealing in the north, and that he was disappointed to find none of his countrymen in residence.

"You *had* thought to find them, then?" asked Andres, his voice still betraying nothing more than curiosity.

Sigurd shrugged. "Someone, at least. Zawaia is known and respected in the north as a valuable marketplace."

That was true, if only in a very limited circle of the more adventurous traders.

Andres' grin widened slightly. It looked genuine enough, but the Icelander knew that sincerity was an easy thing to feign.

"Kind of you to say so. But with your Norse brothers... gone, where shall you turn to for trade?"

The slight pause before the word 'gone' was not lost on the captain but he chose not to press the point, instead giving a vague answer about trusting his skills in the marketplace among the local merchants.

"Expect some hard bargaining. Most of them are Jews. They don't act in collusion, usually, but each knows much of what the others look for, and what they'll pay."

"The same is true of merchants and markets everywhere I'm afraid. Jewish or otherwise," replied Sigurd.

"I imagine so," said Andres with a laugh.

"You're not a merchant yourself, then?" asked Katrine, who shared her captain's wariness.

The Andalusian shook his head as the little group resumed walking at a slow pace. "Not I. I am, or at least was, a man at arms. As

a young man I was a soldier in Cordoba for the father of the current
Caliph. Hisham was a boy when his father died. The real authority
lay with his mother Subh. The old Caliph's 'trusted advisor'
Almanzor lay with her too."

"I've heard the name," said Sigurd neutrally, although he was
intrigued by his new companion's evident delight in gossip.

"An ambitious man, and a clever one – over the years that became
increasingly clear. He forged his own alliances with princes and
emirs around the country, by flattery, bribery or force. He's not a
Berber himself – son of a Yemeni nobleman, actually – but he's
somehow got their loyalty and has brought many over from their
land across the strait."

Many of the references were as yet meaningless to Sigurd, but he
didn't interrupt Andres' flow. Information was a most valuable
commodity.

"I could see the way things were going. Caliph Hisham was
becoming increasingly isolated, as was Cordoba itself. I decided to
depart, and made my way to Zawaia with plans to sail to somewhere
where the air was less bitter."

"No loyalty to this cal-eef of yours?" asked Lars Magnusson, a
barely disguised contempt in his voice. He was a straightforward man
who put a high value on his own fealty and expected as much of
others.

"In truth, the young man has done little to earn it. As a boy his
acquiescence to his mother was understandable, but as he's grown up
he's proven himself unable, or unwilling, to stand up to her and her
consort. I'd have stood by his father to the death, but such loyalty
must be earned, not just expected."

The smile fled from el Espada's face as he said, "Do you know that
al-Andalus prides itself on being a centre of knowledge? There are
universities and libraries all over the country. The library in Cordoba
itself is said to be the greatest in the world. But this Almanzor had
demanded that it be stripped of anything containing knowledge he
declares to be profane. And extends that edict across the land. 'Profane' of course being anything that doesn't fit with his view of the

worlds above and below. If Hisham had raised his voice in protest I'd have stayed with him and supported him with my life. But he just murmured some platitudes about 'respecting traditions' – Almanzor's own excuse for his narrow-mindedness – and accepted the outrage."

Unless the man was a truly gifted liar and performer, Andres el Espada's position in the brewing civil war was clear. He was on neither side.

"So why do you remain? What happened to the plan to sail away from here?" asked Katrine.

The ex-soldier waved a hand. "A man must eat, and passage does not come free for someone who can offer no skills as a sailor. I've taken a contract with Migash ben Asher as his 'assistant' – in truth his guard – and I will honour that for the two seasons it has yet to run. He pays quite well, for a man of his faith and occupation. I live frugally, and by the contract's end I'll have enough to afford my departure."

"Frugally?" asked Anna, plucking the sleeve of the silk shirt.

"This material is less of a luxury here than it must seem to you," Andres explained. "It's true I take pride in my appearance, but the fabric is light and comfortable in the heat."

Sweating in their woollen garments, most of their furs having already been discarded on the boat, the crew could appreciate that notion.

"In your position with this ben Asher, have you dealings with two brothers named Moshe?" enquired Sigurd, on the trail of business again.

"Joseph and Mishael ben Moshe. Competitors of my employer, but decent men. Yes, I can understand your asking after them if you've come here with any knowledge of the Zawaia marketplace. Joseph especially traded often with both the Norsemen who sailed here, and those who made their homes in the little precinct you visited. I can take you to him now, if you wish."

"A welcome offer, thank you. First though I'd rather return to my ships and consult with my other commanders. I confess I wasn't prepared for the... political situation here. Would you meet us at the dock later? You should be able to identify my *Serpentfang*." The captain offered his first smile of the conversation.

"Indeed. I'll speak to the brothers on your behalf, and to my own employer. They'll all be aware of your presence of course. No boat approaches the towers that Almanzor added to the old Roman walls without word rapidly spreading among the marketplace. What have you to offer them?"

The conversation was now on comfortable ground for Saemundsson. Without detailing quantities he listed the catalogue of goods his boats carried. He refrained from mentioning the Irish folk, concerned they might be regarded as touting for work in the soldiery of either side of the local conflict. Andres nodded as he spoke, and promised to see them at the dock after conveying word of the available stock to the three merchants.

The Andalusian bowed smartly, his past as a soldier revealing itself in an instant, and took off along a crowded thoroughfare at a brisk stride.

"The name he gives himself – it means Andres the Sword," explained Katrine, as the man in question was lost to view.

"Well, he makes no secret of his past employment. A man who chooses such a name for himself, or has it bestowed on him, ought to be able to back it up. We'll watch him, when he returns," said Sigurd.

"*If* he returns," came the voice of one of the Lars' behind him.

They'd reached the city gate, and soon arrived at the waterfront. *Stormbearer* and *Red Whale* were already docked and secured to Saemundsson's satisfaction.

Quickly Sigurd convened a meeting of his senior crew, adding Katrine to the group so as to draw on her local experience. He related what had been learned from Gerda and Andres, admitting that neither was a completely reliable source.

"I thought there was trouble afoot, just from the attitude that ratty little harbourmaster gave me when I docked," grumbled *Red Whale*'s captain. Sverrir had scant patience for bureaucracy at the best of times.

"You're not thinking of casting off and heading for home straight away are you?" asked Corri. "We've over a hundred and fifty sailors who want to get out and explore this strange new land they've been sailing for."

"Hmm, I think you betray the thoughts in your own head more than theirs, cousin. But no, I've not come this far just to turn tail without making some effort at a profit, war or no war."

Hrolf looked concerned. "What if many of our crew decide that mercenary soldiering holds more appeal than sailing? The pay may be better, for one thing."

"Aye, but the life expectancy a damned sight less, although admittedly that won't matter much to some," said Sverrir drily.

"I've always said I'll have no one sail with me who doesn't want to be there. Makes them unreliable. We tell the crews before they go into the city, what the lay of the land is. If any want to chance their arms on the side of this Caliph, or his usurper, well, so be it. There may well be some among those from Cahercommaun who think it appealing. We can bear some loss if we must, and I believe we might find a few willing replacements."

Sigurd was thinking of the disaffected soldier Andres. There must be others similarly interested in getting away from the place. Even if they weren't experienced sailors, willing hands could be taught.

"So we sit and wait for these Jewish traders to turn up...?" began Corri.

"No. You were right about not keeping the crews cooped up on this dock. That would be folly. We'll need some to stay as guards, for both the boats and the cargo I fear. And a stevedoring team to handle the goods if the merchants surprise me by arriving themselves, and quickly. The rest are free to roam Zawaia, though we should advise them to travel in small groups. A schedule of shifts, so that everyone gets their turn ashore. Hrolf, that should be a task for you and Cailin."

His adjutant smiled. "She should have it drawn up by now. We thought it would be a sensible gambit, and if you chose not to use it now, well, it's a good exercise for her, and I didn't doubt we'd use it in the future anyway."

Sigurd clapped his trusty's shoulder. "Well thought, all of you," he said looking around the little group. He was well aware he had an excellent command team – loyal but dependable, shrewd and self-reliant. He put a high value on their initiative.

Suddenly they became aware of a commotion on the dock. Hervor appeared at a run.

"Company coming, captain, and I don't much like the look of it," she said.

She led the way smartly back ashore, the commanders close behind with their weapons near to hand.

Striding purposefully along the dock towards them were twenty or so men in formation. They were swarthy fellows in voluminous white robes. Dangerous-looking curved swords hung from their belts, naked steel glittering in the sun. Spiked steel helmets poked from the coils of white fabric encircling their heads.

At the head of the group marched a man whose purple sash marked him as their leader. He was a half head shorter than most of his men, with a beard more carefully clipped than theirs, and a large nose shaped like the beak of a bird of prey.

The officer stamped to a halt in front of *Serpentfang*, standing little more than an arms-length away from Sigurd. He had to look up to meet the eyes of the Norse captain, a fact that clearly irritated him.

"Your arrival in Zawaia has been observed, as have your coming and going from this vessel. Why are you here? Did Thorir Eirikson summon you?" snapped the hawk-faced man.

"Never heard of him," was Sigurd's even reply, which up until very recently was entirely true.

Behind her captain, Katrine was silently impressed at his command of the Berber language he'd been addressed in, and replied in. She'd thought he was an adept student and was pleased to be proved right.

The captain continued in the same level tone. "My name is Sigurd Saemundsson. I have sailed from Hofn in Iceland to barter with the merchants of Zawaia. Do you speak on their behalf... sir?"

He added the last in a voice that clearly indicated he knew otherwise, but was alert to the officer's impolite failure to introduce himself.

A tiny flick of a muscle in the shorter man's cheek indicated that the barb to his honour had struck.

"I am no representative of the dogs of the marketplace! I am Uthman al-Silb, commander of the forces of the hajib, al-Mansur Ibn Abi Aamir, the most holy Almanzor. I hold the hajib's authority here, and I decide who may or may not enter Zawaia."

"The very man I wanted to meet, then. Excellent. My case is plain, commander. I simply wish to trade goods of the north for the – what is the word - desirable products of al-Andalus and its neighbours," replied Sigurd, smoothly diplomatic.

Dark eyes peered at him over the curved nose. "Trade goods only? You have no thought of embarking on any other enterprise?"

"The thought had not crossed my mind."

This too was true until very recently. Saemundsson was genuine in his desire to avoid involvement in a local war, but there was something deeply aggravating about this Uthman al-Silb that was tempting him to change his mind.

"Thorir Eirikson..." the commander began.

"A Norwegian name? Not my country I'm afraid. I'm not familiar with every resident of my own land, commander, far less those of a place a week's sailing distant."

Uthman's eyes narrowed. His knowledge of northern geography was non-existent, but the calm figure before him seemed genuine.

"How long do you anticipate your trade to take?" he asked, trying to match the other's even tone.

The captain made a show of turning away to look at his three boats thoughtfully, even stroking his moustache as he seemed to consider the question.

"This is my first visit to your city, commander. I don't know my way around your marketplace, who I should trust..."

"That is simple! Trust no one!" replied Uthman. It was not said in jest.

Sigurd shrugged and continued, "A wise trader is always cautious.

Thank you for the advice. It reinforces for me that my decisions should not be made in haste. And after weeks at sea my crew has earned some time ashore to relax. With those considerations in mind, I think perhaps, fifteen days should suffice."

al-Silb's black eyebrows shot up. "No! Five at most!"

"Commander, in such a short stay I would be obliged to put my crew ashore in large groups to allow them all to have some time away from the confines of ship-board life. Surely smaller numbers would be easier for you when it comes to... maintaining your authority? My people will be in your streets with coins in their purses – I would rather those coins went into the hajib's economy legitimately than be lost to villains and rogues."

The dark eyes glared. Uthman inhaled heavily while he thought. He may decry the merchants of the town, but he was astute enough to realise that it was the taxes levied on them that paid him and his men. It truly was better that any revenue from the newcomers should be kept in plain sight.

"Let us say ten days. Be warned though, my eyes will be upon you and them at all times. Trade as you wish. Encourage your people to spend freely. Avoid trouble and do *not* seek to become involved in affairs which are not your concern."

The hawk-faced man turned on his heel and strode away with his white robed retinue, leaving Sigurd fuming at his manner, although satisfied with the outcome of the discussion. Ten days were more than he figured to need for business but he didn't want to feel rushed, particularly by the brusque officer.

After a brief discussion each captain returned to his own boat to address their own crew, detailing the situation in the town, and the intended roster of guard duty, cargo work and shore leave.

It wasn't long before the first contingent of sailors were making their way through the gates of Zawaia. The bars closest to the waterfront would do well over the coming days.

They'd been gone only briefly when Andres el Espada presented himself at *Serpentfang*.

After being introduced to the captains of the two knarrs, and being handed a tankard of ale from the cask that Sigurd kept for his own use, the swordsman made his report. Joseph ben Moshe was most certainly interested in seeing what the Norsemen had to offer. His stock of the northern goods that he liked to keep on hand had declined. Andres noted with a grin that news of Joseph's interest had piqued the curiosity of his brother, and also his own employer, the esteemed Migash ben Asher. When word got around the marketplace that all three of these worthies sought to investigate Saemundsson's goods, he was confident others would follow. How that word might get around was implicit in a twinkle in his eye.

There was a warning though that the merchants were reluctant to venture out of their own precinct. Even dispatching their agents was not considered wise. Andres himself did not share that caution, he announced. He would not give any such satisfaction to Uthman al-Silb.

"Ah yes. We've met," said Sigurd drily. Their mutual distaste for the representative of the 'most holy Almanzor' only improved the trader's opinion of the swordsman.

The merchants had expressed a strong desire to conduct their business as soon as possible. Over a hundred Norse swords and axes on the edge of the town made many people nervous, Andres explained.

"Including the hajib's officer," observed Corri.

"Yes," agreed Andres. "And his agitation adds to the concern of others. Uthman al-Silb can be – *rash* in his actions. He is not the deep thinker he pretends to be. So – will you accompany me now?"

Sigurd stroked his moustache as he looked at the sky. The sun was lowering, and he'd observed in recent days that in this region it sank quickly when it neared the horizon.

"I think not. Darkness approaches if I read it right," he said.

El Espada shrugged. "The marketplace has many lanterns. Trade here continues well into the night."

"As it does in many places, my friend. I'm not afraid of the dark, or those who skulk in it. But I confess to limited experience of the wares on offer from your employer and his ilk. Until I have some familiarity with the goods I'm examining, I prefer to look at them in broad daylight. No offence intended."

"None taken, by me at any rate. I'm no merchant, but your position seems very sensible to me!"

"Give me directions to find Joseph ben Moshe, and your ben Asher too, and I'll attend both tomorrow morning. I'll have an inventory of my goods, and enough samples to whet their appetite."

Lingering only long enough to finish his ale, Andres gave the appropriate directions, then bowed and departed for the marketplace. The Norsemen discussed the prospects. They were cautious, but optimistic.

By morning the sense of optimism had improved. It had been a quiet night. Uthman al-Silb's men had been visible by firelight in the towers and along the ramparts of the walls, but gave no sign of hostility. The crew members who'd been into Zawaia returned in their small groups.

Their experiences had been innocuous enough. Katrine's language lessons had certainly made things easier, it was agreed. No one here seemed to have any command of the Norse tongue, or if they did they weren't admitting it.

Pall Jansson was typical of the crew when he noted that very few locals seemed to want to engage with them, beyond taking their money for food ("Too spicy"), drink ("Too thin") and games of chance ("Probably rigged, as they are everywhere").

The only fights reported were scuffles between themselves over some of the games. The worst of them had been resolved when Odd Arisson banged the offending heads together.

Saemundsson was satisfied. He was still wary, but more confident that today he could concentrate his diplomatic skills on trade, rather than local politics.

He let it be known amongst his people, including those who'd boarded in Ireland, that there did seem to be an opportunity – indeed, a choice of opportunities – to seek employment as a fighter. He made it clear though that he would not guarantee anything positive about the terms of that employment and that his own advice would be to look for better options elsewhere.

By mid-morning he was ready to seek out Joseph ben Moshe. Corri would accompany him. So would Cailin, serving as a clerk so Hrolf could stay behind, responsible for all three boats.

Sverrir Bent-knee was to be the first of the captains to enjoy some 'time out'. Sigurd had quietly arranged this in supervising the roster, partially out of respect for his elder commander, and partly because the veteran sailor was unlikely to want to spend long on shore anyway. Aboard *Red Whale* was where the old man was happiest.

Three names were drawn from each of the rostered lists of guards, cargo men, and those allowed into town. The 'sample' trade goods were distributed among these nine to be carried to the marketplace. Katrine chanced to be among that number. Actually, there was no 'chance' involved, Sigurd having seen her name on the list and decided he wanted her linguistic skills close by. He was finding he increasingly enjoyed her company, too, but that was a pleasing incidental.

Twelve was a good number, he reasoned. Large enough for everyone to carry a modest load but still be able to reach for a weapon quickly if necessary, and small enough to be mobile and not look too threatening to any jittery guardsmen.

As the dozen-strong party followed Andres' directions to find the prospective trading partners, Sigurd kept a watchful eye out. Zawaia was an interesting place, and under other circumstances he would have looked forward to exploring it in depth once business had been conducted. Tension was thick in the air though, and he felt it congealing around himself and his people.

Even as they made their way through the marketplace itself, Saemundsson noticed the expressions on the faces of merchants and buyers alike. At best he saw curiosity. but more commonly distrust. Suspicion. Hostility. Fear.

On arrival at their first destination Sigurd had his crew place his samples by the bench from which Joseph ben Moshe ran his business. He kept his cousin, the Irish clerk and Katrine with him. The others were stationed around and outside the stall. They were too distinctive to be unobtrusive, but their instructions were to be alert, not threatening.

Joseph had one of the larger stalls in the Zawaia market. He carried a diverse range of goods but clearly had a particular interest in textiles. His shelves were festooned with bolts of cloth of different textures, colours, and patterns. The display could have been garish and jarring, but the merchant clearly had a good sense for design so the fabrics actually led the eye around the stall and directed potential customers' attention to certain stock.

Sigurd introduced himself. He'd been expected. Andres el Espada had spoken highly of him, he was told. Despite which, Sigurd could not help noticing the merchant's reserve. Perhaps it was just the man's manner, for he certainly thawed when shown samples of the wool from Cahercommaun.

While acknowledging that the northerner would certainly want to look at other options Joseph made his interest clear. He expressed enthusiasm for some of the carved timber he was shown, too. He expected that el Espada's employer would find this desirable, and that it would of course be discourteous not to pay a call on ben Asher's stall. But he did quietly suggest that his own brother would surely offer a better price.

The Icelandic captain received this discreet information with a courteous smile and bow, and gave his cousin Corri a knowing wink when ben Moshe looked away.

Joseph had long since run out of the 'fire inch sticks' from the East, alas. The trader who'd brought them hadn't been sighted in Zawaia for a long time, for reasons that may never be known. None of his competitors had any either, as far as he knew.

After some negotiation, each side's best offers were agreed. Cailin made appropriate notes on a square of hide, surprising the Jew. He accepted Saemundsson's politely apologetic explanation that he did this whenever he did business in a market for the first time, to rein-force his own memory. With a sincere undertaking that he expected to return to the stall later to finalise arrangements (for at least some of the trades they'd negotiated), Sigurd led his group back out into the walkways between stalls.

It was some little distance to the premises of Migash ben Asher. As they walked, one of the crewmen drew nearer to Sigurd and quietly said that he thought they were being followed.

"Shifty fellow. Long moustache and pointed chin. Every time I turn to look at him properly he suddenly becomes very interested in whatever item is nearest. So far I've seen him study a rug, a glass vase and a brace of dead chickens," was the report.

"Well done, Bjarni," commended the captain. "I thought I'd seen a figure flitting from the corner of my eye. Wait and I daresay we'll see what the fellow is up to soon enough. You've a free hand for your axe, eh?"

"Count on it, captain."

A few minutes later Andres el Espada was introducing Sigurd and Corri to his 'esteemed employer'. Despite the swordsman's best efforts at geniality, the conversation was following a very similar pattern to that with ben Moshe. It was clear that the activities of Thorir Eirikson had made an impression in the marketplace, and not a good one.

The stall was smaller than the one they'd just visited, so more of the retinue stayed outside. They could browse the nearby options but stayed alert for their captain's voice. Katrine's lessons in vocabulary were useful as the Norse attempted friendly, or at least diplomatic conversation with the locals.

Joseph had been right in his assessment that ben Asher would be interested in the decorative wooden carvings he was shown. His own stock included many such items. The wood used in many of these had very different fragrances to the northern timbers. The colours were different too, with Sigurd being especially taken by pieces cut from a glossy black wood that was heavy and very hard. 'Damned difficult to carve, but beautiful,' he thought.

What appealed to Migash about the Icelander's samples was the intricacy of the designs. Saemundsson's judgement hadn't failed him when he'd selected pieces for trade. He knew there was a distinctive style to the art of his homeland and its neighbours, but he'd looked for items where the details were especially finely wrought. The better the workmanship, the better the trade.

Shrewdly, he let Corri do much of the talking about craftsmanship and design. His cousin quickly had the merchant entranced with stories about the symbolism of certain motifs, stories which, he explained, ben Asher could himself relate to potential customers to encourage their interest.

While Corri and the merchant talked, Sigurd had a quiet word with Andres. He invited Bjarni to describe the furtive figure he'd noticed earlier.

The swordsman's expression clouded as he said, "Fernando Lobato. His behaviour doesn't surprise me. He's a treacherous rogue. Used to be in the Caliph Hisham's army. Don't trust him!"

"Wasn't that the same army you served in?" asked Sigurd, neutrally.

"Indeed. But it's not his past employment that concerns me, it's his nature. He's the sort of man who would clasp your arm in friendship with his right hand while the left one slips a knife between your ribs."

"Suitably warned then, thanks. I know the type."

Privately Sigurd had wondered if that description might not fit Andres himself. He liked the man, but was still naturally cautious, especially in an unfamiliar and politically charged environment.

Meanwhile Corri's charm had won over Migash, and the offered price that Cailin duly noted was enough to make Sigurd well pleased. The clerk's work intrigued the Jew, who was another who trusted most things to his own prodigious memory. Perhaps though it may be a useful task for his Andalusian 'assistant'.

"I think you may find ink and vellum less cumbersome than that animal skin," ben Asher observed to his visitors.

"Probably," agreed Sigurd. "But vellum is not common at home. The Church holds most of what is usually to be found."

In his mind's eye he saw Katrine av Ord at work in the chapel at Framgord. He caught himself smiling at the image.

Migash may have spotted the fleeting smile. "I could obtain a quantity for you, at a good price. And a supply of sea ink – a fine blend of that extracted from squid, octopus and the small spiny urchin."

Saemundsson's interest was certainly piqued, but his trader's caution was still in place. "I appreciate your offer, but I must wonder whether I might find these things for myself in this marketplace I have yet to thoroughly explore. You are, after all, among the very first I've spoken to here."

"And I am honoured to be so," replied the merchant solemnly. "I must counsel you, though, that you will find many here who will not be so open to trade with you. You are perhaps not aware that others of your fair-haired race have taken sides in a significant dispute here, a position that many amongst us would not wish to be seen to support. Commerce should be above politics."

"Or at least well removed from it, I agree. That's very much my own view, and so I appreciate your advice. You, and all others here, will find that I am in Zawaia only to transact such business as you and I have already discussed."

"Of course, I cannot speak for my fellows, but I am willing to accept that as truth unless it is proved otherwise," said ben Asher with a smile that looked genuine.

After a final exchange of courtesies, Sigurd called his crew together to gather up his sample wares. Notwithstanding the circumstances, he'd be a poor trader if he didn't at least explore some other options while he was here.

The subsequent hours proved largely fruitless, however. There was interest in many of the Icelander's goods, and there were plenty of items that in turn attracted his attention. The advice, or warnings, of ben Asher and ben Moshe proved all too accurate though. Some merchants were diplomatically evasive while some didn't even manage that much courtesy. Even Mishael ben Moshe proved much less willing to engage with the northern trader than his brother.

There was little opportunity for Cailin to add to her notes beyond one or two desultory offers for a small quantity of wool or a few casks of ale.

Sigurd was developing a suspicion, and when Bjarni mentioned again seeing the man identified as Fernando Lobato on the fringe of their vicinity he started to stroke his moustache. He had a quiet word to Bjarni. The blonde crewman nodded, handed his bundle of wool to one of the other sailors, and then moved off casually but briskly down a small passage off the thoroughfare the group were on.

Their expedition continued for a few more minutes. A merchant apologised that he "had no market for northern goods" while another simply glared at Sigurd, grunted, and turned away.

Suddenly Bjarni appeared from between two stalls, one brawny arm around the shoulders of the Andalusian he'd spotted earlier. It looked like the genial embrace of a comrade, but the stocky blonde was strong. Lobato's upper arms were effectively pinned, and it had happened too quickly for him to yet do much to free himself.

Bjarni squeezed, threatening to pop one of his captive's shoulders from its socket, although his amiable grin didn't slip. "This here's my captain, friend. But you know that, don't you? I think you should talk *to* him, rather than about him as you've been doing, eh?"

Sigurd examined the man held pinioned before him. He had the same complexion and hair as Andres el Espada, and was about the same height, but there the resemblance ended. Narrow of face, and sharp of features, he reminded the trader of a stoat. Dark, darting eyes added to the impression. While the fellow had shown some reaction to Bjarni's question, delivered in Norse, the captain remembered his discussions with Andres and spoke in Arabic.

"Talking about me? A strange thing to do, considering we've never met. Why are you so interested in my business, I wonder? You don't strike me as the merchant type, but perhaps you're employed by one?"

The Andalusian scowled, and almost spat out his reply, "I am not one of these feckless money-shufflers! Nor would I stoop to working for any of them! I am a businessman, but in the same business that you truly are."

"Really? What do you imagine my business to be?"

"Oh, I'm sure you've some trinkets and such to add to the weight of your purse, but I know you northerners are really here to sell your swords. When I heard of your arrival, I assumed you'd come in support of the mercenary Eirikson, but when I saw Uthman al-Silb meet with you on the dock then walk away without demur, I realised you must be in the employ of the hajib Almanzor."

Sigurd masked his surprise. That was an interpretation he hadn't expected.

"Why should my allegiance matter to you? Oh, don't shake your head – clearly it does or you wouldn't be scurrying about here warning people off doing business with me." Saemundsson made the accusation more from instinct than evidence, but he got it right.

The Andalusian raised his chin defiantly. "There are those who would pay well to secure support for the Caliph – armed support, I mean. Pay better than that offered by al-Silb. I want a swift end to your charade as a merchant. If you are open to the possibility of hire by the loyalists I could arrange a meeting and broker a deal. Should Almanzor be offering better wages still, then I..."

His voice tapered off. Almost in spite of himself, Sigurd was intrigued. "Then you what?" he prompted.

"Then I would offer my sword arm to fight alongside the Berbers with you. We are, as I said, in the same business. I am just more open about it, and eager to secure the best contract that I can."

The captain of *Stormbearer* addressed his cousin in Norse. "This rascal wants to hitch himself to our fortunes, it seems. I think I'd rather carry a live serpent in my britches."

"Hah – an exercise just about as safe, I agree."

Sigurd turned his attention back to Lobato. "Even if your assumptions about me were correct – and none of them are, I assure you – I've heard enough to know that I would never trust your sword at my side or my back in any conflict. You're an underhanded rogue, sir, and I want nothing to do with you."

At a nod from his captain Bjarni released his grip, spinning the foxy man away from him. The mercenary stumbled before drawing himself upright and throwing out his chest, saying in his own language, "You have insulted the honour of Fernando Carlos Lobato!"

Katrine replied in the same tongue, "We've seen no evidence that you have any."

As the twelve from *Serpentfang* walked on Lobato moved to unsheathe his sword. He glared at their backs. The woman who'd just insulted him – he had a clear stroke at her back... No. Too many others around her. There'd be another opportunity. He'd make sure of it.

Soon after, the Norse had stopped to slake their substantial collective thirst at a bar that serviced the marketplace. Their reception was less taciturn than they'd experienced elsewhere. It seemed Lobato had not preceded their arrival this time. Still, his poisonous words had done a lot of damage to their trade prospects. With time they might prove the truth of Sigurd's avowal of neutrality, but the politics of Zawaia were so tense that it seemed that time was a luxury they wouldn't have.

Reluctantly, Sigurd gave his opinion that they should accept those of the offers in Cailin's notes that were reasonable. Exchange goods as speedily as possible, including making sure that provisions were restocked, and then sail away and let the warring factions settle their own affairs. Anyone who wanted to stay and become involved, on whatever side they chose to be hired by, was welcome to do so.

There was no argument. The day had become dispiriting, so the idea of making such profit as could be taken then moving on seemed sound. Other markets would be more welcoming, and no less exotic, surely.

Sigurd would return to those merchants with whom they'd arranged suitable deals, taking only Cailin and Bjarni with him. The others were to go back to the boats, with Corri to oversee assembly of the goods that were to be traded.

Very soon after those arrangements began being acted upon, trouble was brewing in another part of Zawaia.

A half dozen of the northerners were taking their leisure at a tavern not far from the waterfront gates. The shadow of one of the towers provided shade that was a welcome respite from the sun's heat. Fafhrd lounged on a seat outside the bar, his eyes closed and legs stretched out as he awaited the return of the drinking partner who he'd been conversing with.

Suddenly he was aware of someone sitting down beside him. One eye opened, like that of a sleepy bear. This bruin though had a hand quietly grasping an axe. The grip tightened as he recognised who now shared the bench. It was Uthman al-Silb.

"Is there a problem, officer?" asked the helmsman casually. It was one of the first phrases Katrine had taught them.

"No, no. Consider this a friendly conversation between... men of the world."

"Indeed? Very well. Fetch yourself a drink and we can converse. As best I can. I do not speak much of your language."

"My religion compels me to forego the drink, I am afraid. But I would speak to you about a business proposition."

Fafhrd turned the unfamiliar words over in his head, and then replied in a doggerel mix of Berber and Norse, "You have the wrong man. Talking business is my captain's job."

"Your captain has made it clear to me that he does not wish to pursue the opportunity I have in mind. There have been other men of your country who have sworn allegiance to those I serve..."

"Allegiance?"

"Support. Service," said Uthman, seeking a word this uncivilised lout would understand.

"Ah – paid to fight, yes?"

"Yes. Yes. Your captain says he is not interested. I know you Norse like to fight though, and I find you here with a number of your fellows. I judge you to be by nature a leader..."

Fafhrd couldn't restrain a laugh. "Then you're a poor judge, my friend! I'm no leader. And as to the other, I fight when I must, as any good son of Odin should, but not as an occupation. You'd be better talking to – ah! Right on time – my companion: Hervor Elsdottir. Hervor, my friend," he said reverting to plain Norse, "I think this fellow is trying to recruit an army behind our captain's back."

"Fool. Is his opinion of our honour so low? Ah, what am I asking for? Of course it is," she replied.

"He probably judges all men by his own standards," said the helmsman as he accepted his drink from the walrus hunter and sidled along the bench to make room for her.

The Berber commander flinched away from the contact of the man's hip, staring at the slight figure who now sat down casually. He knew a few words of Norse from his earlier dealings with Eirikson and his troops, but had no idea of what was being said.

"This is a woman!" he sputtered.

"Thank you for noticing," said Hervor with a transparently sweet smile.

"I am seeking warriors, not women!"

"Why? Do we frighten you?"

"Insolent female! There is no place for the likes of you in the holy hajib's forces!"

Fafhrd shrugged. "Their loss, then," he said in rough Berber as he swigged from his earthenware goblet.

The walrus hunter's smile vanished. "And why would I seek a place in a... " She struggled with her vocabulary and settled for, "A crew who cannot fight like me, captained by... a... troll with the face of a bird?"

The officer stood angrily, almost jumping to his feet. He raised his hand to slap her as she deserved, and found the point of a short spear suddenly resting under the tip of his nose.

"He could certainly accommodate an extra nostril," laughed Fafhrd. "I doubt though that it's diplomacy of which Saemundsson would approve." He addressed Uthman again. "I said she was a fighter."

The man with the purple sash was acutely aware that a number of his Berbers were nearby, watching this unsuccessful attempt at recruitment. He knew he was in danger of losing face, both figuratively and literally – the spear point was digging ever so slightly into his skin.

In a low voice he growled, "Our ways are not your ways. I see that." He lowered his hand slowly. "I agree. You would not... fit well in the service of the hajib. But I recommend you do not underestimate the prowess of his forces."

The sweet smile returned as the spear was lowered at the same slow pace as the officer's hand. "Oh, I don't underestimate anyone. Not until they're lying broken or dead at my feet."

Pointedly, Hervor looked away from him and resumed her conversation with Fafhrd. The Berber turned and began to stride away, trying to look as much as possible like a man who'd at least come out even in an argument. Behind him he heard the two laughing, and caught one of the few words of Norse he knew. It was the word for 'coward'.

His already swarthy face flushed. He stopped in his tracks and signalled to his men. These sailors would be taught not to mock an officer of the holy hajib. Their handful of companions would be no match for a squad of his Berbers.

Sigurd was finalising his arrangements with Migash ben Asher, having already conducted a similar conversation with Joseph ben Moshe. They clasped hands on the agreement, and exchanged bows. The captain would send a contingent of his crew with the agreed goods to the stall in the morning, by which time the merchant would have assembled the stock to be exchanged. As a gesture of intent, they'd already exchanged samples of the contracted wares including small amounts of vellum, ink, and ostrich feather quills. Cailin's delight was evident in her broad grin.

As the Norse trio started to depart, Andres appeared at the captain's side.

"May I walk with you?" he asked quietly.

"Certainly," replied Sigurd, intrigued by the man's air of barely suppressed excitement.

The swordsman explained that he'd been disturbed by the poisonous gossip of Fernando Lobato, and disgusted by the willingness of so many to accept it. It was becoming increasingly difficult to abstain from involvement in the simmering internal conflict, and he was deeply unimpressed by either side.

He'd spoken to ben Asher, who had proved surprisingly sympathetic and agreed to terminate the ex-soldier's contract, if that what
was what he desired. A reluctant assistant would always be unreliable
anyway, he reasoned.

"I would sail with you, Captain Saemundsson, if you'll have me. I
admit to no experience as a seaman, but I'm a fast learner."

Sigmund smiled and said, "I don't doubt that at all. Where do you
have in mind to sail to?"

Andres waved an expansive arm and answered, "Anywhere in the
world! North, if you choose to head homewards. South, if you've a
mind to seek more trade. If you do that, I'd strongly suggest due
south. I know Joseph ben Moshe received a lot of goods from somewhere in that direction, and Almanzor draws his forces from the
Berbers to the east. Their brethren of the western coast are believed
to have little or nothing to do with them – a shared history perhaps,
but no more."

"Already you prove your worth, my friend. Knowledge is something I treasure. Skill as a sailor – well, that can be learned by anyone
determined enough. You're welcome aboard *Serpentfang*."

The two men clasped arms as they walked, a definite spring now
in the Andalusian's step. The cheery mood was broken though as
they neared the town gates. A crowd in front of them blocked the
view, but there were definitely sounds of violence ahead. The clash of
steel, and voices raised. Familiar voices.

Even as Uthman al-Silb had called his men to come running,
Hervor Elsdottir had given a loud whistle that served as a signal
among the Norse crew. Four fair-skinned figures dashed from the
interior of the tavern – three brawny men and a similarly muscular
woman. All unlimbered axes or swords as they came. Neither of the
two archers was carrying their bow.

The white robed Berbers slowed their advance slightly. There
were more than twenty of them so the numerical advantage was very
much still theirs, but the sailors were an imposing physical presence.
The die was cast though, because the northerners were charging

straight at them. Great curved blades were raised as the half dozen berserkers smashed into the phalanx like a cannon ball into a wall.

The sailors remained in as close knit a bunch as their flailing weapons would permit, so that the opponents who surrounded them could isolate no one. Even so, they were soon hard pressed by the hajib's troops.

So it was fortuitous that this was the moment when Corri and his eight comrades emerged from the street leading to the marketplace. The *Stormbearer's* captain quickly assessed the situation. With commendable regard for the trader's instincts his cousin had nurtured in him he ordered the merchandise put down in a compact pile and designated one (reluctant) man to guard it. Only then did he give the signal for a charge into the circle of white robes and steel.

The Norse were still outnumbered, but unmatched in ferocity. The fight was like a many-headed living thing, its outline shifting, but the whole moving together as a roaring deadly mass. The Zawaia locals fell over each other to escape to a safe distance. Whatever their allegiance or sympathies, and they varied, no one wanted to be too close to the flying blades.

Uthman swore as the melee brought him within sight of Fafhrd. The helmsman was fighting two handed, parrying with his broad sword and sweeping lethal arcs with his axe.

"So much for not wanting to fight!" snarled the officer.

"When I must, I said," replied Fafhrd in an incongruously mild voice as a downward blow from his axe shattered the leg of a Berber.

The burly man winced as a brief scream behind him told of a sailor going down with a cutlass cleaving fatally through collarbone and chest. Before the Berber weapon could be pulled free its wielder fell gurgling. Hervor had jabbed her spear through his throat.

The impact of Corri's contingent into the fray had not decisively swayed the tide of fighting in the sailors' favour, but it made the battle an even more mobile beast. Instinctively, the Norse moved towards their ships.

Zawaia's gate framed the combatants as Sigurd pushed his way through the retreating crowd. The frustrated crewman guarding the trade goods signalled to his captain.

With a curse under his breath, Saemundsson ordered Cailin and Bjarni to help their compatriot to gather up the stock and get it back to the boats with all possible speed.

"But..." began Bjarni.

"Don't argue! I don't want al-Andalus to be a total loss! Move! And have the ships ready to cast off as soon as we can fight our way aboard!"

The blonde sailor didn't like it, any more than the Irish woman who was more than willing to wade into the fight, but the captain was in charge. He was right, they knew, but when the blood was up it was a damned difficult order to follow!

Satisfied that he was being obeyed, Sigurd drew his broadsword.

"I fight beside you, my captain!" exclaimed Andres, grinning in anticipation.

"As will I," called a voice from behind them. Sword already drawn, Fernando Lobato was arriving at a run. "My welcome in Zawaia has also run out, I fear."

Saemundsson and el Espada exchanged suspicious glances but had no time to debate the matter. More of the Berbers were rushing from the towers and the crew's situation was becoming more desperate. Any sword was valuable. The Icelander threw himself into the fray, bellowing the order, "To your ships! To your ships!" even as his broadsword tore open the side of a Berber too slow to turn.

The blade of Andres el Espada was a lighter and narrower weapon than that of his new commander, but it was immediately obvious that the name he'd chosen for himself was well justified. The sword glittered at first as it danced, but was soon too mired in Berber blood for the late afternoon sun to sparkle on the steel.

Sigurd cursed again as he saw the bodies of two, then three of his crew sprawled in the Zawaian dust. One was Hild, the woman who'd been drinking with Hervor and Fafhrd. Her hand still clutched the handle of the axe that was embedded in the breast of a Berber. The hajib's soldiers were learning quickly that the Norse women were indeed as dangerous as the men.

Roaring encouragement to his companions, Corri was doing his best to lead the way to the waterfront. Blood streamed from a wound to his right shoulder, but the sword in his left hand still swung. His cousin saw him, and tried to get to his aid. No easy task – his way blocked by a knot of white-robed and woollen shirted demons that suddenly swirled in front of him.

Cailin and the others had reached the boats moments before the battle loomed in the gateway. Hrolf and Sverrir acted with speed. Some of the crew were set to rapidly making the longship and knarrs ready to set off. Oarsmen took their places – there wasn't enough wind to fill a sail for any sort of swift departure. Those who could be spared grabbed weapons and were positioned as a wall of steel defending access to the dock. The only people crossing that line would be their shipmates.

Too late it was realised that it would have been wise to keep a contingent of archers among the guards. But there were few in the crew who had much skill with a bow, and that handful was ashore in Zawaia. Somewhere. They would rely on the might of steel at close quarters.

Word of what was happening swept Zawaia like a fire through dry grass. The other Norsemen who'd been ashore came running back to the gates, individually or in small clusters. Fortunately, none had wandered very far from the precinct.

Weapons bared, they smashed into the fight like hailstones. More of Uthman's Berbers also rushed to the scene. The white robed men had no clear strategy beyond slaughter, though, while the sailors had an objective. They were aiming for their ships and the open sea.

Rallying to the cry of their captain, now somewhere in the midst of the melee, the Norse surged towards the dock. Saemundsson himself was crossing swords with a rangy Berber, grimly trying to work his way past the man. He barely heard the growl behind him.

"I will not be mocked..." Seizing the opportunity of the Norseman's distraction, Lobato thrust his sword at the captain's unprotected back. Next he'd find that woman who'd sneered at him and...

The thought was never finished as the Andalusian's head flew from his neck, severed by a single slash of his countryman's blade. Andres had glimpsed Fernando's impending treachery and swiftly turned from his own fight with a soldier.

Lobato's sword did no more than flick Sigurd's shirt as the headless figure pitched forward. A jet of blood from the open neck shot over the Norseman's shoulder and momentarily blinded his opponent. It was all the opening that the northerner needed, his broadsword slashing and soaking the white robe in crimson. He glanced behind, quickly grasping what had happened. There was barely time for a grunt of thanks – the death of the tall Berber had opened up a narrow channel toward the waterfront.

El Espada dispatched his own foe. Executing Lobato had been no more than a momentary distraction, that deadly sweep of his sword seeming just an integral part of the pattern it wove in the air. The smile he now wore was grim – there would be time enough for mirth when they were away from wretched Zawaia. He followed in the wake of his furious captain.

Sigurd's broadsword ripped through the shoulder blade of a soldier who'd been one of two who were causing problems for one of his crew. The woman's own axe caught her other distracted assailant on the upswing, spilling his guts in a gory torrent. With a grateful wave of acknowledgement she staggered toward the boats, the line of Norse guards opening to allow her through.

al-Silb was now in a position to see that line and suddenly realised the strategy he needed to adopt. "Sink..." was all he managed to shout before Sigurd Saemundsson loomed in front of him and their swords locked.

While the blades rattled, the trader's free fist slammed into the Berber's face. The officer reeled back, cursing and almost stumbling over the body of one of his men. Sigurd tried to press home his advantage but caught his feet in the dead man's robes. He fell awkwardly to his knees, his sword hand and sword slamming into the ground.

Uthman caught his own stumble, and despite being off balance slashed his curved blade ferociously towards the Norseman's bare neck.

There was a blur of silk as Andres el Espada flung himself forward. He drove his sword deep into the commander's belly, skewering the purple sash even as the curved edge sliced into his own side. He landed heavily right in front of Sigurd.

The Icelander looked up to see his adversary clutching at the hilt of the weapon impaling him. al-Silb opened his mouth to speak, but all that came out was a gush of blood before he collapsed.

Blood was also soaking the silk clothes of the man who lay before him – the man who somehow managed to grin and say, "It seems I'm not to be a sailor after all, my captain..." before the light in his eyes was gone.

Saemundsson struggled to his feet. He had no time to mourn as another soldier advanced on him. They'd not yet realised their commander had fallen. Even when they did, they'd likely still go on with the battle – their assault seemed largely directionless anyway. An unexpectedly low sweep of the broadsword took the Berber's legs out from under him, literally. Sigurd seized the opportunity and ran for the line on the dock. The last few surviving crew followed close behind.

Lars Longshanks was the last of the Norsemen seen to go down under a Berber blade. Any dreams of mercenary wealth or glory that the young man may have had died with him in the dust of the Zawaian waterfront.

Finally realising the object of the seafarers' run, a group of the soldiers charged after them.

Most of that number stopped hurriedly as the Norse guards stepped forward together. The guards parted only enough to let their shipmates through before their axes cut down the already battered pursuers like saplings. The remaining soldiers stood back, panting, their white robes filthy with dust and blood – their own and their opponents'. It dawned on them that no orders were forthcoming. Not in a language they understood, at least.

Sigurd was barking orders even as he leapt aboard *Serpentfang*. On the two knarrs ropes were already being caught as they were flung from the dock. Long poles pushed the cargo boats out into the water as the oar crews went to work.

The guards backed towards the longship as quickly as they could without taking their eyes off the Zawaia military. At their captain's command they clambered aboard his ship. Bjarni was the last of the Norse to jump from al-Andalus after he'd freed the final mooring rope.

It was only when they were well out into a calm sea that Saemundsson was able to get the three vessels manoeuvred side by side. He'd hoped for a small island, but there were none to be seen, so discussions had to be carried out by shouting from boat to boat. They'd counted their missing, with no choice but to count them as dead even if no one had seen a particular individual fall.

Revenge was often a powerful motivator for Norse fighters, but Sigurd was first and foremost a pragmatic man. There was no practical gain to be had from returning to Zawaia bloody-handed. The shrewd businessman in him was adamant that they head south. He related Andres' advice about trade prospects, and the Berber situation.

"What happened to the man who called himself 'The Sword", anyway?" asked Corri. "I'd more than half expected him to sail with us."

His cousin was silent for a moment before replying, "That was his plan, yes. His plan and mine. He fell under the blade of Uthman al-Silb, a blade that was meant for my neck. It wasn't the first time this day he saved my life."

"And what about that swine Uthman? Did you avenge the swordsman?" asked Sverrir.

"No need. The last thrust of Andres' own sword did the deed." Sigurd briefly and bitterly described the moment.

"So at the last, their blood ran together in the dust before you," mused Corri. "That's the stuff of stories, cousin, and I'll write a fine one honouring him and all of those we lost in al-Andalus, I promise!"

Looking about the three ships under his command, Saemundsson smiled tightly and replied, "Do honour to all who sail with us, Corri, the lost *and* the living. Now, I feel a breeze beginning to stir. Set sails, and let's find the fortune we just earned!"

.ooo.

6

MOROCCO – TRADE WORKS

The southerly breeze that had sprung up very conveniently brought the three ships into a fast moving current going in the same direction.

As the daylight faded, the braziers on deck were lit. The wounded had been patched up, with those who were capable working already. For two sunsets, the mood on the boats was sombre as their losses sank in to the collective consciousness. At the captain's insistence the language lessons continued, on his own boat at least. If anything, the events in Zawaia had reinforced for him the importance of communication for all of them. Members of the crew went about their duties, or sat alone, or in small groups talking quietly.

On their third evening at sea Sigurd sat in one such group. Around him were Katrine av Ord, Hervor Elsdottir, Olaf Vaksson and Bardi Goosefoot. The latter two were among those who'd not been able to leave the boat in al-Andalus. They wanted to know about what had happened in Zawaia, but were tactful, particularly about the fighting.

Bardi was severely pigeon-toed, which hampered him somewhat in battle (his balance was never quite right) and had given him his descriptive name. Broad shoulders made him a powerful oarsman though, and he was as fiercely loyal as any of *Serpentfang*'s crew.

He was genuinely enthralled as the others described the architecture and design work on display. Not much had been visible from shipboard. He'd seen some of the small quantity of new stock that had been hurriedly brought aboard – enough to be intrigued – but it was the description of the exotic tiles and their application that really fascinated him.

It was while the captain was indulging his oarsman by describing in as much detail as he could recall a black-and-white geometric patterned wall that a cry came from the lookout.

"Looks like fire on a shore ahead!"

Striding to the prow, Sigurd stared into the night. His eyes took a moment to adjust after the light of the brazier but yes, there it was. A glow on the horizon that could only come from some sort of settlement. He directed that *Serpentfang* be steered out of the current as much as possible, which proved no difficult feat. As they aimed eastward the character of the water beneath the keel changed as suddenly as stepping from an icebound river to a rocky embankment.

The sail was furled and the boat turned to allow the breeze to blow past without propelling them further.

Instinctively recognising the point of Saemundsson's actions, the captains of *Stormbearer* and *Red Whale* followed suit. Soon all three ships were bobbing in placid water, still some distance from the low dark mass of land that was barely discernible in the starlight.

"We'll make for shore in daylight," was the order.

Watches were set, and those who were able to, slept. There was a palpable sense of anticipation among the crew, from the captains down. Their first venture into an unknown port had not gone well, and now they were about to land in a place of which they had even less knowledge. The Norse were brave, not foolish.

The rising sun stirred everyone into action. Well drilled and disciplined, the oar crews propelled the three boats landwards. At a signal from Sigurd in the prow of *Serpentfang* they slowed as they approached the shore. The captain scanned what lay ahead.

It was a much smaller settlement than Zawaia. A few stone buildings rose from among a collection of huts. As the Norseman watched,
several small boats set off from the shore by the village. By the time
they neared each other, Sigurd could see that there were fishing nets
strung between pairs of the small crafts.

He signalled to Fafhrd at the tiller to give the native boats as wide
a berth as possible. He had no wish to disrupt their activities – he
wanted this interaction to be a positive one. It was a shrewd decision,
as swarthy fishermen waved grateful acknowledgement to the longship as it passed at a comfortable distance.

The knarrs followed in the wake of *Serpentfang*, their crews
receiving similar salutation from the locals. The unfamiliar shape of
the large vessels provoked curious looks from some of the fishermen,
but there was no indication of hostility. Following their preferred
practice, the cargo boats waited a little way off shore while the longship advanced.

Not for the first time, Saemundsson was grateful for the shallow
draft of his boats. There had been a sudden rise of the sea floor and a
broad shelf extended to the coastline. It was this piece of geography
that provided the local fishermen with an excellent supply of such
fare as sole, turbot, eels and crabs.

The longship glided onto the beach. The captain was among the
first to set foot on the unfamiliar soil where a small crowd had gathered. The majority were recognisably of the same race as Uthman al-
Silb's troops, with a few even darker faces among them.

But there were some key differences to the Zawaian soldiery:
many wore long tunics instead of robes, instead of steel helmets
there were turbans and short red flat-topped hats, clothes were in a
wide range of colours and patterns instead of plain white, there
were few weapons visible, and perhaps most importantly, the
majority were smiling. The prospect of trade, it seemed, was
welcome here.

The local dialect was close enough to the Berber that Katrine had
taught for them to understand and be understood. A few different
words and phrases, and what were to both sides puzzling pronuncia-

tions, but there was nothing that could not be overcome by people of good will.

In short order the signal fire was lit, and the two knarrs joined *Serpentfang* on the beach.

The village was called Anfa, and according to local stories had stood in the same spot forever, being rebuilt several times when the earth shook and the homes of men were destroyed.

This cycle would continue long into the future. More than 750 years later an earthquake at the site would destroy the Portuguese colonial town of Casa Branca, only for it to be rebuilt again to serve as an important man-made port protected from the sea by a breakwater.

That lay an unfathomable time ahead. For now, Anfa mostly survived on its fishing industry, slowly but increasingly supplemented by the trade of goods from the southern and eastern interior bound for northern markets. Although very rare, this was not the first Norse vessel to arrive there in living memory.

It was evident that the political strife of the great peninsula had not made an impact in Anfa. There was said to be trouble brewing between tribes in the distant mountains and cities to the northeast – eventually the Almovarids would supplant the ruling Magrawa – but for now this western outpost was not significant enough to be fought over. For as long as this meant the people of Anfa could quietly go about their business undisturbed, they were content.

The tribes were the largest social units in Berber society, but they were only loosely organised, especially in a community such as this. Such administration as there was existed in the form of the jama'ah. This was a gathering of all the reputable adult men, and was held in the village square.

"Not dissimilar to our own Althing," Hrolf observed, with interest.

The parallel development of such administrative structures so far apart seemed to him to be reinforcement that this was the right and natural way for men to govern themselves. The 'authority' of a remote monarchy was an artifice, imposed and sustained by and for the greed of a few.

Discussing this later with Cailin Ruiteach, Hrolf was pleased to have her agree with him. He did find it awkward though when the Irishwoman observed that the obvious flaw, both here and at home, was the absence of female voices at the gatherings.

Anfa's marketplace was not yet a permanent institution. Rough stalls in the streets outside some huts provided most of such everyday goods as the locals required. Otherwise, whenever an opportunity arose the merchants would gather their wares in the village square to compete for the attention of traders who arrived by horse or camel or boat.

It would take a day or two for all of the local sellers to assemble their wares. One in particular, Ya'la by name, pleaded for time that his agent (actually his nephew Jawhar) could return from an assignation with a regular caravan in the foothills to the east. The young man had been gone for three sunsets now and would surely return within one or two more at most. He had a good horse and always made good time. And he would surely return with such treasures as to make the wait very worthwhile for the esteemed visitor.

Ziri, the most senior of the local chieftains and thus the main spokesman, if not actually leader of the small group dealing with Sigurd, smiled at Ya'la's request. However, he explained to the fair-skinned trader, there was some validity to the plea. He knew the caravan that the young man was meeting, and knew that it often yielded unusual items from the far east.

The captain was impressed that the Anfa merchants were so mutually supportive. They were definitely competitive, but also aware of a collective responsibility to make their marketplace as appealing as possible to attract return trade. It was definitely a long-term view.

A few days in Anfa represented no sacrifice for the Norseman. After the drama of al-Andalus and their hasty departure he was happy for the crew to enjoy some time ashore.

It was hardly a bustling metropolis, but most of the northerners came from places not much bigger. Climatically very different, of course, but that could be coped with for a little while, especially with the prospect of good business to be done.

One of the stone buildings served as a tavern of sorts. The owner

Yeddas primarily sold food, but he also kept a stock of the local version of beer. It was brewed from the local maize, and while very different to northern beers it quickly proved popular with the crew. The lack of alternatives helped.

Much of the local diet was made up of the fruits of the sea. That was a familiar situation for the sailors, although some of the flavours and preparation were decidedly different. But compared to the pungency of fermented and dried shark meat – the Icelandic delicacy called hakari – most of the cuisine was easy on the palate. The exceptions were those dishes flavoured with a fiery red spice. They contributed to Yeddas' beer sales.

Despite the welcome that the trading vessels had received, Sigurd insisted on maintaining a guard and minimum crew on each boat. Anfa itself seemed quite safe, but there was no knowing who or what might come from land or sea.

A few of the more adventurous seafarers experimented with activities like riding camels some little way inland. Stories of the beasts' truculence and unpredictability, and of the swift discomfort to tender areas of the anatomy, caused much mirth in the tavern and aboard the boats.

When it was discovered that the bow and arrow were weapons of choice among some of the locals a number of the sailors, Olaf Vaksson among them, invested considerable time in honing their skills with the unfamiliar weapons. Their captains, stung by thoughts of how the brief time in Zawaia might otherwise have turned out, encouraged the exercise. Sigurd even put up a fine decorated leather belt and some good goblets as prizes for a hastily arranged archery contest.

There was nothing like competition to spur a northerner. Most of the awards would stay in Anfa, a young man named Donas being well pleased with his new belt, but the men and women from the boats acquitted themselves well. Both Olaf and Anna Sjelsdottir managed to earn a goblet of their own. Pall Jansson bemoaned his luck that errant gusts of wind had spoiled what would otherwise surely have been winning shots. There was a chance he may even have been right.

Many more of the crew simply enjoyed stretching their legs and relaxing. Katrine made a point of seeking out anyone fluent in any languages beyond what was spoken locally. She was a natural linguist, and even in that short time was able to pick up small vocabularies in a few new tongues.

The sun was high over Anfa when the little team of horses led by Jawhar appeared in the east. The young man was delighted to get such an enthusiastic reception from Ya'la – his uncle had seen samples of the northerners' wool. It got seriously cold at night up in the mountains, and Ya'la knew the material would be highly prized by his trading partners there.

It would be appropriate, Ziri said, if the market took place the next day. Ya'la might have hoped for more time to examine his new stock, but the other merchants had already waited long enough, he conceded.

Andres' advice in the streets of Zawaia proved to be sound. The Anfa marketplace revealed exactly the sort of goods that had inspired the long trip from Hofn in the first place, plus more, and stranger.

There were gold ornaments set with gems and exquisite pink coral. Silks and spices from the east. More of the dark and fragrant woods, carved into both ornaments and weapons. Glassware in dazzling colours, some of it as thin as eggshell – beautiful but impractical for a long sea voyage, agreed Sigurd and Hrolf. Colourful cloth woven, apparently, from a plant fibre called cotton. Hides of animals the Norse had never seen. One was recognisably from a horse, but what horse was ever emblazoned with such wonderful stripes of black and white?

And there was silver. Plenty of it, as jewellery, ornaments and coins, all of which were highly prized by the Norse.

In their turn, the merchants of Anfa took particular interest in bolts of woollen fabric, reindeer antlers carved and uncarved, and a number of the small hand weapons that had come from Iceland or been obtained from al-Andalus.

There was another type of item in the visiting trader's stock that attracted much attention.

Elephant ivory had become scarce in the north of the continent over the past few centuries. The herds had died out as the climate had become drier and the remnant animals hunted to extinction. The ivory trade to the east, through the fabled kingdoms of Nubia and Kush and the routes leading up to Baghdad, was lucrative enough to swallow up such of the great beasts' tusks as were still in circulation.

The walrus ivory carried by Saemundsson's expedition was thus highly prized, despite it being in a form so much smaller than the elephants' tusks. It didn't hurt that Corri was able to quietly convince some of the more credulous local merchants that the sea mammals' teeth were unicorn horns and a 'universal antidote' to all manner of poisons.

Corri's imaginative flair combined well with his cousin's shrewd bargaining skills and they traded well, loading the knarrs with silver and gems and bolts of fine cloth. The silk was a luxurious change from the furs and wool that made up most of the seafarers' clothes, and while the cotton was less extraordinary to the touch, it was a most sensible option for clothing in the heat. A good quantity of spices and exotic hides also made it aboard.

As the daylight waned the trading drew to a close. It had been a busy day for the traders, both the locals and their fair-skinned visitors. Saemundsson was weary. For all that he willingly delegated a lot to his other captains and senior crew, so much of what had been on offer was new and unfamiliar that there'd been a steady stream of "What do you think...?" and "Look at this!" conversations on top of his own sometimes intense negotiations.

Tired as he was though, he was exhilarated. This was what had led him to travel so far. Not the travel for its own sake, or greed for the potential profits to be made. That profit was certainly a welcome prospect of course, but even if he could not have named it, what truly drove Sigurd was curiosity. Things he hadn't seen or experienced before fascinated him. And again, although he may not even have recognised it in himself, he shared with Bardi Goosefoot a

special appreciation of bold, striking designs such as the tiled walls
and floors of Zawaia, and the fabulous striped horsehide found
here.

In return for a token handful of silver coins the captain
contributed a barrel of his own supply of ale to Yeddas' stock that
evening.

While Corri held court inside the stone building, reciting some of
the old tales, with Katrine alongside him practicing her Berber by
translating as he went along, the captain sat in a little circle outside.
The group included Sverrir Bent-Knee, Olaf Vaksson, Ziri and the
still grateful Ya'la.

It had occurred to Sigurd that contrary to Jon Far-strider's advice
he'd seen no evidence of slave trading. Ziri shrugged. Theirs was a
small community, and that was a business profitable in larger centres.
Ya'la confirmed that some of the caravans he traded with on the
inland road included shackled lines of miserable black folks from far
to the south. They were a commodity of no value to him, although
well regarded by some in the northern coastal markets, and in distant
Baghdad.

Ah, Baghdad. Again that name, thought Sigurd. The Anfa
merchants could add little to his sum of knowledge of this place. It
held the same legendary status for them as it did for the Icelander,
although they at least had some more familiarity with the goods
flowing to and from its gates.

It was said to be a round city, grandly designed and built. It was
the centre of trade across the world. It lay on fertile ground, a long
way from the sea. A river called Arvand Rud joined another called
Ufratu, and thus goods were conveyed from the ocean to the south of
the great city. Quite where these rivers met the ocean was unknown.
'A long way east' was the unhelpful consensus.

What was known, though, was that there was an important civi-
lization of black-skinned men to the south. Possibly outposts of Kush
or Nubia, wondered one of the locals. Like Baghdad, these were
places known only by name and reputation. The southern black men
were keen traders. They dealt in slaves, captives from other tribes in

surrounding areas. Their markets were also the sources of many of the items that had most attracted Norse interest.

Rather wistfully, Ziri conceded that Anfa's market was still small. He well understood that Sigurd had reserved a good percentage of his own inventory for other, more attractive opportunities. Graciously he suggested that such opportunities lay further south. He stressed though that the three ships would be more than welcome to come back on their return voyage.

Fired by enthusiasm after the successful trading, Saemundsson and his 'command group' decided when they gathered next morning to set sail for the vaunted markets of the south as quickly as possible.

One final day was spent in the village. Trade goods were sorted and stowed securely. Those that were going to fetch high prices at home were positioned in the furthest reaches of the holds on the two cargo boats. Items that were expected to prove valuable in the southern markets in the near future were, of course, made more accessible.

A supply of the local bows and arrows was also acquired. They were smaller and lighter than the northern ones, but would be no less deadly in appropriate circumstances, and now more of the seafarers were ready to accept the potential value of the weapons.

Provisions were brought on board – some of the local maize, both as grain and coarse flour, and a quantity of dried fish. They were assured that there would be plenty of fresh catch available on their journey but better to take no chances in unknown seas. What Sigurd couldn't obtain as much of as he'd wanted was fresh water.

It wasn't an abundant resource in Anfa. There was enough for their own needs, usually. Times of drought were not unknown, and there were plans afoot for a better system to capture the water of the storms that intermittently struck. But until the proposed cisterns were installed there was only enough to be spared for a few casks to be loaded on each vessel.

Nonetheless, spirits were high as they headed back out into open water.

It seemed sensible to again ride the fast southerly current. With full sail the three ships would make excellent speed without taxing the resources of the oar crews. The air movement from the rate of their travel went some way towards relieving the oppressive heat that was steadily building. Cloth had been rigged to provide some shade on deck, but it also seemed to restrict air movement, trapping the hot air down with the crew.

Only old Sverrir Bent-knee aboard *Red Whale* started to become a little uneasy with their passage. He 'felt' the current through the timbers of the knarr, and realised that they were gradually accelerating to a great speed. There was nothing wrong with speed of course, but these were unfamiliar waters. He set the most keen-eyed of his crew on watch duty, and kept himself ready to alert the other two boats. Sigurd was a fine captain, and Corri too was proving more than competent, but neither had his experience. That experience had honed his mariner's instincts, and those instincts were starting to prickle the scant grey hairs on the back of his neck.

Even as the sun sank, they were continuing at a breakneck pace that worried the veteran sailor. Evidently Sigurd too grasped the value of caution, as *Serpentfang* had her sails furled to reduce speed. The captains of the knarrs followed that lead, an action that Sverrir was quite relieved to take.

Starlight revealed the shapes of some islands away on the western horizon. The current was drawing the boats closer to them, although it didn't seem to be dangerously so yet.

Unbeknownst to the Norse, these were the Islands of Dogs. Named by early Roman explorers for the primitive people who dwelt there apparently worshipping the local wild animals, later people would know them as the Canary Islands, and the swift current as the Canary Current.

There was nothing to prompt the Icelandic captain to steer for the islands. The lookouts saw no concentration of lights to suggest a settlement. The Guanche people then living there were primitive relatives of Berbers who mostly had a Stone Age culture. That would not change much for another three centuries. Such substantial pockets of population as existed were to be found on the more westerly islands, well out of sight of the passing sailors.

Approaching an unknown shore in darkness would be an unnecessary folly. There was no knowing what hazards might lurk in the waters around land. Better to enjoy the safer depths the current was following.

By sunrise, the islands were far behind and lost to view. Satisfied that the ocean ahead looked clear, Sigurd ordered the sails to be raised again, and once more they travelled at a high speed.

Their direction was southwest rather than due south, but frequently their passage brought them to within sight of the mainland shore, albeit sometimes fleetingly. At such times there could be seen neither evidence of substantial occupation nor a river mouth that might offer replenishment of their drinking water. But there seemed no cause for alarm.

That was until the later part of the afternoon. As the sun had fallen from its zenith so too had their following wind dropped. Less obvious at first was the slowing of the current, although the more experienced and intuitive sailors were quick to realise it. Ahead there was another current flowing from the opposite direction. Where they met was an area of leaden stillness.

By the time the sun neared the horizon they'd almost come to a halt, with only the remains of their momentum propelling them onward.

Under oars, the three boats were brought close enough together to allow the captains to converse. The sky was clear. It was agreed to move the vessels to a safe distance apart in case conditions changed overnight, but to otherwise remain where they were.

With the dawn it would be time for the oarsmen to bend their backs and drive the vessels east towards the coast. Once shore was sighted they would follow the coastline until they found a landing site that looked likely to offer some rest for the rowers, and the all-important water.

Those who'd hoped that darkness would bring significant relief from the heat were disappointed. The blazing sun may have gone but the air remained hot and heavy right through the night.

The light breaking on the eastern horizon promised a day of swelter for those on the oars. Still, those oars meant movement and escape. The crews of much bigger, very differently designed sailing ships in coming centuries would pray for such escape after days or even weeks becalmed in similar circumstances. These latitudes would become known as the Doldrums, and break the spirits of sailors for hundreds of years.

.ooo.

7

SENEGAL – THE CALM AND THE STORM

The rowing took hours. Respecting the weather conditions, the captains rotated the teams as often as possible. There was no point in exhausting the crew any more than could be helped. But sweat still streamed from bodies, whether actively at the oars or not. Their limited supply of fresh water was going to be a problem soon if it couldn't be replenished.

It was Sverrir who felt the change in the sea, even before the shore appeared as a ribbon on the horizon. The effort of propelling the boats became even harder. But their hopes lay in the very reason for their new difficulty, as they were heading into an area where a delta emptied into the ocean and the tide was running against them.

As they approached the shore watchful eyes scanned the little islands that dotted the outer edge of the estuary. The rhythm of the oars slowed. Waters like these were notorious for shoals and sand-bars. Even the shallow keeled Norse boats could strike trouble if they weren't careful.

In a cautious procession the three vessels picked their way toward the broad mouth of the river. One island stood out as being some-what larger than the rest, and as they pulled nearer wisps of smoke could be seen rising from the far side of it.

With a signal to Fafhrd at the tiller of *Serpentfang,* Sigurd directed his boats towards the origin of the wisps. Smoke meant settlement.

What they saw as they rounded the island was a village, built on the side of a low hill. Judging by its present distance above the water-line there must be some big tides here. The buildings were a cluster of round huts, each with a conical thatched roof. As a settlement it wasn't even as impressive as Anfa, but it was better than bare earth.

As usual, *Red Whale* and *Stormbearer* hung back while the long-ship slid onto the beach. A few small shallow drafted boats lay nearby, tethered by long ropes to poles driven deep into the sand.

Flanked by Katrine av Ord, Olaf Vaksson and Pall Jansson, Sigurd made his way up the beach. Had it not been for the rising smoke the captain may have wondered if the village was deserted. By the time the quartet had neared the first few huts there was still no sign of human activity.

Then suddenly a small figure dashed through the straw curtain that covered the doorway of the nearest hut. Olaf automatically reached for his sword, and had it half out its scabbard before recognising that there was no threat. The running figure was a little girl.

She stopped before the foursome, panting. Whatever game she'd been playing had left her out of breath. It took a moment or two before she looked up – when she did her eyes widened in her small dark face.

Olaf had left a daughter of about the same age, perhaps five, back in Iceland. Instinctively he smiled and squatted, bringing his face down to the same level as hers.

"Hello," he said.

In reply the girl giggled. Evidently the Norse word and accent sounded funny to her.

A voice called from within the hut, and the little girl shouted a reply. She made no move to run away from the strangers though. A dark skinned woman emerged through the curtain and stood uncertainly watching the tableau before her.

Sigurd smiled and stood with his hands held open to signify that he offered no threat. Katrine and Pall followed their captain's lead, although the latter's smile looked awkward, it not being an expression he used much.

Olaf stayed crouched, wincing slightly when the child tugged at his beard while she spoke in a happy babble to her mother. Katrine listened to the torrent of words and thought she recognised a few that she'd learnt in Anfa. She called out to the woman what she hoped was a polite greeting, and was relieved that she seemed to be understood.

Tentatively, the dark woman approached. Sigurd mused to himself again on the wisdom of applying real effort to communicating. In truth, in this instance the words were less important than the simple trust of a little girl and the gracious way in which her simple welcome had been greeted.

It took the exchange of a few sentences for Katrine to work out which of the dialects she'd tried to pick up in Anfa was most useful here, but the two women were soon able to at least make themselves understood.

At the sound of voices, other people started to emerge from surrounding huts. Nearly all were women and children, with three old men tottering among them. Their attitude was one of curiosity more than fear, which pleased Sigurd. He felt too tired for tension.

With Katrine's help he introduced himself, explaining as best he could where they were from and what they were looking for.

Fair skinned men were not unknown here, but it had been many, many seasons since any had visited. This explained the reaction of the children – those past visits must have been before many of them were born.

The first girl to have met them, Mati by name, took great delight in showing off her new friend Olaf to her companions. The bearded sailor didn't object. He rather enjoyed the attention, even when Katrine quietly suggested to him that at least some of the attraction might have been from the curious fact that his name sounded so similar to the name of the tribe – the Wolof.

With diplomatic caution, the Norse enquired about the apparent absence of men in the village. Mati's mother Mareme

explained that the men were making one of their customary journeys up the river for supplies. Little was actually grown here - this
was primarily a trading centre for boats that made their way up and
down the coast.

That news delighted Saemundsson. It didn't require a long
conversation with the women and the old men before the captain
gave his signal for the brazier to be lit, calling in his cargo boats.

One of the old men, gorgui they were apparently called,
attempted to silence the women and do all the talking on behalf of
his people. Irked by the attitude, Katrine instead made a point of
addressing herself to Mareme and some other women who were keen
to converse.

This seemed to greatly amuse one gorgui in particular, who
clearly put his companions in their place. The grateful Mareme introduced this man as Samba, the village's griot – a word that was eventually translated as 'storyteller'.

Enquiries about the village's chief, called here the borom dekk,
drew wry looks from most of the locals. While they were meeting
with their new visitors, Baye the old borom dekk, was sound asleep in
his hut.

Samba did loyally point out that most of them who weren't
actively involved in caring for boisterous children had been sleeping.
That was the wisest thing to do at the hottest part of the day – stay
inside in the shade, and get such rest as was possible. It just
happened that Baye slept less lightly than others.

There was both diplomacy and common sense in that observa-
tion. Black folk and fair were baking under the sun that was still too
high for the huts to offer much exterior shade. Sigurd told Pall to
meet the knarrs as they landed and have some large sheets of cloth
brought ashore. The boats were to be moored on long ropes, he said,
noting the ties of the small local craft.

He also instructed that only a few from each vessel make their
way to the village. It had seemed a genuine welcome, and he didn't
want to give the impression of an invasion force. He hoped to bring
more of his crew into cooler conditions soon, but only after relations

with the locals were on a firmer footing. Actually meeting this borom dekk, for instance, seemed appropriate.

It was little Mati who suggested a solution with her own preferred way of beating the heat, excitedly begging her mother to be allowed to go into the water. When Mareme smilingly agreed, Sigurd realised that the conditions must be quite safe. No mother would allow her child out into somewhere treacherous or populated by hungry sharks, he rightly reasoned. (In fact there were some dangerous rips around the island, but this beach was well sheltered from them.)

Leading her new friend by the hand, Mati headed for the beach, chattering excitedly and making introductions. "This is Sili, she's my best friend. And Oumy – she's my best friend too. This is Mory. I like him even if he can't swim as well as I can..."

Olaf grinned broadly as most of the babble washed over him. Children were children wherever they were, it seemed. He seldom really missed his own offspring – the sea was his true mistress, but moments like this did stir some wistfulness for their simple affection.

With his captain's happy permission, he shouted a message to his shipmates that they should cool themselves in the shallow waters, as long as some stayed aboard the boats in case any sudden action was required. Soon the sandy inlet was a happy, if incongruous, scene of small black bodies and large pale ones gambolling in the wavelets, tumbling and laughing. Childlike joy was infectious!

The village and the island where it stood were called N'Dar. More than six centuries later a colonial power called France would rename it Saint Louis, and build a large fort there as a base for their own trade operations along the coast and up the Senegal River.

As instructed, Pall brought three of the crew back to the village with him, bearing rolls of cloth. These were slung between the thatches of huts that were suitably close together, creating some patches of shade that allowed the sailors and villagers to sit together as a group without crowding into anyone's home.

Old Baye eventually roused himself (it having been generally agreed that no one would volunteer to wake him, his temper under those circumstances being notorious). The borom dekk was astonished to find N'Dar's population had more than doubled while he slumbered, but warily accepted Samba's assurance that the newcomers meant no harm. Mareme offered a similar endorsement, but that mattered little to Baye. She was, after all, only a woman.

If the chief caught Katrine's low growl it didn't mean anything to him. Sigurd laid what he hoped was a calming, or at least restraining hand on his translator's leg. If the newly arrived Corri noted that his cousin's hand rested there longer than was diplomatically necessary, he wisely didn't mention it.

The men of N'Dar had only left that very morning. Their departure explained the small number of the little local boats on the beach. They would paddle up to Dagana, or even beyond into the country of the Tokolor people, depending on trade. It would be days before they'd return.

"Is there anyone who could or would conduct trade here in the men's absence?" Sigurd enquired.

Baye announced that he had the authority to conduct business on behalf of anyone and everyone in N'Dar, although the sharp-eyed Norse noticed expressions on a few faces that suggested this wasn't entirely true.

That point was largely immaterial though, as there was little in the village to be traded anyway. The paucity of trading stock had meant a diminished quantity of food. Anything interesting, at least - anything beyond the basics that the villagers grew or caught themselves. That, in turn, had meant that it was time for the adult males to set off on their regular journey up-river for supplies. N'Dar could survive on their diet of fresh and salted fish, millet and the few vegetables they grew, but obviously it was preferable to supplement those rations.

"So, what is it that you trade here?" asked Sigurd, as curious as ever about mercantile matters when the gorgui and a few of the more insistent women had gathered in the shade with the senior trading crew.

For local consumption, the main exchange was of various types of fish for rice, meat and vegetables that grew well in the floodplains inland, and for a cheap durable cloth. The boats that plied their trade along the coast bought and sold richer fabrics and items such as gold, ivory, slaves, beeswax and ostrich feathers.

The description of these tall flightless birds stretched the credibility of the northerners, until they saw a few of the plumes themselves. They clearly came from a bird, but it was no surprise that anything big enough to bear that plumage wouldn't be able to get off the ground. Wonders abounded in these parts.

That thought prompted Saemundsson to ask about the exotic hides of the types they'd obtained in Anfa and Zawaia. To his surprise, although such creatures and their pelts were well known in N'Dar, they were seldom traded, and never kept on hand. Leather, or the processing of it, was unclean to the Wolof, signifying something from their primitive past.

Bemusing as that was, the captain hid his disappointment and concentrated on what, if anything, he might profitably acquire. There was little of commercial value, although some gold ornaments were worth bargaining for. A quantity of the locally produced honey was also welcome, both being obtained in exchange for a supply of axes and knives. These were of only modest quality by northern standards, but an improvement on most of the village's tools.

One useful item was a supply of a thick gum, the resin of an inland tree, that Samba explained was particularly good as a waterproof caulk. It was the sealant of choice for the boats of N'Dar, he said. Gratefully, Sigurd set some teams to work patching up places on the keels that had suffered some warping under the hot sun, or been scuffed on rocks as they'd sailed close to shore.

What was most important to the seafarers was drinking water, and that turned out to be abundant. Although the incoming tide could sometimes wash the sea's brine many miles up river, fresh water was still in plentiful supply from a handful of wells dotted about the village. Casks and barrels on all three ships were filled and sealed ready for the next leg of the voyage.

The sun was still strong when several of the women set a fire going in the rough plaza that was the centre of the village. Baye,

Samba and Mareme insisted that the visitors should move from their shaded spot to sit in the plaza. That puzzled the Norse, especially when it seemed the main purpose was to produce more smoke than flame, and the evident intent was to sit amongst that smoke.

It was soon apparent why, though. Down by the water's edge sailors had started slapping at small biting insects that appeared as if by magic as the sun dropped. Mosquitos weren't a problem on the open sea, but here their bites swiftly became a torment, both at the seashore and on the outskirts of the village.

Once he grasped what was happening, Sigurd sent word that the braziers be lit on each boat. Aminata, who was apparently the older sister of Mareme (she was introduced by Mati in a term equivalent to 'Aunty Ami'), handed over several branches of a particular bush. The smoke of the bark and leaves of this plant especially repelled the hated insects. Gratefully accepted, they were immediately dispatched to be added to the braziers.

When sailors began to turn up in the village sporting livid red lumps where they'd been punctured, Aminata made a tsk-ing noise and returned to her hut. She soon returned with a paste made from honey, spit, and the ground leaves of this repellent bush. To the delight of the afflicted sailors this concoction took the heat and itch from the bites almost immediately.

One of the huts operated as a communal kitchen for the village, and from this a meal was prepared for everyone. Several types of fish were prepared, again in ways unfamiliar but quite acceptable to the travellers. The Norse contributed the last of their stock of the ground-maize flat bread from Anfa, and a quantity of dried fruits which were combined with honey, spices and boiled rice to make a surprisingly delicious sweet dish.

There was no beer as such, but there was an ample quantity of a fermented millet and honey drink that bore some resemblance to mead. Sweeter on the palate than the northerners' usual fare, it was more potent than it tasted. In the course of the evening it would relax some of the seafarers rather more than they'd expected.

Good quantities of all of the dishes were sent down to those still stationed on the boats. Those conveying the food noted that they were wading into deeper water to reach their mates than had been the case while they were all frolicking earlier.

Over the meal, Sigurd raised the question of the slave trade mentioned fleetingly earlier. He was puzzled that the village would be left so unguarded by the men when such traders routinely visited.

"Why otherwise?" Baye asked.

The more astute Samba explained that it was only ever strong healthy men who were traded as slaves. Warriors and workers were required, not women, children or gorgui. Every place had plenty of them already.

The Norseman had more than an inkling that this was not universally true. He and Katrine shared a look that said they both hoped N'Dar would not soon fall victim to a much harsher reality.

A different type of foliage was put on the fire as the sun set and the whine of mosquitos decreased. What was wanted now was light and some heat, rather than smoke.

Assorted groups formed around the fire. Some were made up exclusively of sailors chatting amongst themselves about the curious people they found themselves surrounded by. Others were groups of N'Dar locals holding very similar discussions. But there were several where there was a mix of both races doing their best to converse by gesture, pointing, and the exchange of such words as they were able to pick up.

Many of the children were in one group together, with a half-dozen of their mothers, Olaf Vaksson and some other seafarers for whom the little ones triggered fond memories. Giant Odd Arisson belied his threatening size by delicately tootling on a little flute he'd carved. In turn, led by the precocious Mati the children sang their favourite songs. The words and rhythms were strange to northern ears, but the experience was simply joyful.

At another part of the circle, Corri and Samba took it in turns to tell stories. The grizzled N'Dar had earlier managed to explain to his counterpart from *Stormbearer* that the job of the griot was to be "a messenger of his own time, and in doing so become the creator of the future". The knarr captain had stared at Katrine as she'd haltingly assembled those words. It was, he realised, a fine summation of the role of the sagas in his own culture.

So, as he spoke, Corri didn't just tell the old tales as he normally might have. He made an effort to recount the adventures of their voyage so far, embellishing only slightly the story of Sigurd the World-Farer. Just enough to embarrass but quietly delight his cousin.

Both men delivered their narratives slowly, giving Katrine and Mareme the opportunity to collectively translate for their mixed audience. The two women had quickly established a rapport, sharing an intuitive gift for language.

Katrine had mused to herself that it would be very good to take the N'Dar woman with them on their travels, but it was clear she wouldn't be willingly separated from Mati. Not unreasonable, and the child was far too young to be taken along. Although, looking across the fire at Olaf and his group, it seemed likely there would be no shortage of sailors who would look out for the girl!

Faces black and white began to yawn as the fire burned down. Many of the sailors were as sleepy as the children, especially those wearied by rowing. Some curled up where they'd been sitting around the plaza, others made their way to sleep on the soft sand or back aboard, on or below deck according to comfort. A small number accepted invitations to spend the night in a hut. Among them was Bjorn Breakneck, led quietly away by a woman named Astou. Unlike his captain and mentor Sverrir, Bjorn's love affair with the ocean was not to the exclusion of all others.

Guards were set in shifts on the boats, more from routine than real concern.

Although no less tired than many of his crew, Sigurd struggled to sleep. After a while of staring up at the stars, he got to his feet and quietly paced the deck of *Serpentfang*. He wore a fond smile as he surveyed his slumbering sailors.

There was Hervor, clearly troubled by the heat. Face down and naked on a length of cotton, with only a trailing corner of the fabric pulled over her lithe form to provide any pretence of modesty. Her knife and axe were right by her hand though, he noted without surprise. Olaf Vaksson sitting propped up against the mast, snoring with his head on his knees. Dreaming of children – his own or the little ones of N'Dar, the captain wondered?

Looking over onto the beach, he watched those who'd settled into the still-warm sands. It seemed that all had managed to remain above the tide, by now past its peak and falling steadily. They looked like peculiar nesting birds, but comfortable. Doubtless Pall Jansson, for all that he slept well now, would by morning be complaining about the fine white grains making their way into sundry uncomfortable places.

Near Pall lay Anna Sjelsdottir. Sigurd realised that she was curled up with one of the local women – Sindjely by name, he recalled. Mildly surprising, but he was not a man inclined to passing judgement on others on anything but their ability to carry out their appointed tasks. Let the likes of Erp try to dictate morality.

Erp. He thought he'd managed to forget that wretched priest, but there he was, lurking at the back of his mind like an uninvited wedding guest. Was the young rogue having his way with Thordja in her husband's absence? Saemundsson doubted it, he thought she had better taste. It mattered more to him that the priest didn't get his hands on the business holdings. Sigurd spat into the sea, and walked on.

He exchanged nods with Bjarni, standing watch at the tiller beside the sleeping form of Fafhrd. The steersman would take up his regular position in the morning when they set off again.

N'Dar held little appeal for a longer stay. Sigurd realised that boredom, a bad companion, would quickly set in if they tried to wait the unspecified number of days for the men to return. It didn't seem likely they'd be returning with a lot of trade goods worth waiting for anyway. There were traders beating their way up and down this coastline regularly, so there must be markets further south offering better prospects.

The captain looked up at the star filled sky. No clouds between the sea and the crest of N'Dar's hill. He sniffed the air. Sea salt, and the whiff of smoke from the smouldering fire. A faint trace of the insect-repelling smoke still clung to his moustache as he stroked it. Yes, moving on was the right choice while conditions were so fair.

Facing the sky he almost stumbled over a figure lying on the deck wrapped in a dark cotton sheet. It was Katrine av Ord. Sigurd looked down. Her long hair spilled across her face like a dark wave in the starlight. He was no more aware of the smile on his own face than he was of her barely opened eyes looking back at him. Then she opened those eyes fully, and their startling blue glittered. Wordlessly she lifted the sheet. She was more modestly draped than Hervor, but not by much. Sigurd accepted the unspoken offer.

Scant hours later, refreshed by more than the brief sleep he'd finally managed, Saemundsson was among the first to rise. The stars were still out, but the early signs of dawn were visible over the river to the east. The tide was on its way back in and the sun would rise quickly here. All three boats were soon bustling with activity as the shift changed.

Tubs of porridge were prepared on each of the vessels, using some of the local millet they'd obtained and sweetened with honey for a change.

Those sleeping ashore, on the beach or elsewhere, hastily made their way back to their boats. Nobody elected to stay behind, but the numbers increased by two as both Astou and Sindjely chose to remain with the northerners they'd coupled with overnight. It seemed neither had children, or any attachment to any of the men up-river. None that they wanted to continue, anyway.

The captain had some doubts about this, although both women were adamant in expressing their willingness to work at any task they were given. Still, he expected that they'd make landfall again soon and could leave either or both ashore if he saw fit. At least they spoke a local language or two. He would get Katrine busy learning all she could, and passing on that knowledge as rapidly as possible.

If any of the crew had taken any note of the captain and the interpreter together in the early morning, no one mentioned it. Relationships were a fact of life on board a ship. Some were fleeting, some endured. Gossip would inevitably eventually rebound on whoever bandied it about, so only the newest to seagoing life fell into that trap, and they quickly learned their mistake. Couplings between crew-mates only became an issue for the captains if they had an impact on discipline. When that happened it was usually the job of each boat's 'enforcer' to take appropriate action after consulting their commander.

Of course, if the problematic relationship involved either a captain or their enforcer (or both!) things could be tricky. It might require some intervention from those at the head of the other two vessels, thankfully not something that had ever arisen in this company. The matter had crossed the mind of Hervor Elsdottir on more than one occasion, but she was resolutely professional. As far as she could ever tell, her captain knew her only as a completely loyal, reliable and efficient comrade.

Indeed, she'd worked so hard at crafting her image that Sigurd had given up on any other ideas he'd earlier entertained. At best he had moments, such as under the previous night's stars, when he looked at her and thought, 'what a waste...'

This morning she'd dressed early and done her best to shake off some lingering effects of the honey drink. She wasn't alone in feeling below her best after the potent brew, but if anything that only less-ened her sympathy for anyone else showing signs of not working hard enough.

Woolly heads were in such abundance, though, that the tasks of securing goods and provisions still took more time than usual to complete. The new seals had to be checked, too. Samba hadn't over-sold the gum. Whatever cracks and gaps it had been applied to seemed watertight. It had set thoroughly and set hard, although the old griot had assured them that it would flex along with the timber as much as required.

As it was though, all tasks were completed to Sigurd's satisfaction (and thus Hervor's) by the time the tide turned, and they would be able to ride the current back out of the delta.

It seemed that most of the available population had turned out to farewell the Norse. Clearly they'd made an impact, seen most clearly in the row of children jumping and waving at the water's edge as the boats pulled away. Hauling on a rope to raise a sail, Olaf couldn't free a hand to wave back. The children with the keenest vision could see the expression on his face though. Mati knew that the bearded man was smiling just at her.

The sails were going up because there were the first stirrings of a wind coming from the north. The intention was to try to catch the wind to propel them as far as possible away from the area of dead water they'd hit previously, without again taxing the oarsmen too much. Then they'd hug the coast until they found the trading centres they knew must exist in this direction.

What Sigurd and his crew didn't know – indeed, couldn't know, as none had ever sailed this area before – was just how mercurially the weather could change. From dreadful, mind-destroying, seemingly endless stillness to the most appalling of hurricanes, in a matter of minutes. The seas of the Doldrums were, and still are, frighteningly unpredictable.

They'd not long reached the open sea when they saw what the encouraging tail wind was really bearing. It was Fafhrd who spotted it first, looking back south from his tiller, casually checking on the following knarrs.

What he saw was a bank of cloud starting to billow over the horizon to their north. Heavy, black and menacing, it seemed less to be borne by wind than to be forcing a gale on ahead of it. Even as the seafarers watched the storm front advance, they felt the strength of the wind rising rapidly.

The only chance was to turn, and try to make it back into the relative shelter of the delta under oars.

Sails were dropped and furled. Steersmen threw their weight, and the weight of companions, at the tillers, straining to force the rudders to turn the ships around. The oar crews strained against the tide.

Time defeated them, emphatically. The three boats simply could not make haven before the hurricane overtook them.

Sigurd and his crew had battled foul weather before. The terrible conditions around Eirik the Red's Northern Camp in Greenland were so bad as to be legendary. They'd survived them on a voyage north a few years earlier. But this freak event off the African coast was the stuff of nightmare. Neither sail nor oar had any chance of prevailing against the wind and waves.

The storm caught the boats and bore them away from the shore-line wildly. Running aground on that slightly familiar environment seemed a preferable option to the swirling screaming hell they found themselves in.

The three crews had lost sight of each other's vessels within minutes of the massive typhoon having struck. Sometime during the worst of the howling gales and torrential downpour, one of the ships was truly lost. Ironically, it was the ship named *Stormbearer*, with Sigurd's cousin Corri and twenty tons of cargo aboard.

Whether it was struck by lightning, swamped by a giant wave, or foundered on some treacherous reef or marauding sea serpent, Sigurd and his remaining crew would never know. The knarr and all on board were simply never seen again.

For what seemed like a moment there was an unearthly stillness as the eye of the storm passed directly over them. Sailors drew ragged breaths, some emerging from whatever places they'd secured themselves to look out through the rain that still fell. It was then that they realised *Stormbearer* was gone, but had barely time to register the loss before the hurricane's eye had moved on, and hell opened up on them again.

The other two ships were driven south - the direction they'd intended, but at an unguessable speed in unmanageable chaotic conditions. How far they were flung was impossible to tell.

Equally impossible was estimating how long it took for the storm to finally pass over them. It felt like hours. Perhaps it was. By the time the mass of clouds had flown south ahead of them the sun certainly stood much higher in the sky than it had before the disaster struck.

Even after the storm abated the Norse sailors realised that their situation was dire. Hastily tied lashings had been torn asunder. Sails were ripped and many oars damaged. The brass weathervanes of

Serpentfang had been ripped loose and sent spinning to oblivion. *Red Whale*'s side rudder had been smashed.

Yet a terrific current followed in the hurricane's wake. Here the prevailing current should be north, the counterbalance of what they'd ridden days earlier. But in the trail of the massive storm the sea ran a full 180 degrees from its usual direction, although the north-erners had no experience to give awareness of that.

As *Red Whale* held the richest of their remaining bounty, Sigurd refused to abandon her to the racing southbound current that the rudderless knarr was trapped in. *Serpentfang* and her crew were in little better shape to fight the conditions anyway – easier to trust the gods to bring them to a landfall where they might undertake some repairs.

Saemundsson and Bent-knee took stock of their own vessels – the injured and the lost. Some had been washed overboard, such as Lars Magnusson. He'd last been seen trying to grasp a flailing rope to secure the tiller, even his brawn no match for the wave that had smashed over the stern and swept him to oblivion.

Sverrir had lost one of his best steersmen, Arne Arnesson. He'd been huddled at his station when the side rudder was torn to pieces. The tiller that he'd spent half his working life at flailed uncontrol-lably, staving in the luckless Arne's skull.

There were others, on both ships. Men and women whose final moments had gone unnoticed in the nightmare.

For some, the mental toll was almost as bad. The two N'Dar women cowered down in the hold of *Serpentfang*, both on that vessel at the time to share languages with Katrine. They'd known hurri-canes before, but never at sea. Even more traumatised were several of those who'd chosen to join the journey at Cahercommaun. They'd never known anything like that terror, and for some the experience was overwhelming. One's heart had given out, and two more could do nothing more than stare, drooling and moaning, out over the water.

Even the resolute Cailin Ruiteach was struggling. With a mighty effort she got the least damaged of her Irish compatriots together to set about restoring some order to the space below decks. The hardest thing was the stench of vomit, forever now in her head as the smell of uncontrollable fear. Opening exotic perfumes didn't help. Relief only came when the recovering Astou put a flame to small bundles of dried herbs and sticks she'd carefully selected.

The bundles produced a heavily scented smoke that seeped into the ship's timbers, crowding out the more noxious aroma.

The surviving sailors were exhausted in mind and body. Sigurd could only track their southeasterly direction by the sun. The relentless, blazing, burning sun that now seemed to fill the sky. The fair-skinned crew suffered badly.

Saemundsson did his best to arrange duties to permit as many men as possible to huddle in shelter and makeshift shade while running the ships as best they could. The longship was carefully trimmed to run as near as was safely possible to the cargo boat that was wholly driven and steered by the current.

The first tantalising sight of distant land was fleeting, gone before any useful action could be devised. Determined not to be so frustrated again, Sigurd managed to manoeuvre *Serpentfang* to a position where long ropes could be thrown between the two vessels.

It took some superb seamanship, but when land was next sighted Sigurd was ready. The two boats were hauled together, hull to hull. A barrier of leather shields was thrown in place to try to protect the ships' timbers. With the tiller of the longship providing steering, and rowers on both vessels straining their throbbing muscles, the Norsemen were able to take a diagonal course across the current and finally out of its powerful grip.

Much impressed by their effectiveness in his own hold, Saemundsson had more of Astou's little bundles prepared and thrown over to *Red Whale*. She suffered just as vile an atmosphere below the main deck. Sverrir was profoundly glad to be able to make what was, in many ways, the primary work area of his boat, an easier place in which to breathe.

The storm raced on ahead, fortunately not doubling back on itself as they sometimes do. The freak current eased off as the more usual northward flow began to reassert itself. In any case, the waters closer to shore were considerably calmer, and they were able to make their way along the coast seeking a safe harbour.

Somewhere quiet and still, with shade and water. Somewhere where they could recover, and grieve.

.ooo.

8

GHANA – TREES OF LIFE

They were called the Bambara people, and their home was called Denga. To the Norse, they were a gift from the gods.

Was it only a day after the terrible storm that they found themselves sailing into the sunrise as they limped along the shoreline? Sigurd didn't dare to wonder if they'd inadvertently chanced upon the route to the river port that serviced Baghdad. For now, his only thoughts were of survival.

Four times since that storm they'd tried to get to what looked like promising places on the coast.

Once, their passage was blocked by a band of reefs and sharp rocky ridges that rose near the surface of the water, too dangerous even for their shallow keels. It would have been a perilous passage under the best of circumstances, but with their ability to steer so badly compromised, the boats would have no chance.

Then a small fleet of canoes, filled with screaming black men who hurled long spears and brandished clubs, had cut off a foray shoreward. The northerners should have easily overwhelmed such foes, but it was more than their ships that were damaged. Bodies were battered and broken, and spirits little better. They fired a volley of their arrows to keep the screaming men at a distance and then pulled back to more open sea, frankly relieved that the howling mob didn't decide to pursue them.

That night they'd seen the lights of a few fires along the shore, but after the previous two experiences there was no appetite for attempting a landing in darkness. They'd bobbed in the now placid current, gnawing at some dried fish and savouring some of the water from casks that had come through the typhoon undamaged.

A third prospect had looked good in the morning light, almost all the way to land. It was only then that they got a good look at what had appeared to be a large number of floating logs just off shore. One of the logs seemingly yawned, its gaping mouth revealing a set of terrible teeth set in long jaws that could crush bones in an instant.

There were more of the great lizards lying on the shore. No prospect at all of bringing the boats in amongst that lot for repair. Here there really were dragons!

On the last occasion the outbound current of a big river was simply too strong for the exhausted oar crews to overcome. They'd washed back to deeper water as the teams slumped at their rowlocks.

When the cluster of wooden buildings came into view as they rounded a cape, few dared to hope any more. The settlement seemed quite large and well established, set against the backdrop of a tall lush forest that it seemed to have been carved from. It was sitting alongside what from a distance looked like little more than a good-sized stream. There was no telling what reception awaited them, but what choice remained?

A change of direction was now the cue for a change of manpower as Sigurd tried to marshal his rapidly waning resources. Another team shuffled into their positions at the oars. It was Sindjely who took up the position in the prow from the weary Katrine, and now called the rhythm in her own tongue. The rowers dully recited as they sweated, barely registering the words that crept into their brains.

The conjoined keels crunched onto the pebbled shore together, and were quickly surrounded by a cluster of very black men and women. Some of the northerners clutched at their weapons, but as they reeled it was obvious they were in no condition to fight. The spirit may have been willing, but the flesh was far past it.

Fortunately there was no need for the weapons. These people had no interest in conflict. They were simply curious, and at the sight of their strange visitors' obvious distress, concerned.

They were Bambara. Their home, this place, was called Denga. The new arrivals were welcome. All of this they tried to explain as they helped the people from the sea off their craft. Among the new arrivals, the two women of similar colour to the Bambara showed some signs of understanding.

What had been fair skin shone bright red and blistered. Arms hung limply from sagging shoulders and bent backs. Bruises, dried blood, and the distortions of broken bones showed on many of those who almost fell onto the beach. The hardiest, or most stubborn of them, dragged themselves to their full height.

One such was a solidly built man with a rough beard and a long, salt-crusted moustache. He looked into the eyes of the Bambara man who'd put a hand out to catch him, and grasped the extended arm.

"Sigurd," he managed to say, evidently by way of self-introduction, before his knees buckled.

It took a few days for the strongest of the sailors to recover. For many it took longer. Some never truly recovered from the ordeal of the typhoon, either in body or in mind, or both.

One man simply walked out into the sea before anyone realised what he was doing. By the time his intention was clear, he'd walked into a rip that whisked him away as if he'd never been there. Another, a veteran oarsman and fighter who'd been with *Red Whale* for nearly as long as her captain, just stopped eating or drinking. Stopped everything, in fact. He hated the ocean now, he'd told Sverrir a few nights after their landing at Denga. It was Sverrir who found him the next morning, sitting on a log, apparently staring out to sea. The eyes weren't staring though, they were glazed. No sight. No breath. No heartbeat.

As he recovered, Sigurd moved among his crew, offering all the encouragement and support that he could muster. But in truth he was a man at war with himself.

The sailor in his head knew that these terrible things happened at sea, and was thankful for his own survival. The businessman cursed the losses, and began to plan how they might be recouped. The cousin, the friend – they mourned.

Standing one night on the flat roof of one of Denga's buildings, looking out to sea, it was the mourner who was aware of Katrine at his side, an arm around him. He should perhaps be concerned that any of his crew thought he needed to be supported, but damn it, yes, he *did* need that, right at this moment.

"Do you still wonder what marvels are out there in the markets of the world?" she asked quietly. "Because *I* do."

"You want to go on?" Sigurd asked, uncertain of his own answer.

"Yes," the woman replied simply. "When enough of us have healed to be able to manage. When the ships, and crew, are... repaired. I can't speak for everyone of course. I'm one of those who has, well, really nothing to return to, so onward will always be my choice. Others have families and loved ones..."

She left unspoken the suggestion that he was one of those 'others', but Sigurd had caught it.

"I have a wife, yes. And we loved each other once, in our way. That memory will always be there I suppose, but that's what it is, a memory. For a long time now, it's been my business that drives me. Does it drive me home?" he mused, talking to himself as much as to Katrine. "Home, indeed... *Serpentfang* has become home. My crew, my family. Loved ones. Loved *one*...?"

Suddenly he found her finger pressed to his lips even as he'd turned to look at her.

"No," she said. "Not now. You need to grieve and to heal too. We both do. If we can manage that together I'll be more than glad, my dear captain, but for now, no declarations, from either of us."

He nodded, but embraced her anyway, burying his face in her hair and finally letting tears flow. Losing Corri, especially, felt like it had torn a hole in him, and it was a relief to let the pain express itself.

The pair stood together like that for some minutes, until finally Sigurd drew in a deep breath and took a small step away. He rested a hand on the railing that edged the rooftop.

"There is another option to be considered. Staying here. How many might find that appealing?" the captain wondered.

"Make this Denga a home? Not a lot, I'd reckon! You can ask, but I think most will want to either sail on, or sail back."

"I think you're probably right, Katrine. But I not only *can* ask – I must. Those who want to remain, well, so be it. For the rest, it can be a motivation to heal body and mind. The sooner the boats are repaired, the sooner we can set out for... wherever is agreed. If a great majority wants to return to Iceland I'll have to accept that. I can't compel an unwilling crew otherwise. Sailing requires discipline and co-operation. But my own preference is, yes, to go on."

They shared a final hug and a lingering kiss. Then they stepped apart, almost shaking themselves back into their formal roles, and set about assembling the crew to discuss their immediate future.

Chief of Denga was a large, flabby man named Dak. Extremely lazy by nature, he was nonetheless a clever fellow, and generous. The people of Denga were happy to let their guests use the large building that was their equivalent of the longhouse. It was known simply as 'the hall'. All the crew gathered there, with even the most injured pleading that the pallets they were confined to, be carried into the assembly.

With Sverrir beside him at the centre of the room Sigurd outlined the three options that he saw, scrupulously avoiding making his own preference too obvious. Any and all were invited to contribute to a discussion, but very few did.

Red Whale's captain spoke passionately against remaining in Denga. He appreciated all their hosts had done, and were doing, but for a Norseman to quit sailing was to quit life itself, he swore.

One of the Irishmen worst affected by the hurricane sadly replied that, for him, returning to the sea would feel like walking open eyed into the jaws of death. If Denga would have him, he would stay and hope to repay the kindness they'd been shown.

A few shared that sentiment, most of whom were from Caher-commaun. Two Norse sailors, a man and a woman, confessed to having been defeated by the storm. They too wanted to stay, and make some sort of new life here together.

Cailin was emphatically not among the Irish who wanted to stay here. She'd left one situation that was in terminal decline, she said, and had no intention of moving into another. The captain wondered what the big woman had seen or heard, and resolved to ask her later.

To Sigurd's surprise (and silent delight) there was only one who spoke for a return to Iceland. Olaf Vaksson talked about his family. He admitted that until recently he'd only thought of his children in a distant, detached way. N'Dar had changed that, and after coming so near to death in the storm, he was troubled by the thought of not seeing his little ones again.

But Olaf finished by saying that he'd sworn loyalty to Sigurd Saemundsson. Whatever the decision, he would stand by that oath and support his captain with heart and hand.

No one else wanted to speak after Vaksson's declaration. Sigurd allowed a few minutes for contemplation and quiet conversation among the assembly, and then put the options to a vote. Overwhelmingly, the preference was to move on.

The captain smiled his appreciation. Perhaps they would find the way to Baghdad. Perhaps they would find other wonders. He hoped they'd find an opportunity to turn north and perhaps make their way home via the eastern coast of this great landmass they'd sailed down. But they would keep going.

The days and weeks that followed saw the slow recuperation of the crew, and the gradual reconstruction of the boats. The Bambara offered to help, but that assistance was usually confined to the provision of local knowledge and advice. Few actually lent a hand to any labour.

There was no doubting the hospitality of the Bambara. They'd nursed the injured, and tried to comfort those sick in heart and head. Water was plentiful. The swift stream that ran alongside the settlement was much deeper than its width, providing consistently cool clear drinking. Dak's community gave freely of food, such as it was.

Their diet seemed mostly to consist of starchy roots: boiled, fried, or pounded into a gritty paste as the base for a barely palatable gruel. Flavouring came from a variety of berries and leaves from the abundant forest. Sometimes birds would be plucked and cooked, but there was no organised hunting – it was left to individuals to stock their own larder.

Archers among the Norse crew were tasked with helping in this activity when they could be spared from boat repairs. Both the hunting, and the making of new arrows, became significant parts of how the seafarers spent their time.

Likewise, the northerners applied such resources as they could to fishing. This was another haphazard activity in Denga, inexplicably, given the proximity to both fresh and salt water. Had they applied themselves, the locals could have maintained a steady regular supply, just as their visitors did. But there seemed to be no appetite for the effort. For the seafood itself, yes, when it was offered, but again it was left to individuals to seek their own sustenance when the mood took them, and for most that didn't seem to be often.

Beyond shaking their heads, there was little that the seafarers could do, other than feed themselves and offer to share any extra. The main focus had to be on getting *Serpentfang* and *Red Whale* seaworthy again.

The cargo had been stripped from both vessels and was stored in a nondescript wooden building whose owner had died recently. A guard was posted at all times – the least demanding job of all in Denga, it seemed. No one had expressed the slightest interest in the boxes and bundles as they'd been moved to allow access to the interior structure of the boats.

It was the ideal opportunity for Cailin to list every item of their surviving inventory on some of the sheets of vellum brought from Zawaia. Tightly rolled for storage, it was a far lighter material than the cumbersome squares of hide that had formerly been used.

Ropes were repaired. Mercifully few had been lost, and there was less damage than there would have been if they'd been fashioned from anything less resilient than walrus hide. These were trimmed and respliced where necessary. A hardy jungle creeper was found in the forest that promised fair service as a replacement for those lost, if properly treated.

Some of the N'Dar gum had survived the storm and was applied to fractures and splits in otherwise sound timbers. Not all of the planks could be repaired though. The decking had suffered more than the hulls. That was fortunate, as these timbers were considerably easier to replace. When the supply ran low, the local people were able to produce their own equivalent. It took longer to dry, and proved a little less flexible in its final state, but it would be adequate.

Red Whale was in worse shape than the longship. Losing the side rudder had been bad enough, but Sverrir was aghast to realise that two of the great support timbers that gave shape to the keel had fractured. It must have happened when the knarr had been twisted in the grip of the storm-lashed waves. It was ironic that the long straight split logs of the hull had actually weathered the storm better than the ribs that were meant to brace them together.

This was not damage that could be repaired. Their only option was to replace the pieces.

The people of Denga had not been seafarers for many generations. Shipbuilding was a lost art to them. But the forest that fringed their home was rich in many types of timber. Surely something there would do the job?

Sigurd and Sverrir had to hope so. Selecting crew members with requisite knowledge or experience, they sent two parties into the surrounding jungle to examine the timber options. The trees themselves were unfamiliar, but they knew the characteristics they needed. Strength, some flexibility, not too heavy. A Bambara went with each party to assist, not least with identifying local hazards like poisonous berries and the likely hiding places of anything venomous.

All but the most injured were kept busy, and even the invalids had tasks to occupy them, like mending sails and splicing ropes.

Katrine had everyone trying to learn new languages. Astou and

Sindjely taught the language of N'Dar, and proved valuable in bridging the communication gap with the locals. The Bambara tongue was just similar enough to their own for them to find some common words and expressions. These were the first steps to conversations, steps that Katrine av Ord keenly took together with the dark skinned women.

The Bambara had a written language too, although they seldom now used it. It seemed a complex combination of scratches and symbols that defied all Cailin's efforts at understanding. Particular symbols didn't represent particular specific sounds. She could learn what certain combinations stood for, but then find an almost identical set of characters would mean something entirely different. Whatever logic underpinned it was beyond her.

Eventually, once her inventory had been completed, she took her frustrations out with a mallet, alongside other brawny shipwrights bashing newly cut dowels into joints.

The constant pace of industry by turns amused and bemused the locals. They had adopted a lifestyle that ran on doing just enough to get by. Till the soil, sow and harvest as required. Create, construct or repair only when necessary. Eat when hungry, drink when thirsty, sleep when tired. It was not uncommon for the time between those activities to be spent sitting in the shade of a tree watching the small waves roll in across a whole day.

And telling stories. Denga loved stories. Corri would have rejoiced in the place, thought his cousin without a hint of bitterness. He and some of the others did their best to fill the void he'd left.

It was Hrolf the Dark who proved best at this. He would sit in the middle of the hall in the evenings with his shield lying face down in front of him. From the hollow boss in its centre he'd pull out a leather purse. This was a twin to the one in which he kept his set of trading weights – only he knew how he told them apart at a glance.

In the purse were small objects like coins, shells and stones of unusual colour, shape or texture. Each had been collected or gathered somewhere they'd made landfall, even if only briefly to scavenge supplies.

Every piece had a story. Many, like the silver coin from Zawaia, had several. Each night, Hrolf would randomly draw one item from his purse and relate a story from their journey.

The Bambara were fascinated by what they were able to understand, and simply by the sound of the sailor's rich voice as he tried to duplicate Corri's melodic rhythmic style. For his crewmates, the stories brought laughter, excitement, and sometimes tears. Slowly but surely, they also brought healing.

The work progressed. Usable timber was found and shaped. The hulls of both ships were reinforced, and the rudder of *Red Whale* replaced. Sigurd, Sverrir and Hrolf inspected every fitting and fixture. A splint was added to the mast of *Serpentfang* when her captain detected a tiny hairline fracture running lengthwise, less than the length of his thumb.

It was painstaking labour, made all the more taxing by the heat and especially the humidity. The air would become heavy and damp over days, then one night there would be a cloudburst. The thunder of rain on wood panelled roofing would wake them, or the streams of water running through seals not replaced in years.

But by morning, the rain would have passed. The heat continued, and the moisture was drawn back up from the damp ground to stultify the air again. A breeze from the sea brought a little comfort in the afternoons, but the encircling forest cut off any other relieving winds. Perhaps it was these conditions that had nurtured the lassitude that was typical in Denga.

For all that the constant activity was alien to them, some of the Bambara took to staying near to their visitors. The work fascinated them, and some could clearly watch it all day. It was a good opportunity for the seafarers who took to heart their captain's advice about the importance of communication.

Taking his turn at guarding the cargo, Fafhrd sat in the shade of a tree overhanging the abandoned building. He was painstakingly carving a talisman to attach to the new tiller of *Red Whale*. The design was the same as he wore on his pendant.

Sitting in front of the steersman was a Denga man named Mar.

The two fellows were about the same age, but that was where the resemblance ended. Fafhrd was fair and burly. His observer was small, thin and very dark. But his eyes were bright and alert.

Mar was gazing in fascination at Yggdrasil, the world tree depicted on Fafhrd's pendant. He sensed by the Norseman's behaviour that it was an object of some spiritual meaning. For his part, Fafhrd was intrigued by the other man's interest.

They managed a long and painstaking conversation. For Fafhrd, the tree represented the centre of the universe, and the connection of all things. The branches and roots connected the nine worlds: the worlds of mist and fire, the realms of the gods, men, giants, sorcerers, elves and dwarves, and the land of the dishonoured dead who were barred from Valhalla, the great hall in the gods' world Asgard. The great ash tree linked all, and through it elements of each world sustained others.

He was surprised to find that in local tradition, the same tree (or something very like it - Mar pointed at a grand old fig tree as he explained) represented one half of the spiritual universe – the 'world below'. A vine symbolised the 'world above'. To indicate the world in which they currently dwelt, Mar pointed out another type of tree, a grenadine.

Curious, Fafhrd mused, that these people so far from the centre of creation should have such a clear understanding of the nature of the universe. An almost identical thought was in Mar's mind.

Over subsequent days they continued their philosophical discussions, slowly learning fragments of each other's language. *Fu*, Fafhrd learned, was the Bambara's prime creative force. *Fu* had brought forth knowing, *gla gla zo*, which in turn had given rise to physical and spiritual existence.

Fafhrd saw a similarity to the emergence of Ymir, from whose body the earth had been made, out of Ginnungagap, the primeval ice. He had difficulty explaining this concept to Mar, who knew nothing of ice. The helmsman had to settle for something like 'a great emptiness'.

Later, Mar told of how the spirit *Pemba* made the earth and *Faro*

made the sky. After he'd created the heavens *Faro* gave life to the
earth, making in succession plants, animals, water and fish, then
determining the seasons and separating day from night. Then *Faro*
gave order to all the creatures, including men, according to the quali-
ties of their blood. That, Mar explained, was where *Faro* inscribed the
destiny of every tribe.

As well as the local religion, a few of the Norse were able to piece
together some of Denga's own story. Generations ago – the phrase "in
my grandfather's time" was clearly more symbolic than accurate – it
had been a thriving administrative centre for a kingdom that lay an
unknown number of miles inland. A supply of ivory, gold and gems
had flowed down for trade with ships that traversed the coastline.

Then the kingdom had expanded. Cities were conquered, and
new centres established. A new port had been built, far away. There
was a natural harbour there that could accommodate bigger vessels
than Denga's pebble beach. The flow of goods didn't dry up, it
stopped almost overnight. Most of the population had moved on to
pursue their opportunities elsewhere.

Those that remained were the old ones who'd formed some
emotional attachment to the place, or were simply content with the
simple life it offered. A comfortable subsistence that still remained
today, Dak had said.

In many ways it was a relief when the two boats were reloaded,
provisioned and ready to return to the water. For men and women
who were seafarers by choice, the existence here was suffocating.
With only a handful of exceptions they were all eager to be under sail
as soon as they could. Even some still hobbling, with broken limbs
still bound, wanted nothing more than to get away.

Sverrir spoke for a lot of them when he said, "Even being battered
lifeless by a storm is a better option than a slow death of sweating
tedium."

Just as on the day of their arrival, a crowd gathered on the beach
as *Serpentfang* and *Red Whale* were propelled back out into the gentle
surf on the ebbing tide. A few fair faces were among the dark faces of
Denga. Were they wistful? Perhaps, but they'd made their choice and

would stick by it. None of the locals had chosen to take a place on the boats.

As, for the last time, he looked back to the settlement that had saved them, Sigurd sighed sadly. He had come to understand Cailin's disparaging remark at the assembly to determine their plans. This was a stagnant, dying community.

The forest was slowly encroaching on their buildings, and their lassitude would see them fall easy prey to any raiders. The only thing sparing them from attack thus far was the scarcity of their resources – anyone arriving there would quickly realise the situation.

Virtually all of what goods had remained from times past had been spent, admittedly on food. Water was plentiful, and the root vegetables and a few types of fruit. But they'd almost run out of live-stock. The northerners had realised (with shock and embarrassment) that they'd helped consume the last of the settlements' pigs. Other than migratory birds, the Bambara had hunted most of the reason-ably edible wildlife to extinction, for their own food and for trade.

It was the stripping of resources that Cailin had recognised as congruent with what she'd left behind in Ireland.

Here the soil was still fertile, and there was an abundant supply of fish, but the will to exploit them was gone. Perhaps the few Irish and Norse who wanted to stay would be able to inspire some among the Bambara to make Denga thrive again.

Otherwise it would eventually disappear back into the forest. The wooden structures would collapse back into the soil, and the only traces of its existence would be fragments of metal, pottery and bone for future generations to stumble upon.

.ooo.

9

ANGOLA - IRON IN FLIGHT

They'd sailed east for days. Sigurd had privately begun to hope that they might actually find the river of Arvand Rud spoken of in Anfa, and thus Baghdad. He had to conceal his disappointment when the coastline they were tightly following changed direction and they had to continue south.

The heat and humidity remained oppressive. Hugging the land took away some of the benefits of offshore breezes, but the captain was determined not to miss an opportunity for trade and provisions. The shade cloths gave some welcome relief.

In the holds, sailors worked scantily dressed or even naked. On deck though, this quickly proved impractical. Terrible sunburn incapacitated for days the first few fair skinned men and women to try the gambit. Some would never lose the scars.

Cotton and silk were the fabrics of choice. Those who'd not already acquired clothes on their travels crafted robes and tunics. Weird and wonderful headgear was fashioned to protect faces (and thinning scalps).

A number of settlements were spotted and visited as they sailed, but none for any length of time.

Some were ruins, including what had been the city that usurped

Denga's status. There was no way they could tell that the kingdom had long ago fallen, and the people of the new port had been slaughtered or enslaved.

Other more substantial places, cities even, proved disappointing in their own ways.

Some were outposts of an empire whose rulers had, for their own obscure reasons, decided to close their borders to the corrupting influence of the outside world. Water may be taken on board, and such supplies as small traders on the waterfront may sell, but access to the cities themselves, and the markets that once thrived, was forbidden. These were the last days of that empire.

Others were not unwelcoming, but their merchants were simply not interested in Sigurd's stock. They wanted the practical, not the exotic. They already had the fabric, spices, dried foods, even the gold and silver of those up the coast from them. And the northerners' own goods held no particular appeal. Wood was wood, however well carved. They still had ample access to the great tusks of elephants, so sea ivory meant nothing to them. And what use was a heavy material like wool in their climate?

A few places had traders that were interested in some of their goods, but could offer little or nothing worthwhile in return. Poor quality carvings, brittle timber and some ornaments in a substandard gold that squashed easily between thumb and forefinger. Sigurd obtained a few interesting hides to replace those on *Stormbearer*, including some from a bizarrely shaped animal with a neck the length of a tall man, and some leather won from the type of fearsome dragons they'd encountered before Denga.

There was one town where the locals were only interested in the heavy axes and swords the Norse carried. Sufficiently interested that it took the enthusiastic application of those weapons to keep thieving hands off them.

At one point, they crossed paths with a wide-bodied boat ploughing its way under sail in the opposite direction. No one on board answered any of the northerners' hails though. Noticing that the deck was crowded with naked dusky figures chained together at the neck, Sigurd was content to pass the slave ship by without further contact. Not a trade he liked, nor, he was finding, traders he trusted.

Several times they sailed through storms. There had been a natural fear among many, especially when circumstances meant that there was no prospect of seeking safe harbour. But nothing came near to what they'd experienced off the delta, and after riding out a second storm at sea the crew were largely back to their old confident selves.

Even so, when he saw a dark, dangerous-looking cloudbank massing far to the stern, Sigurd chose discretion and signalled for them to head for shore.

They slid the boats onto a small beach between low cliffs. There were several of these in close proximity; the cliffs jutting like a row of pointed dark teeth into the ocean. Even as he ordered the boats to be secured, the captain hoped the natural stone walls would provide good protection from the rapidly approaching storm.

It turned out he wasn't alone in that thought. As sails and shade cloths were being stashed below decks two canoes skidded in on the choppy waves, narrowly missing the longship and the knarr. It was as well they did – the small boats were quite flimsy and weren't likely to have survived the collision.

A half dozen black-skinned people jumped from each boat. They looked at the northerners uncertainly, but clearly had greater priorities. They pulled their own boats well up onto the beach, and then scrambled into shelter among the rocks and clefts at the base of the stony ramparts.

'Local knowledge', thought Sigurd. He had Olaf Vaksson, Anna Sjelsdottir and a few others jump ashore. At a nod from the captain, Sindjely followed. They took long coils of rope in the hope of securing the ships if they started to shift, and found themselves positions among the rocks. They made sure to be well away from the breaking surf that the storm was now whipping up.

The storm was intense, but mercifully brief. Big waves crashed in, but none of the boats were damaged. Not even the canoes, one of which was spun sideways and tumbled up the beach some way.

As the wind dropped and the rain eased, the dark folk emerged to check on their craft. They kept wary watch on the much bigger boats. It was because their attention was thus engaged that they didn't at first see the sailors emerge from the rocks opposite where they'd secured themselves.

They almost jumped as one when Sindjely hailed them loudly. She'd shouted in the Bambara tongue, reasoning that it was the geographically nearest one which she was moderately familiar with. She got blank looks in response.

On impulse, she called a greeting in her own language, and was surprised to get a cautious, barely recognisable reply.

Watching from *Serpentfang*, Saemundsson signalled that none of the others on board were to move. No weapons were in evidence, and he wanted to see what would happen next.

Sindjely walked slowly forward, Anna and Olaf cautiously advancing behind her. Anna took the N'Dar woman's hand and squeezed it supportively. Sindjely turned for a moment and smiled her gratitude – she'd never been a diplomat before.

Two of the canoeists, including the one who'd answered her, stood their ground. Their companions went to the little boats and checked what was obviously an important cargo, tightly lashed in the pointed ends of the craft.

N'Dar language evidently bore enough resemblance to their own tongue for them to attempt a conversation. Sindjely shook her head, and gestured for them to slow their speech. The taller of them, a man with skin the colour of the hard wood Sigurd had been so impressed by, accepted the request and repeated himself slowly, emphasising each syllable. It was similar to N'Dar, but with many different sounds too, including a persistent click of the tongue,

Despite herself, Sindjely laughed. Hers was a language that relied heavily on intonation. To hear vaguely familiar words uttered like this was somehow childlike. Much as Katrine taught the sailors, she realised.

Realising that the man seemed affronted by her mirth she quickly apologised as best she could. He seemed to understand. Good. So much so that he held out a hand in a universal gesture of greeting.

On his deck Sigurd smiled. Perhaps it was simply that they obviously shared a respect for the ocean, but there was something about these people that instantly appealed to him.

With diplomatic caution, the captain joined the little group on the beach. The other canoeists had entered the stilted conversation once satisfied their precious cargo was safe. His own smattering of N'Dar was enough for him to introduce himself and make a polite greeting.

The tall dark man's name was K'pah. He wasn't any sort of leader, he said. Their people didn't have chiefs. Considering some they'd met, this didn't seem such a bad idea to Sigurd.

Sindjely explained that they were traders, but the word provoked a sudden fearful reaction. A few of the canoeists looked ready to grab their boats and take flight. K'pah caught the wrist of the nearest man and indicated the longship. Did they really think they could outpace such a vessel?

Besides, he said, there was something in the manner of this pale man that was entirely unlike the 'traders' they knew.

True, conceded a woman who'd been one of those quickest to react. She released her grip on the edge of the canoe, stood, and with difficulty, asked Sindjely what it was that they traded.

The answers seemed to puzzle the little group. By now Katrine had come to her captain's side. She had the intuitive skill to gently ask questions that untangled the knots of variant words and phrases. Eventually it became clear that the word the N'Dar used for 'trader' had a much narrower definition for these people. It meant 'slaver'.

Katrine's words, Sigurd's demeanour, and Sindjely's obvious freedom of movement all combined to reassure them.

After a brief private conversation, they invited the fair-skins to accompany them to their home. It wasn't far, and perhaps they may have something to trade?

Initially, Sigurd privately doubted this, but on second thought his merchant's instinct kicked in. A different environment, a people he'd not met before, who knew what might be found? One man's mundane object, used every day, might be a treasure to someone who'd never seen it. He'd heard of places where jade or even silver were so commonplace they went unregarded.

His offer to take the canoes on board *Serpentfang* and convey them and their paddlers to their home was politely declined. Once they'd set off, the captain understood why.

The little boats made good speed, so it wasn't too difficult to keep the longship and knarr tucked in at a safe distance behind them. But he quickly had to shift his vessels further out to sea. Sharp rocks jutted up from the breaking waves around the points of the protruding cliffs, more of them around each successive one. The canoes could dart between them, but the Norse boats could never match their manoeuvrability.

The worst concentration was around the southernmost jagged cape, but it was here that the canoes turned sharply. They skipped through a welter of obstacles that stood like black daggers in the surf, then glided past a flat stone ledge towards shore. Saemundsson's boats had to make a much wider turn to follow them, and a buffeting crosswind that struck as they crossed the line of the cliffs surprised the sailors. That explained the paddlers' choice to travel as close in as their impressive skill allowed. They were better equipped to handle waves than wind.

That last stone 'tooth' marked the start of a broad shallow bay, fringed with the same dark stone that formed the cliffs. Here, though, it had taken on the shape of a curving slope, rather than a sheer drop.

Shell fragments, tiny pebbles, and a coarse brown sand made up the beach that the boats were grounded on.

K'pah waved, indicating that their home lay up beyond the crest of the slope, out of sight of the beach.

The trader was puzzled when the canoeists appeared to start carrying their little craft up the bare rock. The mystery was quickly solved when they ducked into a cave, the opening of which was barely visible in the dark stone. Moments later they emerged without the canoes, but clutching the cargo bundles.

Again, K'pah waved for them to follow. Then realising that the much greater numbers would require some organising, he stood and patiently waited for a small group to catch up. That had been the Icelander's suggestion. He didn't want to risk a problem by having his people descend like a swarm on what he gathered was a modest settlement.

Sigurd did, however, allow many of his crew ashore. Stretching their legs was always welcome after days at sea. He did insist on a substantial guard to keep watch on the boats – the broad bay was a little too open for his liking. Sverrir Bent-knee agreed, and was more than happy to stay on the beach and take charge there.

There were nine in that first party to make their way up the slope. Sigurd himself led, of course, accompanied by Katrine av Ord, the reassuring presence of Hervor Elsdottir, Anna Sjelsdottir and Sind-jely (the latter to lend her assistance to Katrine's interpreting duties), Olaf Vaksson and Bardi Goosefoot both equipped to complement Anna's bow if required, and the valued muscle of Fafhrd and Bjarni.

Saemundsson was pleased to find that the 'security' elements of his party turned out to be unnecessary. K'pah's companions had gone on ahead. They'd excitedly given their friends and families a brief description of what had happened during, and more especially after, the storm. So the sailors' arrival caused more curiosity than concern.

As K'pah had indicated, there was no chief here. It was effectively a communal society with everyone having an equal say in running things. Gender didn't matter and neither did occupation. A fisherman had as much standing as a basket weaver, and both were the equals of any of the herdsmen who tended the small livestock kept nearby.

Such an arrangement held a lot of appeal for many of the Norse, particularly the women. Even Sigurd, who held by far the loftiest position of any of them in their own society, could recognise a lot of advantages to this even-handed system. People worked hard and worked cooperatively, for their own interests and the interests of everyone around them.

There might be a danger if cliques formed, or if one group of indi-viduals could somehow come to dominate the decision-making process. 'Odin knew, that happened often enough at the Althing,' mused Fafhrd. He couldn't imagine how his captain put up with the bickering. But there was no obvious indication of it here. Expecting the system to fail would be the typical negative response of someone like Pall Jansson. The nine members of this little group were impressed by the positive.

Several locals offered to guide their visitors around. There didn't look to be much to see – a neat but nondescript collection of conical huts walled by reed mats, occupying a small plateau studded with outcrops of the dark stone of the cliffs and slope. Nonetheless, tact suggested that the offer be accepted, especially after some of the hosts said that the remainder of the sailors would be welcome too, but could they limit their numbers to about twenty at a time? A bigger crowd might be difficult to attend to.

K'pah would remain with the captain and his group, together with an older man named K'rn and his daughter, also confusingly called K'rn. If there was a difference in pronunciation it eluded even Katrine's well-tuned ear. K'rn the younger had also been among the canoeists they'd first encountered.

As conversations staggered clumsily along, Katrine realised that the broadly similar tongue that had enabled K'pah and his group to communicate with Sindjely was not their native language. That was a so far baffling mix of clicks and consonants that landed on the ear like stones in a copper pot. What was shared with the N'Dar was a dialect variation of a very old language that must have once been used and spread by traders all along the coast they'd been following.

She wondered if what the Bambara spoke was actually closer to the ancient form? Perhaps the kingdom they'd once been part of was the source of the language. Or perhaps they too had absorbed it from someone else – someone older.

The word that the members of the community used for themselves was Khoikhoi. The linguist had worked out that it simply meant 'the people', or perhaps 'the *real* people', to distinguish themselves from others they encountered.

Certainly there were such others. Most especially the slave

traders mentioned before. Some came by sea. The descriptions of some of those – swarthy and hook-nosed - reminded Katrine and Sigurd of the Berbers and Arabs of Zawaia. More often they were taller, much darker men. The details of their appearance struck the Icelanders as being like their new friend K'pah. He was a little taller, darker, and more broad-shouldered than his companions.

Noticing their reaction the man admitted that yes, his mother's father had been a Ba'tu man. He stated quite openly that his grand-mother had been impregnated by force, and that it was only the generous spirit of the Khoikhoi that had seen his mother raised communally alongside their own children.

K'rn the elder explained sadly that the Ba'tu were the most consis-tent of their attackers, and had been for many years. Sometimes they'd come from the sea, but more often, a wave of raiders would come overland from somewhere to the north or northeast.

That was the direction where the Khoikhoi routinely posted sentries. At any sign of trouble the sentries would sprint back to the village shouting a warning so the Khoikhoi could gather to defend themselves.

As Katrine explained this to Hervor the lithe fighter shook her head in bemusement. As a defensive plan this had so many flaws she was amazed there were any of the Khoikhoi left! They must make up in ferocity what they lacked in strategy, she reasoned.

The 'guided tour' had taken them beyond the outskirts of the village proper. Amongst the huts there had been strips or troughs of greenery: narrow gardens of leafy vegetables and short hardy fruit trees. Out here there was fertile soil in greater quantity, blown in on the winds over millennia to settle among the stony outcrops and give a base to small fields. These fields were now home to the cherished livestock of the Khoikhoi.

At any alarm from the sentries the herdsmen would drive the small number of beasts into the village where they too could be protected. A challenging procedure, yes, but less difficult than getting replacements, declared K'rn the elder.

The greater part of the 'herd' was twenty or so goats. They were kept for the milk, explained the younger K'rn, with the meat only eaten if an animal died or was killed accidentally.

The remaining livestock were beasts of a very different sort. Very different from anything the northerners had ever seen. They looked like several different animals had been cut up and their parts reassembled at random.

Fascinated, Saemundsson cautiously approached one of the five animals. It flicked its ears but made no move away, clearly used to human contact. Standing almost eye to eye with Sigurd, the body shape resembled a rather portly horse with a longer than usual neck. The face was reminiscent of a calf (the large dark eyes perhaps, thought the captain) but with big flexible ears and short, hair-covered horns rising straight up from its brows.

Most remarkable of all was its skin. The body and neck were a deep brown, the face much lighter, softening to grey around the throat before darkening again around the muzzle. By far the most striking element was the skin of the legs and rump, marked with horizontal white stripes that merged into solid white around the ankles. The trader couldn't help but think of the beautifully patterned horsehides he'd seen earlier on their travels.

Then the creature revealed its final surprise. It poked out its purple tongue, the length of Hervor's forearm, and licked at the inside of its ear.

Who could do anything but laugh? Bardi in particular was delighted, almost doubled over with mirth, but also appreciation for the bizarre but beautiful animals.

They were called o'api, and they originally came from forests far to the north. These five were the last generation of a small herd that had been traded for, long ago. The meat was apparently very good, much prized by the forest people, but it was the skins that had made them valuable. Sigurd wasn't the first trader to be enamoured of their novel beauty.

Such animals hadn't been seen in this area for many years. If they'd ever been native no one remembered it, and none had been sighted, live or dead, among the passing goods of K'rn the elder's lifetime, or his parents. His daughter suggested that the animals were dying out from overhunting. Remembering the way the people of Denga had treated their local resources, this seemed sadly plausible to the more thoughtful of the Norse.

Hearts were light, and even Hervor's guard was down as they started back toward the village along a different route than the one they'd taken to get out to the small 'pastures'. The older K'rn led the way along a passage between two tall outcrops of stone. The shade was a welcome relief; one reason the Khoikhoi had chosen this path. The little group chatted as they walked. Bardi Goosefoot was stretching his limited vocabulary to learn all he could about the o'api from the elder Khoikhoi.

Suddenly a little shower of pebbles fell from above. There was barely a moment to look up and register a pair of dark figures atop one of the outcrops before boulders came crashing down.

The attackers had almost gotten their timing completely wrong. Perhaps the unexpected white faces had disconcerted them – most of the intended victims weren't far enough along the passage to fall into the trap. Most, but not all.

K'rn probably never knew what hit him as a stone struck his skull. As the first rocks tumbled Bardi had turned and thrown himself back to shove his captain clear. He might have made it to safety himself had he not overbalanced in his effort to save Sigurd. Saemundsson watched helplessly as one boulder landed on Goosefoot's cursed legs moments before another crushed his ribs and spine. The captain rolled away quickly, caught only by a few small rocks and pebbles.

One of the attackers was in the act of notching an arrow to his bow. He didn't hurry. Their victims had been caught by surprise and had no cover to hide behind.

Hiding was not a consideration for the Norse. Anna and Olaf had aimed and fired their bows before their assailant had even drawn back his own arrow. Rage gave them deadly accuracy. The two black men fell, one tumbling from the outcrop to land sprawled on the boulders he'd helped stack then lever over the edge.

Led by K'pah, Hervor and Bjarni scrambled up a cleft in the rock face, weapons drawn. The two Norse archers had bows at the ready while Sindjely's keen eyes scanned for any sign of further attack.

Sigurd and Fafhrd bent their backs to the task of getting to the victims. The two strong men lifted boulders as best they could, to allow Katrine and K'rn to haul first Bardi then the old Khoikhoi clear of the rocky debris. The young woman stayed remarkably calm, even as she wiped blood from her father's face.

It was clear that both men had died almost instantly.

Hervor called down to her captain. The top of the outcrop was clear. Beside the body of the man Olaf had felled, there was almost nothing to be found. Two dropped bows and some stout poles that had obviously been used to position the rocks and launch the deathtrap.

"There is an easier way down over here," called K'pah. "We will meet you at the end of the passage, yes?"

Sigurd signalled agreement.

The captain took the lead, Anna beside him with an arrow at the ready. Then came Katrine, K'rn and the watchful Sindjely. Behind them Fafhrd bore the weight of their slain comrades, one draped over each brawny shoulder. At the rear was Olaf, trying to walk backwards as much as he could, his bow like Anna's ready for instant use.

As they clambered over the fallen rocks Sigurd stopped briefly to examine the body of the man killed by Anna's arrow. There was little to be learned. Taller and darker than the Khoikhoi he was evidently one of the Ba'tu who'd been described. He retrieved the shaft, handed it to his archer, and then tossed the corpse aside.

Their three companions were waiting for them at the end of the passage.

"They must have somehow got past a sentry," said K'pah bitterly.

"Maybe with only two of them they were able to get by without being seen," suggested Katrine.

That was plausible, although if they were to have looked for the sentry in question they'd have found him face down in a bush with an arrow in his back. The unfortunate fellow had been relieving himself just as the Ba'tu stealthily arrived, and his distraction was fatal.

"Where there are two, there will be more. We must prepare our defences."

"Yes, K'pah," agreed K'rn. "I must do the work of a sentry and have the animals brought in."

Her actions were as good as her words as she sprinted away. There would be time for grief later, she hoped.

"Should I go after her?" asked Anna. "I'm armed, and I can match her speed," she said confidently.

"Good idea," said Sigurd. "Be careful, though – I don't want to lose you too. See you at the village!" he called as the long-legged archer was already running.

The remaining eight made their own good speed back to the village, where K'pah immediately explained what had happened. There was clearly a system born of long practice in place as the Khoikhoi sprang into action.

Reed mats were pulled from the walls of huts at one end of the village. These were attached to what had looked like a random assortment of green branches about two huts nearest the access point to the beach, an area well dotted with tall stones and rocky outcrops. Suddenly there was an enclosure into which the children and the old folk were ushered. This was where the livestock would be driven, too.

Short bows and spears were pulled from huts. Hastily armed men and women clambered onto the tallest of the rock formations. Others set themselves in concentric semicircles that emanated out from the mat enclosure, each line a thrown spear's distance from the next.

The Icelander nodded. He understood the system. It made as much use as possible of their scant resources. But he had an idea. Briefly he explained it to K'pah, who immediately set a group of villagers to work on a task that frankly baffled them.

Hervor was sent down to the boats with a detailed message. The boats were to be put a little way out to sea as quickly as possible, with crews ready to defend themselves if a raid came from the ocean. He didn't expect that, but then, nobody had expected the deathtrap either.

Before launching though, Hervor was to assemble twenty or so good fighters. The contingent of archers was to be divided between the two ships and this group. As the boats were prepared to move off, this fighting force was to be brought back up to the village, where they would join the Khoikhoi defenders.

Sigurd looked over at the body of Bardi Goosefoot, laid out in the enclosure. It was one thing to avoid being caught up in a local war as they had been in Zawaia. This was an act that *did* require avenging.

As he waited, Sigurd quizzed some of the old Khoikhoi. He wanted to know who and what they were up against. Knowledge was power.

When some of the Ba'tu tribes overran a village, after the initial onslaught they would enslave the survivors. Eventually they'd interbreed with those not sold off, gradually absorbing them into their race. Not so this group. They would kill every one of their victims that they found in their way as they pillaged food and anything else they liked. It was run or die.

If these Ba'tu ever decided that they wanted to occupy this site instead of just raiding it at whim it would be the end of the Khoikhoi, they knew that.

There was a sudden commotion as the herdsmen arrived, driving goats and o'api before them towards the enclosure. The first of Hervor's small 'army' were just arriving from the beach, and the sight of the outrageous animals was enough to stop a few in their tracks.

Still smarting from the loss of her shipmate, Hervor chivvied them on impatiently. "Get a move on! It's just a funny-looking horse!" she shouted, getting her species identification completely if forgivably wrong.

K'rn and Anna arrived immediately behind the herdsmen, the archer having been determinedly guarding their backs. Sindjely sighed with relief, even as K'rn went to find her father's body. There was still no time for grief, not with the village to defend, but she did at least want to make sure the corpse was out of sight of the marauders.

They were coming. Everyone in the village was sure of it, and they were right. The two men killed at the rocky pass had been an opportunistic scouting party who, after surprising a sentry, had stealthily advanced. They'd seized the chance for a trap to claim several lives at once on a path clearly well travelled.

When the two scouts failed to return to the main party of raiders there was a brief, puzzled conversation among the forty-strong group. To lose one warrior may be considered a misfortune, but to lose both to a lowly sentry beggared belief. The best way to find the answer was to press the attack. Holding their bows before them, arrows already notched, they advanced at a steady walking pace.

Several of the Ba'tu had raided this village before. They knew how the game worked. To them, it almost *was* a game. One group of attackers would breach the first ring of the defence, perhaps the second on a good day, killing as many as they could. Behind the melee of their advance a smaller second group would quickly loot as much as possible from the surrounding huts. They were particularly fond of the bundles that had been brought up from the sea, but would take anything that could be eaten or sold.

Once they'd sustained a few casualties of their own, the first wave of marauders would back up, a covering fire of arrows ensuring they weren't pursued. Even laden with their spoils the long-legged Ba'tu could travel swiftly, and would be quickly away leaving the villagers to count their losses, and begin to restock before the next raid.

As they neared the outskirts of the village, they separated into their two groups.

There was the dead sentry. Good. They passed the deserted paddocks, as usual. They didn't follow the path through the passageway, taking the more open route that was more accommodating of their numbers. So they never found the bodies of their comrades, or knew what had happened there.

A little ridge marked where they stopped, steadied themselves, and charged confidently. They wore breastplates of tough leather, hardly worthy of the term 'armour' but enough to resist the arrowheads of the Khoikhoi from anything but close range.

Here was the secret of the Ba'tu ascendency. Superior technology. The Khoikhoi tipped their weapons with bone and stone. The Ba'tu worked iron. As yet, still in limited amounts, but enough to make arrowheads far more effective than those of their comparatively primitive victims.

The first hail of Ba'tu arrows flew. One pierced a Khoikhoi leg, but most were deflected or blocked by the line of Norse shields that suddenly, shockingly rose up from the rough rampart Sigurd had ordered thrown together. Mostly sand and saplings, it wouldn't withstand much impact, but it had done its job of hiding the Khoikhoi's reinforcements.

Even as the Ba'tu were releasing their arrows they got their second shock. Fair-skinned archers knelt shoulder to shoulder with their dark allies behind the line of shields, and their arrows were tipped with iron. Sharp, hard iron that ripped through leather, skin and bone.

It was mayhem in moments. Some of the first wave of Ba'tu fell immediately. Others turned to flee. More behind them continued to charge, their view of what had happened obscured. The second party – the looters – collided with their panicked fellows. Then as they too turned to run, the last element of Sigurd's trap was sprung.

He hadn't just supplemented the front line of the Khoikhoi defence. Four Norse fighters armed with axes and swords had been stationed in each of two huts on the flanks of the Ba'tu raiders' regular, predictable entry point. Any would-be looter would have gotten the last surprise of his life, but none even got that opportunity.

The flankers strode from their huts and into the small throng of Ba'tu. The ugly clubs which the Ba'tu wielded were little defence against the sailors' blades. Hervor led one quartet, a grim Bjorn Breakneck the other. Bardi Goosefoot had been much respected by his crewmates, and was being brutally avenged.

Clambering over the low rampart, the other Norse fighters and some of the Khoikhoi front line joined the fray, Sigurd and K'pah among them, the latter armed with Bardi's axe.

The Ba'tu fought for their lives with frenzied desperation. A dying raider managed to thrust an arrow into a Norse leg even as he collapsed. In the close quarter fighting the clubs did do some damage. An oarsman dropped his sword and reeled away, clutching a broken arm.

In the midst of the melee, Sigurd and K'pah stood almost back-to-back. The latter half turned and swung the axe to deflect a Ba'tu club aimed at Sigurd's head. It was an unfamiliar, unwieldy weapon for him though, and the raider was able to bring the club thudding down onto the Khoikhoi skull instead. He had no time to celebrate. The captain's broadsword sheared through the shoulder of the arm that held the club, and the Ba'tu man bled to death quickly.

The bloodshed was over in minutes, although it felt longer for those in the thick of it. Only three of the Ba'tu survived and managed to flee. Eventually they made it home to relate their own warning: that this particular village was now protected by demons, and was never to be raided again!

The second, third and fourth lines of Khoikhoi defenders stared open-mouthed, as did those behind the enclosure. They'd never seen slaughter like it, and already sincerely hoped never to do so again.

An eerie quiet fell over the little battlefield. The Khoikhoi and their allies gathered their wounded and their one lamented slain. Some of the locals began to disassemble the enclosure and herd the animals back to their small pastures.

Sigurd noticed that they took a wide path around the scene of the uneven battle – no, call it what it was, a massacre. He felt no remorse. He knew these Ba'tu would have killed them just as mercilessly if they'd had the chance. But he also realised that death on such a scale was new to the villagers. A good thing, he thought, as it would almost certainly have been their own slaughter they'd experience.

But he respected their distress. He asked one of the older women he'd spoken to earlier what they'd previously done with the corpses of dead enemies.

There hadn't been many, he was told, but those few were taken out on the canoes and dumped as far out to sea as possible. He nodded. It seemed a reasonable solution.

Quickly he found Hervor, and explained what he wanted done.

"Even before we get ourselves cleaned up," he stressed. "Let's give these folks their village back, as well and as speedily as we can."

His enforcer nodded. She knew the fighters would want to get the blood and dirt off themselves as soon as possible – she took the same pride in her appearance – but she also understood her captain's thinking.

The bodies of the Ba'tu were swiftly gathered up and carried down to the beach, stacked like logs on the sand. The ships had been signalled to come back in, and *Serpentfang* was soon loaded with a grisly cargo. Hrolf understood.

He had the longship driven out to a point well beyond the breaking waves, where the sea was deep and dark. The bodies were pitched overboard with no ceremony or regret.

"Let the fish have them," said Hervor, noting with satisfaction the first few grey dorsal fins cutting through the water towards the spot.

Back at the village, clean sand was being strewn on the site of the conflict. At least it would look less like the floor of a charnel house.

Gradually, the Khoikhoi came out of their state of shock. As they did, the overwhelming feelings were first relief, and only later, triumph. It was, the community agreed, an occasion for a feast, to which their new friends, allies, saviours, were of course invited.

Not this night, Sigurd said. There was an important task that had to be done before any celebration of a victory.

The captain himself supervised and helped with the collection of a large pile of driftwood, assembled at a point some way along the beach from where the boats were moored. The timbers were placed some way below the high tide line. Meanwhile, Katrine stayed in the village and quietly explained what was going on.

Cremation was familiar enough to them, but the concept of a funeral pyre was something new. As its significance sank in, K'rn boldly asked if her father and K'pah could share Bardi's final rite.

Katrine took the request to her captain. Wisely he consulted with both Sverrir and Hrolf. Fafhrd was brought into the discussion too, as they knew Bardi Goosefoot had still in many ways been a follower of the old traditions.

The Khoikhoi had fought alongside them in battle. Well, K'pah certainly had. K'rn had died with Bardi, at the hands of their foes. It was their deaths that had precipitated the conflict. Yes. The two men would be laid with honour beside their crewmate.

Now the Norse were able to clean their hands and hair of the blood of their enemies. Being well groomed was important at the ceremony. Anything less would be grossly disrespectful.

That night, as the flames and embers bore the spirits skywards, sailors and Khoikhoi alike sat around the fire and sang their own old songs. Hrolf told stories of the pigeon toed seaman – many funny, all of them affectionate.

Older Khoikhoi spoke of past deeds of both K'rn and K'pah. They were a community without a leader, but if they'd had one it would probably have been the broad-shouldered man, his Ba'tu ancestry irrelevant.

By morning, most of the remnants of the pyre had washed out to sea. Another tide would sweep away the rest.

Sverrir and many of the crew were in favour of an early departure, but Sigurd demurred. He understood the significance of ritual, and realised how much a victory feast meant to the village. Historically they'd had few to celebrate.

Happily, the Khoikhoi believed that a feast was an event for the middle of the day, under a bright sun and clear sky. The boats would still be able to catch enough of the ebbing tide to depart without great effort.

It was only when the meal itself began that the sailors discovered what had been in the treasured bundles brought from the canoes. A rich fish stew was the staple of the banquet, but the high point was the presentation of the Khoikhoi's favourite culinary delight: lobster. Impressive crustaceans they were too, large and equipped with claws that looked capable of severing a hand, never mind a careless finger.

More than a match even for the fondly remembered Icelandic lobsters caught near Hofn!

The capture of these delicacies was to have been a cause for celebration in itself. But the destruction of virtually the entire force of Ba'tu raiders – *that* was something else.

Among the cheer and bonhomie, Sigurd worried about the future of the village. They'd wiped out one group of marauders it seemed, but surely there were others. He'd equipped them with a new strategy, but did they have the tools to use it?

The Khoikhoi had no iron for axes, swords or arrowheads. There was no chance of leaving behind any of their ships' own stock of weapons – often he'd wished he had more as it was. Even if they could, the fate of K'pah showed what could happen to someone who tried to use a weapon without practice or training. Training that the Icelander had neither the time nor inclination to give.

The village was too small to sustain the seafarers' presence for long. He knew many of his people were anxious to be away. There was no real trade to be had here. He stroked his moustache. No, they must go, and let the village stand or fall according to its own destiny.

Such musings made the captain gloomier than the feast deserved, but he put on a brave front. Still, he wasn't sorry to soon be boarding *Serpentfang*.

But as the longship's mooring rope was being untied, the sight of K'rn running out through the shallows surprised him. She reached up toward him, holding a roll of hide that she thrust into his hands.

"Thank you," was all she said before running back to shore, but she said it in clear Norse.

Where was Katrine? She must have had something to do with this... A correct assumption, but the interpreter was standing at the other end of the ship. The Khoikhoi woman had spoken to her the night before and she knew what the gift was. Knew, too, that her honourable captain would never accept it without trade unless forced by circumstance.

As the prow cut through the waves, Sigurd unrolled the skin. It was a little discoloured by age, having seen service in the home of both K'rns, and of the K'rn of a generation before, but it had been well preserved and was instantly recognisable. He had an o'api.

Fafhrd looked over from the tiller, saw the gift and smiled. In Valhalla he knew Bardi would be smiling too.

.ooo.

10

SOUTH AFRICA – SUCH A SIMPLE THING AS A BUG

Still they pressed south, tracing the coastline. Still they pulled into anywhere that looked like the trade might be good, although it was never as good as Sigurd wanted. Still they gathered supplies and fresh water where and when they could.

Still there was no sign of a route to the fabled Baghdad. Perhaps it never existed. A dream or a fiction. Perhaps it lay on the other side of a doorway to some other world.

The weather was cooler. The sun still blazed during the day, but at least there was relief at night. Not cold, certainly not by the standards of Iceland, but enough for the wool and furs to start being appreciated again.

As they battled on, Saemundsson realised that the settlements ashore were getting fewer, and smaller.

"Have we reached the limits of human habitation perhaps?" the captain asked Hrolf the Dark in weary conversation one evening, the two men standing with Fafhrd by the tiller. Their hair flew wildly in a crosswind that was gradually gaining in strength.

"Odin knows, we're near our own limits," was the steersman's rueful reply.

Sigurd understood. It felt like they were getting a poor return for the labour they were all investing. There'd become a dispiriting sameness to the places they'd landed in recent days. If there was a difference, it was only in their becoming steadily less appealing. The three men stared out over the stern.

"Turn about?" pondered Hrolf. "Make our way back? At least we'd know what we were sailing into..."

Even he didn't sound enthusiastic at his own thought, but he pursued it. "We at least know now the best of the goods we're likely to find. We can look for more of those."

"Enough to make up for the loss of *Stormbearer*? We've seen nothing that'd turn that sort of profit," answered the captain bleakly.

He tried to avoid letting his gloom show, especially around anyone in the crew. Morale was hard enough to maintain without negativity coming from above. But he was tired, and these two men were his oldest friends, especially now that Corri was gone.

All three gazed north, in the direction of Iceland. Looking back as the sky darkened and evening fell.

It was blonde Bjarni, standing at look-out in the prow as the first braziers were lit, who cried, "Lights on shore! On the cape away south-west!"

He'd been looking ahead. That was, after all, his job in the lookout post, he pointed out to Fafhrd later that night.

Serpentfang headed toward the light.

Over on *Red Whale*, Sverrir had been standing in his usual position on the ocean side of amidships. It was, he said, where he felt closest to the water and best able to gauge its mood. He'd been having a similar conversation to Sigurd's, as it happened. His confidantes had been Bjorn Breakneck and the side tillerman, Egil of Dalir.

On the death of Arne Arnesson during the storm, Egil had become the senior man at that tiller. He was another who'd sailed with old Bent-knee for years, and would speak his mind when asked.

All three had been of a mind to carry on, despite the poor results of recent times. In part, it was out of loyalty to Sigurd. But it was also out of bloody-minded intransigence. None of them wanted to ever have to say, "I gave up." Besides, Egil was a gambler of long experience, and reasonable success. Every run of bad luck ended, he said. Only those who persevered found fortune. Walking away on a losing streak just defined you as a loser.

There were some flaws in this logic, but before they could be explored, their own lookout called of *Serpentfang* changing course, and saw for herself the twinkling firelight that had prompted it.

Although there were heavy clouds over the land, the sky above the ocean was still quite clear. The crosswind evidently kept the clouds pinned to a mountain they could see some distance behind the shore.

It was something close to a full moon that shone brightly. In its glow, sailors on both vessels realised that they were sailing into a school of large sharks. They knew the big predators well, of course. They were a common enough sight from the North Sea down, but they'd never seen them in a dense crowd like this.

The keels actually bumped the backs of some of the great grey fish passing under them. Anyone going overboard wouldn't have time to drown.

But even with the distraction of the sharks underfoot, as it were, Sverrir was puzzled. There was something going on with the water. He couldn't yet tell what, but the veteran's mariner senses were on high alert.

As they approached, the sailors realised that the cape they were aiming for was at one end of a substantial bay. Using the crosswind they changed course slightly, intending to round the point and land in the bay. Sverrir's sensitive feet tingled.

The course change brought good news. Further along the bay side of the point more fires were burning. Too many for a handful of wandering hunters, as they'd encountered in the recent past.

It wasn't firelight though, but moonlight, that saved them from potential disaster. A couple of momentary flashes of white as water broke on something submerged dead ahead. Strong arms hauled on the tillers, the rudders steering the vessels hard left. Propelled by the fast increasing wind, the two ships passed perilously close to a massive rock. It was barely visible as they went by. Even their shallow keels would have found the treacherous mass if they'd tried to turn a few seconds later.

Over the years, as this seaway became busier, hundreds of ships and thousands of lives would be lost to this one hazard, and the great white sharks that abounded. The area would become known in several languages as 'Danger Point'.

They were still a little more than a mile off shore, but pressed by the wind that distance was eaten up quickly. Indeed, less able captains than Sigurd and Sverrir would have struggled to bring their boats in safely.

But they made the beach intact. Fortunately the sand was soft. The normal routine of having the knarr hold fast off shore was out of the question here.

"Do we make for those fires now?" asked Hervor, pointing to the western edge of the bay.

"In the morning," replied Sigurd as he stroked his moustache. "I don't like meeting people for the first time in the dark if I can help it. But post guards on the sand and on board, just in case the locals aren't as courteous."

The guards were refreshed (or in some cases annoyed) by a couple of heavy overnight showers.

Not long after sunrise, a few curious figures did make their wary way along the fringe of the beach. At the same time, Sigurd was assembling a small party to head for the settlement behind the night's fires. The captain himself, and Katrine, as usual. Bjorn and Astou from *Red Whale* – this time Sindjely could remain at the boat, in case she was needed to try to converse with any locals who turned up there. Two archers and two swordsmen. That should be enough.

The two small groups met some way from the longboat. It was impossible not to see the resemblance between these locals and the villagers alongside whom they'd fought the Ba'tu.

The language was similar, too, a baffling collection of clicks, consonants and grunts. It was quickly evident that the Bambara language that had served them further north was of no use here. They'd have to rely on the tiny smattering of Khoikhoi that Katrine had managed to pick up in their short stay.

A connection with the northern villagers was confirmed by the discovery that these folk called themselves Khoe.

Painstakingly Sigurd and Katrine managed to communicate that they were interested in trade. The concept at first seemed baffling to the locals, but Katrine persisted. She demonstrated the exchange of one item for another, first with Sigurd, then with one of the more confident Khoe. She repeatedly used the Norse word for trade, and could see the idea sinking in.

The Khoe were interested in the big boats that had been moored on the beach, but were intimidated by the numbers of the fair skinned sailors, so they were happier to lead the small party back to their village.

Less populous even than the home of the Khoikhoi, it sat like a ribbon on the slopes above the water. It comprised a few thin lines of shacks, built in the same way as those of their northern counterparts: green branches stuck in the ground and tied at the top, then wrapped in reed matting. There wasn't so much as a central plaza for them to gather in. They simply squatted in an apparently random area in front of one of the rows of huts, overlooking the sea.

The place had a name, but it was unpronounceable even for Katrine and Astou. As near as they could make out, it translated to 'the place where clouds gather' – a reference to the apparently permanent mantle draping the mountain that loomed behind them. That had an equally unmanageable title, but was readily understand-able as 'sea mountain'.

In many ways these Khoe seemed less developed than the Khoikhoi, although they shared the same communal, concordant societal structure. They kept no livestock, and their scant gardens were used only for two or three types of root vegetable. There was plenty of fruit among the trees that occupied the slope behind the village, although the variety was limited in some seasons. Their livelihood came from the sea, and the great majority of that in the form of shellfish and edible seaweed that regularly washed ashore.

'Cloud Town' (as the Norse quickly took to calling it) had some canoes, but these hugged the shore. The dense concentration of sharks in deeper water was not an unusual phenomenon, and the flimsy canoes offered little protection against any hungry giants. It was bad enough when any of the great-jawed predators swam into the shallows – why go out *to* the monsters?

The Khoe knew the sea, though. They spent their lives watching it and eking their living from around its edge. One grizzled Khoe whose name sounded something like K'sd (or perhaps he had the equivalent of a lisp) remarked that the ocean changed 'out there'.

Bjorn's attention was immediately caught. He remembered Sverrir's sense of something happening in the water.

"Changed how? What does that mean?" Bjorn asked.

K'sd shrugged and replied, "Different."

Clearly there was nothing more useful forthcoming, but Bjorn would be sure to talk to his captain. He'd be trying to learn more from anyone else, too.

Perhaps it was a reflection of the weariness that had been evident in the recent shipboard discussion, but Sigurd decided not to immediately set back out to sea, as they'd done recently from places that, frankly, had more in their favour than Cloud Town. Or perhaps there was something in the comment K'sd had made that he wanted to investigate further.

A day – they could wait a day, while they tried to learn something of what lay ahead, 'around the next bend' as it were. The Khoe didn't object. They were more curious than afraid of their visitors. They seldom saw anyone of any other tribe. If the Ba'tu made it this far south they'd wipe out the villagers and take over Cloud Town in a single raid, thought Sigurd. Not that there was any obvious reason why they'd want to.

A local woman named K'bt suggested the newcomers might eat with them later. They shared a communal meal under the trees when the sun was at its highest. That seemed a sensible suggestion, and a welcome one. The captain did explain, with some concern, that there would be many mouths to feed. His crew numbers must have been close to the total population of Cloud Town.

K'sd and K'bt were unconcerned. The bounty was good at present. They had plenty, and would find more as they needed it. Nonetheless, the sailors conferred and agreed that they would contribute something from their own provisions.

It was, in effect, a day's 'shore leave', not there was much to be done. 'Mingle and learn what you can' was the instruction. The language gap would obviously be a problem, but the northerners were becoming used to communicating with new people by a combination of sign language and a few mutually recognised words.

A guard detail was posted on the boats. Although it seemed an unnecessary caution, it was not a habit Sigurd was willing to break. A few of the crew were tasked with checking and repairing the fishing nets as required. If the catch here was as good as K'sd indicated (which seemed likely, otherwise that number of sharks wouldn't be lingering) then they should make the most of any opportunity to boost their own stocks when they could.

For most though, the morning was simply a chance to stretch their legs on dry land for a little longer than usual.

Cailin Ruiteach was one of those who were particularly glad of the opportunity. She'd adapted well to life at sea, but did enjoy the simple pleasure of walking on a surface that didn't roll and rock underfoot. Precisely the sensation that veteran sailors like Sverrir most missed when ashore.

The Irishwoman had a figure that was the epitome of feminine beauty to the locals' taste. It might have been flattering to someone else, but the clerk simply found the attention annoying, especially when she found herself being followed as she walked.

As she accompanied Hrolf and some others on a walk along the sands of the bay she became aware of a trio of local tribesmen following close behind her. They were nattering loudly in their native tongue – the words were meaningless to both Norse and Irish, but the tone was clear. The foremost of the men was obviously showing off his 'wit' at the expense of the woman they trailed.

Hrolf was considering whether to intercede on her behalf. Had she been Norse he'd have known not to, but he was still learning what was the best course of action around the feisty redhead. The loudmouthed local was less considerate and decided to show off his boldness to his friends.

The man caught Cailin by her long braid. That was a mistake, not least because it meant she knew how close he was. She spun and planted a brawny fist in the centre of his face. He let go of her hair – a natural reaction to having his nose smashed.

His companions fell about laughing as he sprawled on his back in the sand. Furious he grabbed the hard wooden club he'd worn on a rough string from his shoulder. In an instant, the point of Hrolf's sword was digging into the wrist of the hand that held the weapon.

No words were needed. The dark timber was quite hard, but would be no match for the metal blade. The tribesman uncurled his fingers from the haft of the club. Hrolf nodded approval of the action, and flicked his head to indicate that it would be a wise move to find a different direction to walk in.

Chastened, the fellow's cronies helped him to his feet. They bobbed at the knee, evidently the local equivalent of an apologetic bow. Hrolf glanced over to Cailin.

Fist still clenched, she took a pace forward and growled. Her assailant jumped back, doing his own knee bending even as he wiped at the blood streaming from his nose. Satisfied that her point had been made, she folded her arms, but continued to glare as the three men scurried away. Hastened by her baleful stare, they weren't to know that within a few paces they were little more than blurry retreating objects to her.

"I'm glad *you're* with *us*, Cailin Ruiteach!" declared Hrolf approvingly.

"As am I," she replied with a grin.

The shared meal was a casual affair, with everyone sitting cross-legged on the ground under a canopy of trees overlooking Cloud

Town. Mussels, clams and crabs were the main fare, but each group learned a new eating experience from the other.

Salt pork was a novelty for the Khoe, for whom meat was mostly confined to the occasional antelope that wandered out of its range and came too close to the village. Most animals kept clear of Cloud Town, and the locals had, over many generations, become fishermen, not hunters.

The salt pork's texture was strange and unfamiliar, but the flavour appealed to most who tried it. The seafarers had a similar reaction to the locals' favourite delicacy – grasshoppers grilled over an open fire. There were grasshoppers in the north, but nobody had considered roasting and eating them.

As they all crunched and chewed, Sverrir and Sigurd at last were managing to get a sense of what had been meant by the ocean changing 'out there'. The winds became stronger – they'd already had some experience of that – but there was more. Further from the shore these winds could fall away suddenly. The waves, though, could be high and choppy, changing direction from moment to moment, it seemed.

The two captains looked at each other, an idea forming in both heads at once. When one of the older Khoe fisherwomen mentioned that the waters to their east were much warmer than hereabouts, the suspicion seemed confirmed. It was the confluence of two currents. Old Bent-knee had been feeling the stirrings of the current they'd ridden approaching the area where they converged. If they hadn't turned for land they would have found themselves in the middle of it.

But a different current might mean many other different conditions, especially if there really was a significant change in water temperature. The two men started to discuss the possibilities.

Suddenly Pall Jansson, sitting a little away from the captains, swatted a large yellow insect that had been crawling along his leg. Casually he tossed the stunned creature onto the fire alongside some of the roasting grasshoppers.

A shocked silence immediately fell over the Khoe. Many of them stared wide-eyed at him, though he was blissfully unaware as he chewed at a piece of pork.

K'bt urgently whispered to Katrine, who then called over to Pall in worried explanation, "You've just killed their most sacred thing!"

"What?" asked Jansson, puzzled. "It's a bug. They *eat* them, for Thor's sake."

"They eat grasshoppers. That was a mantis. In their stories, it was a sacred yellow mantis that created *everything*."

Pall did something he very rarely did, and it was the worst thing he could possibly do. He laughed.

"Don't be ridiculous! Who ever heard of worshipping a bug?"

The words had barely left his mouth when a Khoe club hit the back of his skull. It almost defied belief that Pall Jansson died laughing.

Several of the crew jumped to their feet, drawing axes and swords to avenge their shipmate. Some Khoe did likewise, bravely willing to pit their clubs against the superior weapons.

"No!" bellowed Sigurd. "Weapons down, all of you!"

The Khoe were huddling together, some fearful, some belligerent.

"We back off! Down to the boats. Orderly. No one runs, and watch your backs!" commanded Saemundsson, standing with palms open.

He wished there was a proper chief he could try to talk to, but had to settle for trying to address the whole tribe at once. He didn't know any Khoe words of apology, but did his best to express regret, and explain that his people had known nothing of the Khoes' ways.

"But everyone knows the yellow mantis created life!" shouted one. And to these villagers, that was true. 'Everyone' meant anyone they'd ever met.

Hervor was ushering the crew in accordance with Sigurd's order, although several were reluctant. She was one of them.

"Why run? These people are no threat. We could wipe them out without getting tired," she said quietly as she neared the captain.

"We could, yes, but why? What would be the point?" Sigurd asked in response.

"To avenge Jansson, that's why!" snapped Sverrir beside him. "You were quick enough to want vengeance for Bardi Goosefoot!"

"The Ba'tu killed Bardi for no reason but an act of war. This is different. If a small child strikes you in its temper tantrum because you've trodden on a toy and broken it, do you take up a sword? Pound his small head with your great fist? You can call it an act of revenge for these people – unwitting as it was, Pall killed one of their gods."

"It was a bug, Sigurd!" exclaimed Sverrir.

"Not to them! How would you react if someone came on board *Red Whale*, seemingly in peace, and then burned your carving of Njord that stands at your prow?"

"But Njord is the god of the sea..." the old captain began to protest, stopping suddenly as he realised Sigurd's point. He was stubborn, but not stupid.

The captain knelt and picked up Jansson's body himself. The man could be difficult, but he was crew, and should be given a proper farewell at the first opportunity. He made sure he was the last to back away. Elsdottir remained at his side with her knife drawn in case anyone thought to take advantage of his being hampered by the corpse over his shoulder. As they made their way onto the beach she muttered under her breath. Sigurd didn't catch the words but recognised the tone.

"We're not running away from a battle. You said yourself, they'd be no challenge," he said quietly. "The slaughter of the Ba'tu is still fresh in my mind. There's no good reason to slaughter this whole village, and that's what would probably happen. It's not as if the place is desirable enough to want to stay here, but neither do I want to leave a wasteland in our wake."

The tide was just about at its highest. Getting the ships out to sea would be a quick task, and they would continue east to see where this warm current would take them.

The Khoe didn't follow them to the beach. Many were still in shock at the killing of the sacred mantis, others were acutely aware of the folly of running into the swords and axes of the fair-skinned ones.

A few made a hero of the man who'd clubbed the mantis-slayer.

Others, more pragmatic or thoughtful, realised how close they'd come to being killed themselves. Sigurd's clumsy speech had made an impact on some of them at least.

Clearly it was a complicated thing, this dealing with other people from other places. Better to avoid it in future if they could.

.000.

11

MADAGASCAR – TALKING TO THE ANCESTORS

The strong winds swept the two boats rapidly east. Sigurd tried to keep the coastline in sight off to their north, but this new current pulled them steadily away from land.

It had become little more than a fringe on the horizon. Oars and tillers were worked at mightily in the hope of preventing the shore from being lost to view, but the efforts were futile. *Serpentfang* and *Red Whale* were gradually dragged in a northwesterly direction, but the land had seemingly disappeared.

The moment was seized to return Pall Jansson's body to the ocean. It wasn't the funeral pyre of a warrior, but he'd hardly died a warrior's death. Nonetheless, there was respect and reverence as the corpse, wrapped in a cowhide from their northern home, was slipped over the side as gently as possible.

Then suddenly, the land was there again, another dark serrated line in the distant north. It was a target, and the Norse crews aimed for it. The ships at first were more like ponderous logs than flying arrows, but steadily they fought through the current. At last, they were cutting across the water in the way they wanted and the land began to look larger.

Sigurd and his crew couldn't know it, but they'd shot past the end of Africa and were now coming into sight of the huge island later to be known as Madagascar.

It was the south east corner of the island that lay ahead. The heavily forested slopes at first didn't inspire much hope, but... surely those were the smoke plumes of some human habitation rising from amongst the green?

Anna Sjelsdottir was on lookout duty in the prow of the longboat, but it was the sharp eyes of her now constant companion Sindjely that spotted the subtle change in shape at one point of the shoreline that still lay distant. Anna peered. Her N'Dar lover may have the keener vision, but *she* had the experience at sea. That was... surely? Yes! It was a dock. A real, man-made dock!

The news put Sigurd in two minds. The structure implied a more developed settlement than the dwindling villages of recent times. That should mean better trade opportunities. But their last experience had rattled him, probably more than he'd realised. A simple misunderstanding had cost him one of his crew. Perhaps more significantly, he felt he'd had to strain to maintain discipline – something that hadn't happened in a long while. What if there was another mistake? Another confrontation, with better armed, more belligerent opponents?

The truth was that the events of Cloud Town had, for most of the crew, actually deepened their respect for the captain. Especially after word of his reasons for the withdrawal got around. And both Katrine and Hervor made sure that it did, as did Bjorn Breakneck on *Red Whale* once Sverrir had recounted the conversation to him.

Clearly the boats had been sighted, as there were people starting to gather on the dock. Where they were coming from wasn't obvious though, as there only appeared to be a couple of low buildings at the waterfront. The walls of them were made of a dark earth that from a distance was barely visible against the backdrop of forest.

The normal routine was resumed. The knarr kept her position a little way offshore while *Serpentfang* was manoeuvred alongside the dock.

The people on the dock were cautious, but more curious than

aggressive. The fair skins of the new arrivals were quite unfamiliar, and their ship was utterly unlike anything they'd seen. But surely they must be from somewhere nearby, because the head on the long neck at the prow was clearly an image of one of the crocodiles that lived in the estuarine rivers of their island.

While the complexions were unfamiliar, at least not all of the words were. Among the confusing babble shouted from the strange ship as it pulled in were coherent sentences in Arabic, so obviously these people were merchants. That had been the language of many generations of merchants who'd come here. A dialogue was soon established.

Sigurd remained wary, but their reception certainly indicated that these people seemed more interested in trade than confrontation. That was very much his own preference. Nonetheless, before calling in the knarr, he wanted to see the settlement itself, and gauge the people in it.

Leaving Hrolf in charge of the ship, Sigurd assembled a small party to investigate. Katrine, of course, as translator. Thord and Thjodrek, two imposingly large seamen with axes and swords to match, and Hervor Elsdottir. The captain reasoned that, on balance, his enforcer was more likely to be of value at their destination than in guarding the longship.

It proved an unnecessary precaution, as they were made genuinely welcome. The place was called Madagasikara, although it was never clear if that name applied to the town they were taken to, or the surrounding land. Perhaps both.

Led from the beach up a path cut into the lush forest, the trading party found themselves in a substantial settlement.

It looked like a clearing had been slashed from the forest years before to make way for a village. As the village expanded to a small township, more trees were cleared. The clearing of forest for one or another 'trade' purpose would eventually become a most divisive issue, as some of the islanders (and many people overseas) would come to recognise the costs of destroying the environment and habitats of so much that made Madagascar unique.

Most of the square buildings appeared flimsy, but rose up from stone foundations, at least. The exceptions were a handful of solid-looking squat windowless stone structures at either end of a central plaza.

In recent years trade had started to thrive. Arabs were becoming regular visitors, bearing goods from the continent's interior, like gems and silver, mined in the south of the mainland, hence the fluency in their language.

Much of the lead in talking with the newcomers was taken by a man named Ramboasalama. He introduced himself as a driana, which they rightly took to mean a sort of nobility.

Satisfied as to the security of their situation, the captain sent Hervor back to the longship to arrange the signal to call in the knarr. There was just a moment of hesitation before she moved to obey.

"I can go with you to protect you," offered the local noble.

"I do *not* need protecting," Elsdottir replied, glaring back at the man before storming back down the path to the dock.

The other four Norse exchanged glances and tried very hard not to chuckle out loud. Ramboasalama looked puzzled.

"I merely meant that the forest can be dangerous," he explained. "There have been reports of an antamba prowling nearby."

"My friend, I have no idea what an antamba is, but if one crosses the path of Hervor when she's annoyed, what it will be is endangered!" said Sigurd, grinning.

The antamba, or giant fossa, was something like a cross between a cat and a mongoose, about the size of a wolf, and was already well on the way to being endangered. Within a few generations any that survived were lurking in the high mountain forests, their sighting the stuff of legends.

Hrolf and Sverrir were well acquainted with how their captain liked things organised. The crew was soon divided into teams to variously go ashore, stay by the boats on stevedoring duty as required, and a small number to discreetly stay on guard in case the situation should suddenly change. After all, it had happened before.

Physically, the local Merina people were quite unlike those of the great mainland to their west. They were shorter, with skin the brown of good leather, and eyes that were more narrow than round and that turned up slightly at the corner.

Their own language, too, was quite unlike any the sailors had heard. Fortunately, the shared familiarity with other tongues meant communication was not a major problem. Katrine was, as ever, the conduit for more complex matters, but by now quite a number of the seafarers could maintain at least a simple conversation when they came into town.

Sigurd and the crew spent a substantial part of what remained of the day exploring the substantial Madagasikara marketplace that was based in and around the plaza. In its earliest days the town had traded mostly in timber and foodstuffs like rice and beef from the strange hump-backed cattle they herded up in the hills. Now it was developing into a genuine centre of commerce as traders sailed in from the south and the north.

Ah, the north. Somewhere in that direction lay Baghdad, and one of the merchants of Madagasikara confirmed that, albeit not entirely helpfully. Yes, the river called Arvand Rud met the ocean somewhere to the north of here. The question 'How far?' got only shrugs in reply. He'd been told by a trader, who'd heard from a gold merchant who'd heard from a slave ship captain...

Hervor was with her captain when he was told this frustrating snippet of information. It was clear from her expression that she shared his irritation. Watching the exchange, Ramboasalama rolled a lock of his long black hair between his fingers. It was an unconscious action, the equivalent of Saemundsson's stroking of his moustache.

"I shall ask my grandfather about this tomorrow," he promised. "In his time he was the cleverest of our traders. He will know."

Sigurd thanked the nobleman for his gracious offer. After a gentle nudge from her captain, so did Hervor.

As the town's first-ever visitors from the Land of Ice, they would of course be introduced to the queen at a small ceremony this evening. That prompted a burst of serious grooming activity from most of the Norse across the rest of the afternoon.

They were normally fastidious about their appearance, but the long time at sea with human interaction limited mostly to tribes with very different ideas about what looked attractive, had let the standards slip. Beards and moustaches were cleaned and trimmed. Hair was washed and braided (with a few exceptions like Hervor and Sverrir for whom washing was quite sufficient, thank you). Clothes were repaired, or in some cases new finery was taken out for the first time. Even some of the more interesting oils and perfumes were applied.

After all the careful preparations, the Royal Meeting itself was something of an anticlimax. The crew was lined up in ranks, most of them looking quite dashing. Queen Rangita was carried out into the square on a litter borne by four brawny young Merina men. They must have been required for the weight of the gaudily decorated litter, as there wasn't enough of Her Majesty herself to need all of the strength of any one of her bearers.

The queen was a wizened little figure, with a face like a rather dark walnut and the physique of an underfed prepubescent child. Her eyes were bright, alert, and calculating though.

It was the royal attire that was most disappointing to the more fastidiously turned-out crew though. She wore a headdress of feathers that would have been bright in their day (but that day had been decades earlier), and a robe seemingly sewn together from panels and strips of whatever fabric had caught the regal eye on any day she'd been in the marketplace. The colours and fabrics didn't match, and the patchwork itself was random. Either the robe had been made for a different, much larger woman, or the queen had lost a very great deal of weight.

Diplomatic to the hilt of his broadsword, Saemundsson bowed and introduced his crew to the monarch. The old woman gave a long look over the assembled Norse, her gaze lingering approvingly, or even lecherously, on a few in particular. The litter was placed on the ground, but she didn't lift herself from her chair.

"A fine body of men. And women. Although a bit pale for my own taste," she said in perfect Arabic. Her voice was surprisingly strong and clear considering the spindly frame it came from.

She rapped the shoulder of one of her bearers with knuckles like brown beads and ordered, "Food and drink!"

The fellow nodded and strode away towards one of the larger buildings around the square. It must have been a prearranged signal, as even before the man had reached the doorway people were coming out of the building with platters of food.

"Tell them to relax," the queen said to Sigurd, waving toward the crew. "Now, sit with me and talk. My sister's boy has told me something of you, but I'd like to hear it from you."

"Certainly, your Highness," answered the captain, dismissing the assembled crew with a gesture.

There was a distinct lack of seating options, so Sigurd settled himself cross-legged on the ground beside the old woman.

"Call me Rangita," she ordered. "I'd rather feel that you were talking to me, not the title."

"Yes ma'am – er, Rangita. Thank you. Er – your sister's boy?"

"Ramboasalama. Quite a bright lad. Bright enough not to be too ambitious, when he'll be better served by being patient, if you understand me?"

The captain nodded. He realised immediately that there was no power lurking behind this throne. Despite her appearance Rangita was clearly shrewd, intelligent, and ruthless when she needed to be.

Earthenware beakers of good quality red wine were brought to the pair, as a conversation got under way.

Very shortly though, Sigurd asked, "Rangita, do you mind if I call my interpreter over to join us? I'm afraid my Arabic is not as fluent as yours, whereas hers is excellent."

"Of course, of course. 'Hers' you say – is this the one my nephew has his eye on?"

The captain was genuinely baffled, and admitted as much, prompting a grin to split the wrinkled royal face. Katrine was called over, Rangita watching her nephew's face as the translator approached.

"No. Not her," the queen said softly.

Sigurd was more relieved to hear that than he hoped he let show. With appropriately diplomatic smiles and bows, Katrine av Ord was introduced by her captain and sat on the ground beside him. Wine was immediately brought to her.

"The people serving – they're of a different race to you, Rangita, yes?" she observed.

"Indeed. Well noticed, young lady." To Rangita, almost everyone would be 'young'. "They're Vazimba. Mountain tribe. They lived down here on the coast generations ago, but moved when the Merina came."

Sigurd looked more closely. The individuals in question were distinctly even shorter and darker than most of their hosts, with Rangita herself being one of the exceptions.

"Not all of them moved," observed the captain evenly.

"No, quite right. Some stayed and became part of Merina families. Both of my grandmothers came from such a line. Others have been brought down from the mountains by force. My... predecessor had ideas of becoming actively involved in the slave market. Such traders regularly stop here, and bought and sold between themselves in our marketplace." The old queen shrugged. "There was no desire to make slaves of our own people, so a number of the Vazimba were captured. It wasn't a success though. They were... unappreciated by the passing traders. Too small compared to what they can get over on the mainland, and inclined to think for themselves."

"So they became your slaves instead?" asked Saemundsson, keeping his voice as neutral as possible.

"No," replied Rangita, neither offended nor defensive. "They leave, they make their own way back to where they came from. They stay, they work. There are, of course, certain jobs they aren't permitted to do."

Conversation turned to trade in goods other than human flesh. Rangita had an eye for beautiful things, but what was, to the Icelanders, an eccentric approach to what to do with them. Her royal robe, she explained, had been passed to her as a long rather simple white thing with some gold thread sewn into it. She'd added pieces of materials that she valued because of their colour, or texture, or price. Not that, as queen, she was ever expected to pay for such things of course. The same was true of the decoration of the 'royal carriage', which explained the rather odd mix of baubles, ornaments and jewellery hanging from her litter.

Eccentric and frail as she might appear, this was a woman who was very accustomed to getting her own way. Taking and holding a throne, even here, required some steel in the character. The captain of *Serpentfang* recognised and respected that.

With a gracious and understanding little bow of his head Sigurd said, "I trust that there'll be something amongst our wares that appeals to you at tomorrow's market, Rangita."

The old woman looked at him, puzzled. "I'm sure you'll have something for me. I believe you have some amber with you – rare here and much prized by our passing traders. I like the colour of it, myself. But there's no market tomorrow. Tomorrow is the Feast of the Ancestors. No trading then – everyone knows that."

For a moment Sigurd thought of Pall Jansson, and how the expectations of what *everyone* knows could vary considerably from place to place. The unforeseen delay in trading was irksome, but he couldn't let that show. He chose his words carefully, and Katrine translated with equal diplomatic caution.

"I must admit, the Feast of the Ancestors isn't known of in Iceland, and I can only assume we haven't chanced to be in the right place at the right time for it in our travels. Could you explain about it please? I'd hate for any of us to inadvertently cause any offence."

Rangita's response was vague. Not deliberately so, but she struggled to explain something so intimately familiar to someone with no knowledge of it. Many of the terms she used were in the Merina language, apparently having no Arabic equivalent. They were quite untranslatable, even for Katrine who did her best, and remained resolutely diplomatic.

After quaffing her fourth beaker of wine in quick succession, the aged monarch suddenly announced that she was tired and that, in order to do justice to her responsibilities tomorrow, she would now retire.

Her litter being borne back to the building that apparently served as a palace – really an administrative building with a more than comfortable apartment attached – was a signal for the Vazimba serving staff to clear away platters, and for the rest of the Madagasikara locals to take themselves back to their homes.

The seafarers, for their part, returned to the boats for the night. Whatever the more imaginative of them may have wondered or dreamt about the forthcoming Feast day, the reality of the strange ceremony would still come as a surprise.

A good proportion of the crew elected to stay near their ships the next morning. They had a sense of something supernatural about this Feast thing, and many a sailor wanted nothing to do with spirits or ceremonies that weren't his or her own. So it was only the innately curious (like Sigurd, Fafhrd, Katrine and Cailin) and the dutiful (Sverrir, Hrolf the Dark, Hervor and Bjorn Breakneck) who made their way up the path to the market square.

The area had already been cleared out. Someone, probably the Vazimba, had been busy since first light. Straw mats were laid out all over the square. Several of the locals were already there, some of them laying out flowers, food and drink. Many more were visible around the darkened doorways of four stone buildings that stood at opposite ends of the square.

Rangita appeared, again borne on her litter. But while the litter still had all its ornaments, the queen herself was in a simple white tunic, her concession to colour being a strip of multi-hued woven fabric worn as a sash around her waist. At the edge of the square her litter was put down. The aged monarch got up from her chair and walked, a little unsteadily, to a mat in the middle of the square, where with surprising flexibility she lowered herself to sit cross-legged. She clapped her hands above her head twice.

At that signal people started to emerge from the stone buildings, carefully carrying white bundles of various lengths. The buildings were mausoleums, and the bundles were bodies wrapped in linen.

The shrouds were carefully removed. They would soon be replaced by fresh wrappings, but before then, the cadavers they contained were the focal point of the Feast.

Some of the bodies might have been vaguely recognisable to a close relative. A few years deceased, withered, dried, but still with some skin and hair. Many were little more than skeletons with some desiccated flesh still clinging to their frames. Others weren't even that intact. Lengths and fragments of brittle bone that lay among dust that had once lived and breathed. How they could still be rewrapped was almost unimaginable.

But most bizarrely of all, on this one day, these disintegrating specimens were treated as if they were still alive. Food and drink were set beside them, they were chatted with. And most importantly of all, they were asked questions. This was the day when the guidance of the ancestors was delivered.

The Merina people knew, without doubt, that when something was asked of an ancestor, the answer would shortly appear in the head of the questioner.

The queen was chatting casually to a figure that bore a startling resemblance to her, although that was probably more a reflection of Rangita's apparent decrepitude than the state of preservation of her father.

Who sat where in the square appeared to reflect the social status of the ancestors being consulted, with the queen's family at the centre, drianas and the wealthiest traders around them, and the Vazimba and other lowly families around the edges. The seafarers discreetly wandered about the square, or sat a little away watching.

Ramboasalama called the quartet of Sigurd, Hrolf, Katrine and Hervor over to where he sat with three baskets of food and what appeared at first glance to be a bundle of sticks on a nest of linen.

"As I promised, I shall ask my grandfather how to reach Baghdad for you," the nobleman said with great solemnity.

Eyebrows were raised but Sigurd did have the presence of mind to say an equally solemn "Thank you".

The Merina prince was even more gratified by the smile he got from Hervor. He rested his right hand on the little pile of ossiferous remains of his father's father and started to speak in his own language. Only the word 'Baghdad' was recognisable to his little audience. After some time his voice trailed off, and he sat quietly with blank eyes staring into an unguessable distance.

Then he began to speak again, softly, in the Merina tongue. Then his voice became stronger, the language switched to Arabic, and his dark eyes seemed to regain some life, although he still stared out into the distance rather than looking at anyone.

"Some days to the north east of here is an island – Dina Morgabin. It lies directly south of the ancestral home of the Arabs. It is a long voyage, many days of open sea, but once reached the eastern end of the Arabs' coast doubles back on itself into a great gulf of water. Into the northern tip of this body of water flows the river called Arvand Rud, from which the sea-going traders of Baghdad make their way south and east."

The driana trembled slightly for a moment. He shook his head, and then looked at Hervor, then Sigurd.

"Did that help?" he asked.

The four Icelanders looked at each other, bemused. It was Katrine, who had most clearly understood the narrative, who replied.

"I think so. Perhaps. You mentioned a place to the northeast called the Western Island."

Ramboasalama tugged at a lock of his hair. "Did I? I'm sorry – there are a number of islands in that direction, so I'm told. Did my grandfather say anything to identify any one specifically?"

Saemundsson was stroking his moustache. "No, but if I understood you - er, *him* correctly, that may not be much of a problem. My thanks, Ramboasalama, to you *and* your honoured ancestor."

"You have my thanks, too," said Hervor, well aware of the looks she was getting from the Merina noble, who was, she admitted to herself, a fine figure of a man.

The captain got to his feet and said, "Come, my friends. I think we should let the prince have the chance to converse with his grandfather privately."

The driana smiled gratefully. He did indeed have something he wanted to ask his ancestor about, or rather, someone. When that particular someone allowed her hand to brush his broad shoulder as she stood and walked past, Ramboasalama fancied he already knew the answer to his question.

The four Icelanders quietly discussed what they'd just seen and heard as they walked slowly towards the outskirts of the plaza. They were joined by Fafhrd, who was coming from another part of the square.

"It's intriguing, isn't it Captain?" asked the helmsman.

"A good word for it, my friend," agreed Sigurd.

Hrolf chewed a stray length of his moustache. "Do you think Ramboasalama knew that stuff already, and just wanted to make a bit of a performance out of telling us? Or is there something to this ancestor thing?" he asked.

Sigurd's own moustache was getting a thorough stroking. "I think that if someone believes in something strongly enough, they might shape their reality to fit their faith."

That got a quizzical look from Fafhrd. Sigurd explained further.

"It might be that the information was locked in his head – something heard long ago, perhaps, and it takes the ritual to draw it out."

They'd reached the edge of the plaza. Sverrir and his enforcer Bjorn were sitting on a log that did service as a bench outside one of the lightweight structures at the perimeter.

"Not keen to sit outside any of the ancestors' homes?" asked Hrolf jokingly as he gestured toward one of the mausoleums.

The grizzled sailor grunted. "Hmph. Just keeping out of the sun, that's all," he replied.

"Lot of strange bloody nonsense, as far as I can see," was Bjorn's considered opinion. "Here, Captain, take my seat," he said, sliding off the log and planting his backside in the dirt.

Suddenly he swore and jumped to his feet, clutching at his left hand. Just by where he'd sat on the ground was a glossy black creature, a few inches long. It had eight legs like a spider, but also a pair of large pincers, which Bjorn assumed had caused the sudden sharp pain. Then he saw the thing's tail, curving up over its body and ending in a large, vicious looking point from which a drop of yellowish liquid still hung.

It was the crew's first experience of a scorpion, and it wasn't a good one. Within moments Breakneck was swaying unsteadily, and collapsed back onto the makeshift seat clutching at his throat.

At a sprint, Hrolf fetched a beaker of water. Bjorn could barely swallow it. The merest trickle felt like a sharp blade slicing his throat. The victim slipped forward from the log, landing on his knees, bent double. His eyes and nose were streaming and he was clearly struggling to breathe.

By now, some of the locals had noticed the situation. One of the Vazimba spotted the scorpion and cried, "Halandevo!" A woman ran to fetch help from an older man on the far side of the plaza. He was evidently a medicine man or shaman, for he immediately dashed to his hut, returning quickly with a small clay pot.

Sigurd and Fafhrd were struggling to hold Bjorn upright, even on his knees. The man's skin was fast becoming hot to the touch. Hervor dipped a length of cloth into the beaker of water and tried to mop the red, sweating face, but as soon as the fabric touched his skin Breakneck groaned terribly.

The shaman chanted a few words, then spat into the little pot. Chanting again, he mixed his saliva with the green substance sticking to the clay with his fingers. He managed to make himself understood, asking where his patient had been stung. Katrine knelt and held up Bjorn's left hand. The wrist and base of the hand were already swollen and dark.

Even as the shaman started to smear the poultice on the wound, he knew it was too late. It was very rare for the halandevo's sting to be fatal, but he had known it before. Bjorn tried to reach for his own throat with one hand, and then grabbed at his chest with the other.

The scorpion's poison was enough to make anyone ill, often seriously so, although the shaman's concoction was very effective at drawing it from the wound and starting a healing process. However Bjorn Breakneck suffered from an allergy that nobody there could have known about, including the man himself. Anaphylactic shock had killed him in bare minutes.

The shaman bowed his head and gestured apologetically. Sigurd put a hand on the older man's shoulder, trying to make it clear that there was no rancour at him. On the contrary, the captain knew he'd done all he could to try to help.

Fafhrd lifted the body, cradled in his strong arms. He followed Sigurd as the two captains sorrowfully led the way back down the path to the beach.

Having just been told of what had happened, Ramboasalama ran after them. He grabbed the trailing Hervor's shoulder.

"Can I do anything?" he blurted.

"Not right now," the woman murmured. Unconsciously she reached up and squeezed the dark hand on her shoulder – a very different reaction to how she might usually have behaved.

News of the sudden death rippled through the plaza like wavelets in a pond. There was no question of the Ancestors' ceremony being cut short, but conversations with the departed were mostly not as extended as they might have been.

At the queen's prompting, there was some delicate questioning of the few Norse who hadn't already followed their captains downhill. Was there anything appropriate the Merina might help with? Despite the obviously accidental nature of the death, Rangita felt a sense of responsibility. It was her community, and furthermore she *liked* these traders from the distant north. They showed her respect, unlike many of those who passed through Madagasikara.

So, soon after Bjorn Breakneck's sudden death, Ramboasalama led a group of Merina carrying lengths of cut firewood down to where the two ships were moored.

"I understand you have a death ritual that involves burning," the driana called over to Sigurd. "Our queen offers this wood as a gesture of respect."

It was an outstanding piece of diplomacy, from both the queen and her nephew.

Bjorn's pyre could hardly be built on the dock, but the Merina provided ample timber for the construction of a floating platform. As darkness fell *Serpentfang* towed the structure out to a safe distance, where with great solemnity it was lit by Fafhrd as he and Sigurd said some appropriate words.

Most of the crews of both boats were assembled on the dock, together with a good number of the Merina, not all of them by royal command.

For all that it had been an ignominious passing, Breakneck had been well respected (if not always universally liked, considering his role) especially on board *Red Whale*. And after Queen Rangita's show of support, Saemundsson could hardly do anything else but give the knarr's enforcer a full ritual send-off.

The longship returned to the dock. Sigurd, Fafhrd and their team of oarsmen joined the small crowd watching the flames reflected on the water.

"It is a very moving ceremony," said Ramboasalama approvingly.

He was standing closely alongside Hervor Elsdottir. So close that their arms and shoulders were pressed together, although neither gave indication of noticing. They gave no indication of moving apart, either.

On the other side of the driana was his aunt, the queen. "Don't fancy being burned, myself. Be a bit awkward come the Feast of the Ancestors."

Standing near the queen, as decorum seemed to require, Sigurd had to suppress a chuckle at that remark. Beside him was Sverrir Bent-knee who was too absorbed in his own grief to have heard the remark.

"A stupid, futile, inglorious damned death!" swore the knarr's old captain.

His own captain laid a gentle, sympathetic hand on the veteran sailor's shoulder. Sigurd knew his old comrade had wanted to pass on the captaincy of *Red Whale* to Bjorn. Sverrir had no children – none acknowledged by anyone, at least – and had seen in Breakneck much of what he would have wanted to see in a son. What he saw in himself. Determination, loyalty, hard work and a passion for the sea.

To lose the younger man to such a fate, on land yet, galled the old seaman's heart.

The flames died down as the pyre drifted away. In sombre quiet, everyone retired to sleep, save for those few of the crew who were on watch. No matter the circumstances, that was one routine that Sigurd did not compromise.

On the following day, the plaza was returned to its usual self, a quietly bustling little marketplace. The locals bartered amongst themselves there with whatever they produced: beef, milk, vegetables, fish, leatherwork, woodwork, even a simple form of cloth made from the soaked and pounded bark of a particular tree. The Merina merchants also traded with each other according to mood or whim for goods that had been obtained from the regular traffic of outsiders.

One such vessel had called in several days earlier, on its way south along the mainland's eastern coast. Primarily a slavers' ship, there had also been a good supply of various spices and long tusks of elephant ivory, some of which had been obtained by the Merina in return for their good timber.

Such ivory was evidently less scarce in the east than on the western coast of the continent, although it was still quite rare and highly prized. The presence of the impressive tusks overshadowed the sea ivory of the Norse when they arrived in the marketplace, but they had other goods that were very much appreciated.

High on that list was their stock of amber. Most of the smaller communities they'd visited had shown little enthusiasm for the unfamiliar material, but here it was recognised as highly valued in the bigger markets, therefore a desirable thing to have. It didn't hurt either that Queen Rangita expressed considerable enthusiasm for both jewellery and ornaments crafted in the translucent gold. Sigurd was shrewd enough to ensure that she was presented with attractive samples of both, not least as thanks for her contribution to the previous night's ceremony.

Rangita also gratefully received a quantity of her favourite fabric from the seafarers' stock – the fine wool from Cahercommaun.

It seemed a surprising choice at first. The pristine white was far removed from the extravagant colours the queen normally seemed to favour. Her nephew quietly explained to Hervor later that Rangita increasingly felt the cold of the night air (hardly surprising, given her frame). A blanket and shawl of the Irish wool would be very welcome, in private if not on public display.

At one point an argument broke out between two of *Serpentfang*'s oarsmen. It was a trivial thing, over a carved wooden baton both men wanted to buy. Clenched fists and Nordic growls were alarming the small merchant who'd displayed the woodwork.

Suddenly Katrine av Ord strode between the two, and gave both an open-handed slap to the back of the head.

"Behave yourselves!" she snapped.

"But he..." both men began at once.

"Quiet! What sort of impression do you reckon you're giving of our ship, and everyone on it? Of our *captain*? You can knock yourselves senseless as far as I'm concerned, but do it privately. If I find you carrying on like this in public again I'll kick your arses so hard you'll have to row standing up!"

Both oarsmen dropped their heads, and their hands. The interpreter gave a few coins to the merchant and was handed the desired baton. She looked at it appraisingly, smiled, and then broke it in two over her knee. She held out a piece to each of the would-be combatants.

"You're both capable carvers. Spend some time and effort cleaning up the broken ends and you'll both have something decent to remember Madagasikara by. Something better than bruised knuckles, a bloodied nose, and my boot print on your backside."

The two men took the proffered pieces, each saying an embarrassed and somewhat bemused 'thank you'. Katrine nodded and walked away casually.

Hervor Elsdottir caught the translator's arm as she passed and smiled.

"Very well done," the enforcer said approvingly. "I was on my way over, but you saved my having to interfere, thank you."

"Quite alright. When I saw the two idiots carrying on like that, I just thought of how hard Sig... the captain works at being diplomatic when in a market, and I just thought I had to step in."

The two women shared a long look into each other's eyes before Hervor's smile broadened and she said, "Yes. I understand. Thanks again."

They clasped arms and walked their separate ways.

Elsdottir's wandering took her to a stall where a wizened little Merina merchant was selling spears. They were long wooden shafts with their points carved from the same piece of timber, in different shapes for different types of hunting and fishing.

Olaf Vaksson was standing at the stall, carefully balancing one of the weapons across his palm. He looked up at Hervor's approach.

"These are well made, my friend," he observed genially. "I think they're more for throwing than the close action of the one you carry. They're well weighted and balanced though, I think."

Hervor respected Olaf's judgement, but was interested enough to want to make her own assessment. She took a spear and, like Vaksson, balanced it across her palm, nodding as she did.

"Feels good, yes," she agreed. "But there's only one way to be sure. Would you mind if we tried these out?" she asked the merchant.

The wizened man blinked in surprise. Merina women did not normally handle weaponry of any sort. He cautiously gestured agreement, motivated as much by curiosity as possible sales (and a certain amount of instinctive fear, or at least respect).

They were near the edge of the plaza. Olaf grabbed a couple of the bags of sand that were used to keep streams of rainwater from running into doorways, and set them up on another of the logs that served as seats. He and Hervor stood well back from their targets, holding their spears lightly.

Both had chosen weapons of the type used for hunting antamba, or creatures of that size. There were few predators on the island, and some of the other local animals were protected by religious significance. Not all of them though, and some made for good eating on the rare occasions they strayed near enough to be brought down.

The little merchant was about to remark that his potential

customers were considerably further away from their targets than a hunter would normally be, but thought better of it. These Norse were bigger than the Merina, he reasoned, although in Hervor's case not by very much. *And* she was a woman, so...

Whatever precise implications that fact may have had for him evaporated in an instant when she hurled the spear. It flew fast and straight, and with enough force that its tip poked out of the back of the dead centre of the sandbag.

Olaf's was only slightly less accurate, piercing the top left of his target. He grinned at his companion.

"I told you they felt good," he said as they retrieved the spears.

Unnoticed, watching at a discreet distance, the driana Ramboasalama suddenly realised he was standing with his mouth open in a most undignified manner. He closed it quickly, but the image of Hervor's lithe figure launching that spear with such power and accuracy would stay with him for a very long time.

That evening, Sigurd sat on his o'api hide by a brazier on the deck of his longship, contemplating what had been a successful day's trading. The loss of Bjorn Breakneck was a blow, but otherwise he would take away good recollections of this island.

Seated beside him in what was becoming her usual place, Katrine noticed over his shoulder that Hervor was standing a little away, looking uncharacteristically undecided. The interpreter met her eye and gave a small nod before getting to her feet.

"Someone to see you, my dear captain," she said, before strolling to the stern of the longship to chat to Fafhrd and Bjarni.

At the captain's beckoning, his enforcer came to him and sat down. She drew a deep breath. What she wanted to say wouldn't come easily.

"You'd like to stay here, eh?" asked Sigurd simply, trying not to smile as she visibly deflated. "I don't object, if it's a considered choice, but I'd like to hear your reasoning."

Another deep breath before Hervor answered. "A combination of things, I think, captain. I must admit I'm getting weary of this voyage, and the prospect of a long journey north with no sight of land has less appeal than it might have when we left Hofn."

"We could find an alternate route. These traders who come down the coast of the mainland are coming from the same general direction. Logically, if we follow their trail we should find the Arab homeland and ultimately Baghdad," suggested Sigurd.

"Grind north as we ground south? Relying on flyspeck villages where someone might get killed for swatting a bug? Risking having to land among river dragons twice a man's size? That's no more appealing, I'm afraid. But it's more than that. I *like* this place. The people have a sense of honour. That wrinkled little queen inspires me, believe it or not. Women have authority here, if they're strong enough to seize and hold it."

"Do you see yourself as a queen? I can imagine it – but woe betide any other tribe, or ship full of traders, who tried to cross you!" said the captain with a good-natured laugh that Hervor joined in on.

Sigurd continued, "I think you may have an entry point into the existing royal family if you'd prefer to take such a path instead of a more, let's say, forceful approach."

His enforcer blushed, not a common sight (and one not spoken of when seen), before she answered quietly, "He's an attractive man, yes. Being a prince of sorts is certainly a bonus."

"I think he's a good man, too, from what I can tell in the short time we've been here. I also think he's quite taken with you, too, if I'm any judge."

In that, Saemundsson was entirely correct. Ramboasalama could best be described as 'smitten', rather to the amusement of his royal aunt, who had viewed relationships as transitory affairs of convenience and lust for most of her long life. It would require all his willpower to maintain his noble dignity when Hervor Elsdottir later told him of her reciprocal attraction.

"I think you're not without an admirer too, captain, and closer to home. If I may speak plainly?" the enforcer asked.

"If not now, when? Go ahead."

"I might have worried that in leaving I'd be somehow failing in the duty I've sworn – to protect you, the ship, your honour... Not that there's ever been reason to doubt this crew! But I've seen enough lately to know that there's someone else on board who can fill that role." Seeing a slightly blank look on the captain's face she explained, "Katrine av Ord is ready, willing and able to kick arse on your behalf."

"Really? I mean... ah... I haven't seen..."

"Well, I have. She's not just a bloody good translator and a warm attractive body. She respects you as well as cares about you, and will take no nonsense from anyone. You're safe with her, I'm willing to bet," Hervor stated emphatically.

Sigurd surprised her by taking her hand as he looked into her eyes and answered, "I've long ago learned to trust your judgement, Hervor. Another reason why I'm not pleased to lose you. You have my gratitude for many things, not least your honesty. And you have my respect, which is why I won't argue with your decision now I've heard you explain it. I didn't think you'd be rushing into something without due consideration, but I wanted to give you the chance to hear your own thoughts out loud, as you've so often done for me, my friend."

"Thank you, cap... Sigurd. I'll go and pack my belongings together, so I can be ashore before you catch tomorrow's tide."

The two clasped arms, then the woman stood. As she did, she coughed slightly.

"Chill in the air tonight," she observed, with some justification.

She had no way of knowing that she carried the first traces of a disease that would decimate her new people. She herself would survive to a good age, ruling first alongside Ramboasalama and later alone for several years after his death. But the illness-diminished community would never be able to rise to the dominance she'd privately aspired to – an ambition she'd discreetly not shared with her captain.

As the Norse ships cast off from the dock next day, Hervor Elsdottir stood arm in arm with Ramboasalama, both of them beside Queen Rangita's litter. Her last conversation with Sigurd that morning had been to emphatically back his decision to sail north-east, not back toward the mainland.

"Don't crawl up that coast like an insect on a mangy dog's back. Trade can get silver and gems here with a bit of patience. And persistence," she'd added with a meaningful tap of her knife's hilt. "I'll make sure there's plenty that's worthwhile here for you to trade when you return. Go north, captain. Find this river. Baghdad beckons! I'll wait for you."

.ooo.

12

MAURITIUS – THE BIRDS THAT
WALK AWAY

They knew where they were going. Northeast, to find a place the Arab traders called Dina Morgabin. It should only be a few days sailing before they headed due north from there. The voyage after that would be a long one, but once they hit land it would be easy. Turn to the east and follow the coastline patiently into a great gulf extending northwest. At the northern end of this gulf was the mouth of the river that was their destination: Arvand Rud, gateway to Baghdad.

Reaching what they assumed to be Dina Morgabin was achieved without great difficulty. They saw the smoke before they saw the island – a great black column of it.

"I thought the place was supposed to be uninhabited," said Cailin, standing in the prow of *Serpentfang*.

Sigurd stroked his moustache. "If that's the smoke of a settlement, it's a very unusual one. I've seen something similar before, a long way to the north. You don't have active volcanoes in Ireland?"

"I've heard about them."

"Not something you want to get too near to, my friend. A good thing it looks like this one's on the far side of the island from us," observed the captain with a smile.

The two ships were aiming for a white beach, fringed with palm trees. As they neared the shore, the sailors saw a lot of sharks in the water – not in the same numbers as they'd encountered off Cloud Town, but at least as big. They were bull sharks and tiger sharks, both dangerous.

As the beach loomed, the Norse started to become acutely aware that sharks weren't the only creatures here with bite. The boats had barely touched the sand when they found themselves beset by swarms of mosquitoes.

Any piece of exposed skin suddenly seemed to be a target. Sailors swatted frenziedly, but for every mosquito killed it seemed five more would take its place. Oh, to have the fragrant foliage of N'Dar!

"Captain, this is unbearable! Do we need the fresh water that badly?" pleaded Cailin, expressing the sentiments of everyone on board.

"No! Well, yes, but there must be other options!" said Sigurd, giving an emphatic signal to withdraw the boats. "We'll make for the far side of this island!" he called.

But as they rounded the southern end of the island, the cause of the great column of smoke became all too clear. The volcano that dominated the southeastern corner of the island was active, with a flow of lava pouring into the ocean.

The Norse had no choice but to keep heading northwest to avoid the steam and noxious gases cloaking the coastline. Even more aggravatingly, the superheated water around where the lava met the sea was playing havoc with the currents, and they found themselves travelling at a much greater rate than Sigurd or Sverrir particularly wanted.

The unexpected acceleration had a positive outcome, though, as they soon came within sight of another substantial island. It looked like another gigantic volcano rising from the sea, but this time without an ominous column of smoke.

But while there was no lava discharging into the ocean, what they did find was a series of coral reefs that seemed to ring the whole island. It required patience, and some good seamanship, but on the eastern coast of the island they found a gap in the reef that could be safely negotiated, bringing the boats in to a long wide sand beach.

A broad plain swept back towards a series of rugged mountains. Dense forest covered much of what could be seen beyond the fringe of white sand. Where they beached was close by a stream, not wide but flowing quickly with clear fresh water.

Perhaps it was the prevailing winds, or perhaps the water didn't sit and stagnate here as it evidently did on Dina Morgabin, but the air was mercifully free of biting insects. Sigurd was happy to allow most of his crew to leave the boats and relax. After the casks had been refilled, many took the opportunity to bathe in the stream. It was hot in the sun, but there was plentiful shade for resting in.

Some of the more naturally curious of the visitors explored some way into the fringe of the forest. Among them were Fafhrd and Bjarni, who returned to the beach not long after, bearing broad grins and a brace each of the strangest fowl any of the crew had ever seen.

They were the size of large turkeys, with stubby wings and a large hooked bill that looked like a strange woodworking tool.

"They're the stupidest things!" laughed Bjarni. "We walked into a clearing where there were several of them wandering about. I expected them to take off, but no, they just ignored us. I killed one with my axe, thinking it looked like good eating, and still the others didn't react. One of them actually walked up to me! So I just wrung its neck – neat and tidy! It was only after we grabbed a couple more that the rest moved off into the scrub. Even then, they just walked away, more like they'd lost interest than they were actually afraid of us."

"Well, they look substantial," agreed Sigurd. "Let's get a fire going and see how they taste. Fresh fowl will be a welcome treat for every-one. If they're good, it sounds like we can readily get more to take with us."

It turned into a substantial feast on the sands. There was abundant fruit, and eels that were caught and cooked to supplement the dodos.

After a lengthy consultation with Sverrir and Hrolf, the captain made an announcement to his gathered crew. They faced the prospect of several days at sea, or even longer, before they'd hit the coastline that would lead them on to Baghdad. They should enjoy this opportunity – eat well, and rest, before they set off again on the morning tide. The water was already on board. He wanted some more of the local foodstuffs gathered.

The oversized fowls couldn't be preserved, but if boiled, their flesh would surely last a few days, before they went back to dried and salted meat, and whatever fish they could catch. As he'd expected, there were plenty of volunteers to go hunting. 'Hunting' almost seemed too grand a word, as the most difficult part of the exercise was finding the birds. Killing them was no challenge at all.

Before long there was a substantial pile of dead dodos near the cooking fire. Sigurd ordered two large cooking pots brought from the boats and filled with water. The birds were plucked, chopped up and set to boiling.

Otherwise, it was a lazy afternoon in a tropical idyll. As the sun went down, people stretched out to sleep on the beach by the fire, or on board ship, according to preference. The prospect of a long sail wasn't daunting for the Norse, but the captain's consideration in offering this one 'night off' was appreciated.

Late in the day, there came two significant discoveries. First, Hrolf returned from a stroll in the forest, where he'd been idly gathering fruit and berries. Over his shoulder was a thick fallen branch, at first glance ordinary enough, although the obvious effort in carrying it gave a clue that it was heavy. The true importance lay under the thumb-width of bark. The heartwood was dense and black.

Smiling, Hrolf displayed the broken end of the branch to Sigurd and said, "I think I've found the source of that timber you're so taken with, captain."

Excitedly, the merchant examined the find. Yes, Hrolf was right – this was the wood called ebony in its rawest form. He tapped the black wood with the knife he'd been using to pry away some bark.

"A wood this hard, what could snap off a branch like this?" he asked. "Some powerful animal? We've seen no tracks..."

"Another tree, I think, captain." Hrolf explained that he'd found the branch protruding from under a log he'd sat down on. That log was the bough of another tree that, judging by the charring at one end, had been struck by lightning. It must have caught the limb of its neighbour as it fell.

"Hmm. I wonder how much damage we'd do to our axes trying to cut down some of these?" Sigurd mused.

Hrolf looked uncertain. "Feel the weight of it. I'm not sure how much we could carry even if we could bring down logs of it. And I'm not sure we have the tools to dress it properly. The best of our wood-working equipment was, ah, on *Stormbearer* – I'm sorry."

"No, no. You're right. And probably our best carvers, too. Still, I'm sure this wood is valuable for trade, even in its rough form. The light's starting to fade, but tomorrow we can scour the forest around us. If one branch can fall, there may be others. And we may be able to take some smaller trees, if their wood turns out to be substantial enough."

Then Egil of Dalir arrived back from a one-man foraging expedition upstream. He'd overeaten, and wanted to walk off the feeling of bloatedness. In his wandering he'd stopped to relieve himself by a tree, and looking up, noticed something surprising.

It was a satchel, made from an unfamiliar leather. It was weathered, clearly having hung from that branch for a considerable time. But it was still intact. The overhanging tree had given it some protection. They could only guess that its previous owner had been going about a similar business to Egil, then been called away hurriedly, forgetting his or her burden.

But who was that previous owner? They opened the satchel with some difficulty, the leather having become brittle. There wasn't much inside, but it was more than enough to be revealing. Some small dark stone cubes, each of a different size – plain but effective measuring weights. A small glass container, its insides coated with the dried residue of dark ink. Dry and falling apart but still recognisable, a plume from one of the large flightless birds that they'd heard about on the western coast. The stains on the end of the shaft, the same colour as that coating the inside of the glass, confirmed what the feather's use had been. And rolled up in the bottom of the satchel, two pieces of parchment. The satchel had belonged to someone with a role very like Hrolf's.

With great care the parchments were unrolled. The material was fragile, and the edges cracking and crumbling. One piece was blank, obviously being carried for later use. The other had only a few words on it, as if the writer had been interrupted just as they'd been starting their task.

Cailin was sitting with the rest of the Irish contingent, deep in conversation. Hrolf went and called her away to examine the new find. As soon as she was told what it was she hurried, arriving at the captain's side two paces ahead of the man who'd fetched her. Katrine av Ord was already there.

"It's Arabic, but you knew that, yes? It's not ancient, but it's old," observed the Irish scribe.

"Fifty years at a guess, by the way this character here is formed, see?" Katrine pointed out.

"Yes, thank you, ladies," said Sigurd as patiently as he could. "But what does it *say*?"

"Ah – sorry. Not much really. It looks like the start of a journal entry. 'Arrived at Dina Arobi. Weather calm. Have started to take on...' And that's where it stops," Katrine read.

The captain stroked his moustache and said, "Dina Arobi. I wonder if that means here?"

"The Isle of Desolation. I suppose it could, although it doesn't look desolate, does it, with all these trees around?" asked the Icelandic translator.

"Desolate of life, maybe," suggested Hrolf. "I mean, there's those big stupid birds, but no sign of much else. Certainly no people."

The Irish woman nodded. "That could be it. It almost seems a waste, doesn't it?" she mused, her voice trailing away.

The stars, scattered across the night sky like a million flecks of silver on a black cloth, weren't in patterns familiar to the navigators of the north, but still made a beautiful canopy as they rested. It was a night for quiet contemplation.

Some lay alone, others in comfortable companionship. Sigurd

was lying on his back, on the o'api skin, his hands clasped behind his head. Katrine was beside him, sharing the hide and the roll of cloth that was doing service as a pillow, an arm on his chest and a hand on his shoulder.

A few small clouds drifted above them, obscuring little patches of stars so it looked like there were holes in the fabric of the universe.

"Are you alright?" Katrine asked softly.

"Mm. Yes, thanks. My mind's wandering."

"Memories of Iceland, or imaginings of Baghdad?"

"Both, and neither. Other memories and other imaginings too." He gently stroked her hip. "A bit of a headache, too, sorry."

"Don't apologise, my dear captain. I'm pleased it's not just me."

They closed their eyes, and eventually drifted off to sleep.

There had been a little of the ships' ale consumed the night before, but not enough to explain the collective seediness that seemed to affect the crew in the morning. Not debilitating, but uncomfortable for many, the captain included. So perhaps his clarity of thought was a little impaired when Cailin asked to speak with him privately, immediately after he'd sent several small teams into the forest to look for good sized branches of the black-hearted wood.

He was able to focus through the headache enough to say, "Yes, of course," although there was a hint of reluctance in his voice. But the Irish woman was not to be denied.

"Captain, I've been asked to talk with you on behalf of the folk from Cahercommaun. They – we, I'll be honest – have concerns about the prospect of a long voyage with no sight of land. I know that you and the crew are undaunted, but none of us were raised to the sea in the way that you all were. I know the memory of that storm still weighs on some minds, too. Then, Hervor Elsdottir's decision to remain on Madagasikara prompted some thought... To put it simply, we'd like to stay here."

Caught completely off-guard, the captain's only immediate response was to raise his eyebrows. The big woman continued.

"There's no shortage of food. There's water. There's a forest full of raw material for building shelter. If you're willing to leave us some supplies, and especially tools, I think we can make a little community here, even make a start on an industry using the black wood. And who knows what else we'll find when we start looking properly?"

Sigurd stroked his moustache, although Cailin noticed a very slight tremble in his hand. Finally he said, "You seem to have given this a lot of thought in only a little time."

"Oh, Captain Saemundsson..."

"Cailin, we're friends. If you can't call me by my name by now, I'm disappointed in both of us."

"I'm sorry – Sigurd. I suppose I was trying to keep this conversation formal, given what I'm asking..."

"Don't. This is the time to be talking as friends. As a friend, I don't want to see you go, because I value you..."

The clerk blushed. "Thank you. But as a friend, then, I've got to be honest. I'm exhausted from the travelling. Most of us are. We knew we were sailing into an uncertain future, and did so willingly. This is no paradise we've arrived on, but there are enough resources here to scratch out an existence. We're not born sailors, Sigurd. We do what we can on the boats. We pull our weight, I hope..."

"You do, Cailin, all of you."

"But it was never meant to be indefinite, was it? We wanted an opportunity, expecting to sell ourselves into labour or servitude somewhere, anywhere better than where we were. Well, this is certainly better, and we wouldn't be working for anyone but ourselves. It's no reflection on you, or the crew or the boats themselves, but there are some who feel they've a better chance of survival on this island than once more taking to sea and following the sun."

As soon as the timber-gatherers returned, the captain called everyone together. He explained the proposal that a small settlement would be established here on the island. There was some evidence that traders did land here, at least occasionally, he explained. Often enough for the place to have a name, if not an especially inspiring one.

"Then we'll give it a new one!" shouted one of the prospective new settlers.

The captain smiled and nodded. "A good idea. Something like 'New Ireland' I suppose."

"No!" exclaimed Cailin, emphatically. "We were all glad to see that place disappear over the horizon. I've too many rotten memories of it to celebrate the name."

"What about Sigurd's Land, for the man what's brought us here?" suggested one of the women who'd expected to spend her life in some form of servitude, and was overjoyed at the prospect of a different fate, however challenging.

The suggestion drew loud acclamation, both from those who'd left Ireland and those who'd already been crewing the boats. Saemundsson was deeply touched, and acutely embarrassed as he continued his address.

"Well, whatever it's to be called, it won't be easy. I've spoken with Sverrir and Hrolf – there are some supplies we can spare to help with getting established. Axes, knives, casks, cooking pots, that sort of thing. We'll need to keep plenty on board though, for the long voyage north." He paused and looked around the gathering. "I've always said, I'll have no one on my crew who doesn't want to be there. This is an unusual situation for everyone. Two rare, indeed extraordinary opportunities lie before you. Sail on with me for the greatest marketplace in the world, the legendary city of Baghdad. Or stay here, and be a part of founding something new. There are few in the world who can say they've done either!"

After a few moments of hubbub, the captain spoke again. "I understand – this is not something to be decided in an instant. We've waited this long to reach Baghdad. Another day can be spared. Talk among yourselves, and make your own decisions. Those coming north, we'll sail on tomorrow's tide."

He finished by explaining that the day would be spent dressing the black wood that had been gathered, seeking more, and providing assistance to the new settlers by clearing a space to live, felling timber for building, and helping to construct some basic initial shelters.

"After all, I'd like a roof over my head when we visit on our way back from Baghdad," he explained to Cailin a little later. They both grinned, despite their persistent headaches.

That aggravation continued to bother many over the day. Sverrir was more than usually tetchy when he took his captain aside to grumble that they shouldn't have opened up the possibility of remaining.

"What if too damned many of 'em take you up on the idea? What if we don't have enough crew left to sail north? What then, eh?" Bent-knee asked querulously.

His own discomfort made Saemundsson less accommodating of his old companion than usual.

"What if, what if - what if you let *me* worry about that? I have a crew of sailors, not builders. They'd never be here otherwise, would they? Oh, we might lose a few, but most of them would no sooner give up the sea than you would!"

Red Whale's old master walked away grumbling.

Saemundsson's assessment proved correct. Less than a dozen of the Norse crew elected to stay behind, a loss easily absorbed when spread between the two ships.

The general low-level malaise that seemed to be affecting so many reduced the amount of work that was achieved across the day. That, and the prospect of losing people who'd shared the remarkable experiences of the uncounted days past, cast something of a sombre pall over the evening meal around what should have been a cheery fire.

Good starchy tubers had been dug up, and cooked well with the roasted dodos that had been gathered during the day. The quality of the food was excellent really, but the celebratory atmosphere one might hope for at the launch of a new community wasn't quite there.

The aspiring new citizens of Sigurd's Land chose to spend one last night sleeping amongst their erstwhile travelling companions. They'd start work on the shelters in the new clearing tomorrow. But another night under the stars, on beach or on boat, seemed in order.

It would be good to report that by dawn, the vague unwellness many felt had dissipated, but that wasn't the case. The departure of

Serpentfang and *Red Whale* went surprisingly smoothly, considering the amount of wincing that accompanied the effort. It was as though everyone was determined to put on a brave face, each group wanting to leave the other feeling positive about their collective future.

In all, there were about thirty people making up the population of Sigurd's Land. They were a good mix of genders, with a range of skills and experience. They stood on the white sands for quite some time that morning, waving farewell to the two ships. Cailin stood tall amongst them, silently wishing she were able to see her departing friends much more clearly. Eventually though, they all turned away from the sea. There was a lot to do if they were to make their new community thrive.

It started well. The headaches passed, along with other symptoms that caused some early difficulties. Light wooden shelters, thatched with palm leaves, were adequate temporary cover in the clearing until more permanent structures could be built. The former sailors constructed a robust little boat, modelled somewhat on the canoes they'd seen, that could take them along the coast to seek out more supplies. A first garden was established, with the transplanting of some of the tubers they'd identified.

Tragically, it did not end well. Within weeks of establishing their new settlement a timber-felling expedition led many of the little group into an infestation of tiny black sandflies.

The insect bites were at first only annoyingly itchy, but they'd carried a terrible disease that would one day be called *Leishmaniasis*, or the black fever. Those bitten became feverish and lost all energy. Over a few weeks, without their knowing it, the victims' spleens swelled and their immune systems shut down – all they were aware of was the terrible abdominal pain. When a rainstorm struck, they didn't have the strength to take proper shelter. Within a week, pneumonia had killed them.

The handful of survivors, an inconsolable Cailin among them, gathered up the tools, cooking utensils and as many provisions as could fit and squeezed onto the canoe. They had no idea what had killed their companions, but it was obviously something to do with the island. The only option they could think of was to try to make it back to the thriving trade centre on Madagasikara where Hervor had made her home.

It was a desperate gambit, doomed from the outset. The Merina people never sighted the canoe and all aboard. The fragile evidence of the fleeting settlement that had been Sigurd's Land soon disappeared. The dodos wandered the Isle of Desolation mostly undisturbed for another few hundred years.

.ooo.

13

CHAGOS ISLANDS – THE WELCOME AND UNWELCOME ROCK

T he blight of illness was not confined to those who'd stayed on land. Within two days of sailing from the island, those suffering from headaches suddenly started to suffer from a high fever. The handful who weren't afflicted were soon exhausted from trying to make up for their sweating, trembling crewmates.

Then, just as suddenly as it struck, the fever receded. But a new symptom took its place. Terrible, debilitating pain in all the joints: hands, feet, knees, hips, and even the spine. The sufferers, including the two captains and all the experienced helmsmen, for days spent most of the time lying curled up awkwardly, trying not to be underfoot of the few trying to run the ships. The foetal position that typified how they lay gave the disease its name in later generations – chikungunya virus. It was a Ba'tu word, ironically, given their previous unhappy encounter with that race, meaning 'bent up'.

Perhaps half of those affected developed a painful rash that added to their incapacity. Moving *hurt*, both on the inside and the outside.

It was left to those few not laid low to keep food and water up to everyone, nurse the sick (although in truth there was little that could be done), tend to the sails – there was no prospect of rowing – and steer as best they could.

The greatest problem was that on only the second day of the virus' destroying the usefulness of most people on board, they sailed into a powerful current that caught both boats and dragged them northeast, instead of northwards.

Even those who knew what was happening, or could focus enough through their own pain to be aware that they were travelling forty-five degrees off their intended direction (Sigurd included), could do nothing about it. There simply wasn't the fit manpower available to change course.

For days the boats limped on under a baking sun that added to the misery, especially for those suffering from the rash, which was made even more painful by the incessant sweat. Though the fever had passed, a great thirst remained, and rationing their fresh water was a painful necessity for the ailing captain to insist on.

It took a week for most of the crew to recover enough to make any effective contribution to the running of the ships. The joint pain that had hit so suddenly was much more gradual in receding. There were some who showed little or no sign of improvement.

Sverrir Bent-knee was amongst those. His walk was little more than a hobble, and his crew saw the pain etched on his face whenever he tried to grip something to steady himself. His hands were curled into claws that he couldn't straighten.

They were on an open sea, with only the vaguest idea of where they were in relation to land. A lookout's cry of "Land ahead!" was as welcome as it was unexpected.

They'd chanced upon a small archipelago. A scattering of coral atolls and tiny islets, like crumbs thrown on the water. They aimed, as best they could, for what appeared to be the largest of them, little more than a line of trees – tall palms above denser foliage.

Propped up by two healthier crewmen, Sigurd scanned the shore for a place to land. They followed the coast north, then east around a sharp point where the waves broke threateningly. Suddenly there was a gap in the tree line, and they realised it was an opening onto a lagoon. The idea of a sheltered location suddenly held great appeal to the captain's weary brain, and he signalled for them to make for it.

Serpentfang slipped through a little patch of clear water, a manoeuvre that really was much more a matter of luck than good seamanship. The knarr was following some distance behind.

Had Sverrir Bent-knee been in less pain, he would have felt the dramatic changes in the current under the keel. Had there been a more experienced hand at the tiller, the cargo vessel may have more precisely followed the track of the longship. Had so many of the crew not been sick, and exhausted, there might have been quicker reactions and a chance to avoid disaster.

None of those circumstances were in play though. Plunging down into the trough of a wave near the opening of the lagoon, *Red Whale* crashed onto a large spike of reef that lay just below the surface. The coral shattered, but so did the hull of the knarr.

Water poured into the hold and burst up onto the deck. It took mere minutes for the boat to break up and founder. Tons of cargo tumbled into the deep trench adjoining the reef, along with smashed sections of the knarr, and some of the crew. Many more were too exhausted or too sick to save themselves from drowning quickly, Sverrir amongst them.

Egil of Dalir clung to the reef briefly, counting on luck to bring a piece of floating debris that he could cling to and ride to safety inside the lagoon. When he felt something bump his leg his hopes soared. He groped for whatever it was, eventually managing to turn his head to see. The sightless eyes of Astou seemed to stare back at him pitifully as her body rose out of his reach on a rolling wave. Egil's involuntary flinch was enough to break his precarious hold on the fragment of coral, and he disappeared under the next wave.

Dark triangular fins appeared, cutting the surface of the water as the sea's great scavengers moved in to feast.

The tiller, with Fafhrd's carefully carved talisman still attached, was wedged by a wave into a cleft in the reef. It stood above the surf like a grave marker.

Those on board *Serpentfang* looked back in horror from the lagoon. Those who were able took to the oars, trying to drive the longboat back to where they could pick up survivors and salvage some floating cargo. But the current they'd ridden into the lagoon now worked against them, the much-reduced team of rowers unable to make headway against the incoming water.

With heavy hearts, they laid down the oars, and using the wind and current managed to slide onto a narrow strip of rough white sand that was the bleached and weathered remains of the coral forming the atoll. All they could do was wait and hope for any of their friends, or cargo, to wash close enough to shore to be saved. It was a forlorn hope. Two bodies washed in, and one small keg of Irish ale.

The sheltered lagoon did, at least, provide some security for *Serpentfang* while her crew recovered from the virus, a process that took several days.

Over the course of those days, as their strength returned, they walked the length and thin breadth of the island. It was shaped like a distorted hairpin, the narrow gap the longship had made it through being the only break in the ribbon that poked above the ocean.

Driftwood was gathered and built into a pyre for the two sailors they'd found. They'd died in battle with the ocean, surely the most formidable opponent any Norseman ever faced. As the embers flew up, all those around the fire knew that they carried more souls than the two on the fire.

The ale that had washed ashore was past its best, but nobody cared as mugs and goblets were lifted, and friends remembered.

But with the dawn, they had to look to their own survival. Fresh water was found in pools, filled by the rains that regularly swept over the archipelago. There were coconuts in abundance, their flesh and juice a welcome supplement to the crew's diet. And there were fish. Nets cast in the lagoon brought in both reef fish and food fish, including some fat tuna.

In several hundred years, a small colony would be located here, attempting to grow enough coconut for trade to sustain itself. Later still, the island would be called Diego Garcia, and leased as a military base to a people called 'Americans'. Such ideas would have been beyond fanciful to the Norse, for whom this rock offered barely enough provision to sustain life and continue their journey.

When their strength returned, at least to a moderate level, they were able to row back out of the lagoon. With no idea of their location, or what lay in any direction beyond the hazy knowledge of where they'd been, far to the southwest, Sigurd made the only decision he thought possible. Follow the prevailing current and winds. Due east, away from this desolate spot that had saved half their number, and doomed the rest.

This time no-one wanted to stay behind.

.ooo.

14

COCOS ISLANDS – OF WINGS AND WEARY WEATHER

East. Ever east. Through sun, storm and rain. Whenever they reached a point where they were sure they could stand no more of one sort of weather, it would suddenly change to another, that soon became just as unbearable in its own way.

One day, a drenching squall of rain passed over *Serpentfang*. The longboat slipped through the tail of the little downpour like moving through a curtain. It had brought brief but welcome relief from yet more searing heat.

Looking aft from the stern, the rain looked like a massive sheet of water suspended from the sky. Sigurd and Katrine stood with Hrolf the Dark and Olaf Vaksson gazing back at the unusual sight.

Suddenly a shape burst through the veil of the rainwater. It was a huge bird, white with grey wings edged in black. But what wings! Each was the size of a ten year old child! They didn't flap. The magnificent creature soared, gliding closer to the longship, but seeming to hang back as if content to follow, rather than fly over the mariners.

They'd seen such great birds from a distance, but never at close range. The Wandering Albatross was unknown in the sailors' North Atlantic home.

As they sailed on over the next few days, the albatross flew behind, straying for an hour or so at a time but always returning. It almost seemed to adopt the boat in some way, swooping and diving to pluck fish from the water in a manner that drew some laughter and applause from the tired, dispirited sailors. When Anna Sjelsdottir tossed a particularly unappetising piece of dried eel over the side of the boat the bird swooped low and fast, snatching up the morsel just as it hit the surface of the sea. The crew had precious little food to spare, but small pieces that were beyond even a sailor's hardy (and desperate) constitution were seldom rejected by their airborne companion.

At one point, Olaf idly mused aloud on whether to get his bow and use the bird for some target practice. Perhaps a contest among the ship's archers – the winner to get the plumpest portion of the bird's meat? He was more than half joking, but Fafhrd reacted sharply.

"No! I think there is something... special about the creature. I think the man, or woman, to kill such a bird would be, let's say, tempting fate," said the steersman.

There was nothing specific in his faith to prompt such a thought, but Fafhrd was a man who thought deeply about many things, and who trusted his instinct for the supernatural.

For the best part of two more days, the weather was as mild as they'd seen since leaving Madagasikara. But then, mid-afternoon, a rain front loomed over the northern horizon. Soon it did more than loom, bearing down rapidly, propelled by a swirling mass of dark cloud. It was a tropical cyclone, and it was a big one.

Apparently with one eye on the fast-approaching cloud and winds, the albatross gave a keening *wee-oh* sound and wheeled away back towards the west. It may have spent the first months of its life withstanding fierce storms and bitter cold in the Antarctic, but flying in a cyclone was quite another thing.

Had Sverrir still been with them, perhaps his experience and sea-sense may have given them a little more warning. Only perhaps. And that additional warning would have still been of little use on an open sea. The tropical storm could hardly be outrun.

Sigurd ordered the sails brought down and stowed, and all cargo made as secure as possible. He could see and feel what was coming, and knew that their only option was to ride it out as best they could.

The sun would have been high in the sky by the time the cyclone struck *Serpentfang*, but the mass of black cloud meant that there was no way of the crew knowing that. The longship was tossed like a stick in waves that roared and rose and crashed about them. A heavier, less flexible vessel would have been pounded to pieces, but the Norse boat rode above the worst of the troughs. Both the mast and the tiller cracked, but somehow neither broke. And this time, no one was washed overboard by the water that smashed across the deck.

Fafhrd had one arm wrapped around the crook of the tiller and one arm gripping the hull that he was pressed hard against. As the sea lifted the longship high, he was able to look out through the downpour for a moment. Trees! There must be some land ahead. Should he aim for it, or aim to avoid it? Realistically, could he do either in these conditions? The boat was in the hands of Njord the sea god, or whatever Supreme Being ruled here, certainly not under the control of a Norseman exhausted in body, mind and spirit.

They shot past the clump of palm trees on a small atoll, just as the worst of the cyclone started to move on ahead of them. Very soon though, two more tiny islets appeared in front of them. Miraculously the boat shot between them like a well-aimed spear.

Almost immediately the sea was discernibly calmer. Still rough, but the waves were less precipitous, and mostly travelled in the same direction! They were inside an atoll, broken up into more than twenty little islets and outcrops of coral. *Serpentfang* was actually riding the crest of a wave, like a Hawaiian surfboard of hundreds of years hence, into the heart of the atoll.

As the wave broke beneath her, the shallow keel skated towards the two-mile shelf of sand at the southern end of the circular atoll. There was one final rough moment as the side of the ship tore along a large knoll of coral with a terrible rending sound, then a long, wave-propelled skid up the sand that was still submerged.

Their forward motion finally shuddered to a halt not far from a line of coconut palms, on a narrow strip of land that was still above the water line. Eight hundred years later, an enterprising Scotsman would try to establish a settlement here, before turning his attention to the slightly broader and more tractable isle further north along the eastern edge of the atoll.

For now though, the Norse sailors were simply content to be out of the maelstrom. The monsoon winds and rain still raged about them, although diminishing slowly. Brawny seamen leapt into the breakers with ropes to haul the boat further up, towards relative safety.

When that was achieved to Saemundsson's satisfaction, everyone hunkered down in whatever shelter they could squeeze into on the boat and waited for the storm to pass.

Soon enough it did, and the tropical storm was replaced by blazing tropic sun. As the tide receded they were able to assess the damage. It was significant, but not terminal.

Seawater had poured into the hold of the boat, so all of the cargo had to be unloaded and laid out at the highest part of the island to dry. Some was beyond salvation – much of the spice and fabric was ruined, but the sun and sea wind may be enough to save some hardier materials and wood products, Sigurd hoped.

With Hrolf at his side, the captain cast a critical eye over the area where the coral had torn at the keel. A long gash had been gouged into the timber, almost but not quite penetrating all the way through the planking in a few places.

Even more concerning was a great crack they found running through the rudder. How it hadn't split in two during the cyclone was a mystery.

"I reckon that bird of Fafhrd's must have cast some good fortune on us right enough," said the dark man.

Sigurd said nothing, only stroking his moustache as he pondered his options. Soon, he sent Hrolf with a small group to reconnoiter the islet they'd beached on, and any others they could safely get to.

The sun set rapidly here, and there was a small fire burning on the beach by the time the scouting party returned.

"Precious little to report, I'm afraid, captain. There are a few decent sized pieces of driftwood, but otherwise the only timber in any quantity is from these palm trees. There are some shrubs and low growing things, but all the wood seems to be soft. No sign of any animals. Quite a few birds of different types," Hrolf said.

"Nothing like those big dull-witted ones we found to the west?" asked Anna hopefully.

Hrolf the Dark allowed himself a wry laugh. "No such luck. A few sea birds that a good archer might be able to get for us though. I think fishing will be our best option. Again. And coconuts. There's no end of a quantity of them!"

"Better than nothing, I suppose," admitted the captain. "What about fresh water?"

Hrolf shook his head. "No streams of any sort to be seen. We found a couple of shallow pools full of rainwater. If we can cut through the tangled mass of fallen palm fronds and shrubs along the centre of the islands, I believe we might find some more."

After a moment of stroking his moustache, Sigurd announced his plan. "Two small teams – one to go in each direction from here. Take swords to clear a path where possible, and casks to carry whatever water can be found. A couple of good archers in each group. And bring back anything that looks like it will burn. Another group to unfurl the sail, check it, patch and otherwise repair it as much as possible. Our most important job is to repair the ship as best we can."

"That'll be tough with no decent wood here, and we've not much pitch left for what needs sealing," observed Bjarni.

"I'm hoping that some of the shrubs will provide something to fill that gouge in our hull. Even a moderately soft wood that will swell in the water, enough to make a decent seal, would do. We can brace it in with some of the wood we brought from Madagasikara, or even from home," the captain replied thoughtfully.

"Our trading timbers?" asked Hrolf in surprise.

"I don't see any options, do you, old friend? We're going to have to use the same stocks for jobs like reinforcing the mast and tiller, and putting a couple of braces across the rudder. I'd love to replace it, but we've nothing of the right size or shape."

"What about the black wood?" asked Katrine. "It's certainly hard enough."

"Mm, it is that," agreed the captain. "Difficult to work, though, with the tools we've got. Thjodrek, you're a good carpenter – what do you think?"

"Don't reckon there's much give in that stuff," the big man said slowly. He was a more than capable craftsman, but not imaginative by nature. "Should be good for bracing, I'd guess," Thjodrek continued musing. "Hardest part will be pounding rivets through it without splitting the wood. Can only try, I suppose."

"There might be an alternative," suggested Sindjely. "In N'Dar, almost every join of wood is made by lashing the pieces together. Could that work on a boat?"

"It certainly might!" replied Sigurd. "We've still got plenty of the walrus hide rope – it's ideal for a job like this."

Saemundsson was right about their stock of the cord plaited from the thick skin of the 'red whale'. Highly prized in their homeland as being extremely tough and weatherproof, it had attracted little interest as they'd travelled south. The texture and natural greasiness were just too unfamiliar to most of the traders they'd met. Fancy goods and ornaments could be exotic, that was part of their attraction, but utilitarian items needed to conform to some familiar fundamentals.

A frugal meal was prepared from the surviving stock, and consumed around the fire. More bursts of rain passed over during the night, so most everyone slept in the shelter of the boat. They were all used to being soaked, but it was somehow comforting to take advantage of shelter when it was possible to do so.

The next daybreak was cloudy but fine. Everyone was set to the task that best suited his or her own abilities. One additional group was added to the previous evening's planned disposition: a dozen set off with nets and spears to gather fish.

Despite the showers that intermittently washed over the islets, it was a productive day. The scant remaining pitch was worked into some of the ruined wool, and used to caulk the worst cracks and splits in the hull.

Branches of a cottonwood tree were deftly trimmed to slot into the gouge torn in the planking. Thjodrek took a length of attractively carved Merina timber, and reluctantly cut and split it into pieces. Then those pieces were riveted in place to secure the cottonwood, laid diagonally so the 'patch' might better flex with the hull in rough conditions. Pitchy woollen caulk was smeared around the inside edges of the new panels and around the ends of the rivets. This was *not* a conventional way of repairing a longship, but they were hardly in a conventional situation.

It cost time and effort, cursing and swearing, and dulling the edges of several blades, but pieces of the hard black wood were worked into shapes to splint the mast, tiller and rudder. These were then lashed into place with the tough hide cords.

By comparison, the repairs to the sail were straightforward. It would be serviceable, though suffering from wear and tear, and ideally Sigurd would have replaced it – if only he'd had suitable material to replace it with.

The beach fringes were completely stripped of driftwood. With care, they could have decent fires for three nights with enough left to keep the shipboard brazier lit for some time.

A bare half dozen casks were needed to contain all the fresh water that could be found. Another expedition would have to be sent out in the hope of finding more.

The fishing folk brought back a bonus: they'd netted a moderately sized turtle that would provide good meat to supplement the plump brown sea birds the hunters had killed.

Oh, and there were coconuts. Lots and lots of coconuts.

With the repairs largely done in good time, the next day Sigurd was able to send more crew to forage for water along the length and breadth of the atoll. During yet another midday shower, the sound of raindrops hitting water drew Olaf and his companions, on a western islet of the atoll, to a hole that acted as a natural cistern. The regular rain had brought the water up to a level where it could be bailed out without too much difficulty. Indeed, Vaksson realised, they could fill more casks than the three they had with them.

It was only when he went to retrieve those additional vessels that he realised that they'd made an awkward error of judgement. The rising tide had isolated them. They'd waded to the island waist deep across a sandy causeway with a few coral stumps. They could swim back, but not laden with the casks.

As the senior member of the little party, Olaf accepted the responsibility and, leaving his companions to mind the casks they already had, swam and ran back to where the boat was beached. With considerable embarrassment, he explained the situation to Sigurd.

To Vaksson's relief, the captain showed no sign of irritation. Some amusement perhaps – for some that might have been worse, but Olaf knew how to laugh at himself. More casks were gathered, with ropes to lower them into the natural well if required. A handful of crew who were capable swimmers were sent to take these supplies and join the group on the western isle. Their mission was to fill the casks without delay and return as soon as the tide had gone down enough for them to cross back safely.

It went smoothly. Saemundsson was relieved. They had enough water to boil that evening's dinner. This was regarded by all as a more appealing way to prepare turtle, another one of which had been caught. And with the caulking sufficiently dry, it meant they would be able to row out on the next day's tide. Coconuts had a limited appeal.

.ooo.

15

ASHMORE REEF – THE PRICE OF TRADE BY SEA

Who would have thought there was so much water in the world? It was as though the whole of Midgard was one gigantic sea, and the lands to which men clung were little more than a handful of stones cast by capricious gods.

A love of sailing was one thing, but this had ceased to be sailing. Routine dulled into the necessities for existence, and a threadbare existence at that.

Nothing but ocean, in any direction. Including the east, into which they continued to sail, sometimes at pace, other times at little more than a leaden drift. Unfamiliar stars above, on the nights when the clouds were scant, gave no comfort to the sailors.

They netted fish as they sailed, but beyond that their supplies were again dwindling, and Sigurd had to ration carefully the remaining provisions. Hope, and health, were fading.

One might wonder at folk from Iceland succumbing to the common cold when sailing on tropical southern waters. Perhaps it was the frequent drenching by rain, both at sea and on their brief landfall on the atoll. Combine that persistent dampness with the dramatic temperature fluctuations between day and night, and a diet that lacked a lot of vitamins - perhaps there may be the explanation.

The sad truth was, though, that sickness spread among the crew over the days that followed their departure from the atoll of coconuts. Headaches, earaches, fever, streaming eyes and noses – on top of the persistent sunburn they'd all had to live with, it was becoming a miserable existence.

Half a dozen of the seafarers died. A man and a woman passed away in their sleep. Another of the women was found in the hold, slumped over a small pile of surviving fabric, as if craving one last moment of comfort. Two more men died on the oar benches, not rowing, just sitting propped up by the handles of their oars. And one more, perhaps his brain baked by the sun, wordlessly threw himself overboard late one afternoon. He sank as silently as a stone.

The other corpses were also consigned to the ocean. There was no other option.

The day after the sixth of these dispatches – each ceremony becoming more perfunctory than the last – was another of those where the sea reflected the beating sun like a bronze mirror. There was some wind from the northwest. It was enough to generate a little speed and sufficient relief from the heat for most of the Norse to be on deck, catching such of the zephyr on their skin as they could.

Sindjely was at the front of *Serpentfang*, her chin resting on the lip of the hull near where it swept up into the now badly weatherworn figurehead. She peered, tilting her head and squinting into the glare on the water ahead.

"Do I see... sails?" she wondered aloud.

A dozen pairs of eyes tried to stare in the direction she indicated, all struggling similarly with the sun's reflection. For a few blessed moments a shred of cloud scudded across the solar orb, and yes! They were sails! More than a dozen small white triangles in the north-northeasterly distance.

The captain signalled to the tillerman on duty, to steer a course to intercept the little fleet. Fafhrd was sleeping below, one of the latest victims of a cold that had his head feeling like it was immersed in a pail of warm water.

"What if they're hostile?" croaked Hrolf, himself an earlier victim of the ailment and still nursing a throat that felt like he'd been swallowing sand.

"Then we fight or die," answered Sigurd bluntly. "But where there are boats in numbers I think there must be land not too far away."

"Especially such small boats as they look to be," observed Katrine. "They could hardly carry a lot of provisions for a long voyage."

Saemundsson thought of their own shrinking stock of provisions. Making contact with whoever was under those white triangles might well make the difference between life and death, he realised.

At the approach of the longship, the fleet dropped their sails, bobbing in the water as they awaited the bigger vessel's arrival. *Serpentfang*'s sail was likewise lowered as she glided into within hailing range.

The boats were small and narrow, pointed at either end so they could evidently travel forward or back without turning, using the paddles Sigurd could see resting inside their low hulls. The smallest of them, surely holding no more than two men, were little more than canoes with a single mast to bear the sail. Even the biggest of the boats, perhaps a third of the length of *Serpentfang*, although it boasted two masts (one fore and one aft), had no deck.

Sigurd kept the longship at a cautious and respectful distance, just close enough, he hoped, to be clearly seen and heard. He stood at the side of the boat, palms open in a gesture of peace, and called greetings in as many languages as he could think of.

None seemed to provoke a reaction amongst the men in his floating audience – he did notice that there appeared to be no women amongst them – who nattered and shouted across to each other in a tongue he couldn't identify.

They were quite small men, lean and lithe with brown skin and glossy black hair. Suddenly the resemblance dawned on Sigurd. These men were very like those, far to the west, who had ceremonially dined with their dead ancestors. He looked at the small boats from which they traded. Sturdy enough in their way, he supposed, but surely not able to withstand the vast open waters that had claimed *Red Whale*, and that *Serpentfang* had barely survived.

He tried calling a greeting in the Merina language. That invoked a different sort of quizzical look from some of the nearest of the brown men. Some progress at least? The captain called Katrine to his side. Typically, in their short stay there she'd mastered more of the Merina vocabulary than anyone else in the crew. Not enough to be called fluent, but enough to explore whether it was understood by these sailors.

Her efforts drew more puzzled looks from the small sailors. Part of that was surprise at seeing a woman on a boat. They were already taken aback by the appearance of the new arrivals in their waters – skin and hair of such colour were simply unknown to them. But the woman's words... The words themselves were unfamiliar, but there was something about the sound of them, a few in particular, that stirred vague recognition. Or perhaps recollection.

One of the smallest boats was paddled alongside the Norse ship. One of the two-man crew stood and reached up with one hand.

With the other he patted his chest and grinning, said, "Agung!"

Correctly assuming that was the man's name, the Icelander captain reached for the outstretched hand and said, "Sigurd," as he pointed to himself.

Just as their hands clasped a wave rolled under the little boat and with half the crew standing, nearly capsized it. Agung lost his footing, but with a firm grip on the Norseman's arm almost ran up the side of *Serpentfang* and jumped onto the deck. He landed like a two-legged cat and burst out laughing.

That was infectious – the northerners had had little to laugh about for quite a while, and suddenly it was as though a pressure valve had been released.

Exchanging names was a good start. Preventing the laughing man from falling into the sea didn't hurt either, even if it hadn't quite been intentional. What followed couldn't be called a conversation, but it was at least an exchange of ideas.

The concept of 'trade' was key. Agung got that quickly. He was also able to quickly grasp the need for water to drink, when he was offered a meagre amount in a mug. He called over to some of his cohorts, in his own boat and several others. After rapid discussion – the speed of their speech bewildered even Katrine – there was a flurry of movement as men jumped between boats.

Agung was able to convey a request that two more of his companions be allowed to board. Sigurd nodded agreement. The larger craft was paddled alongside, and a pair of lithe fellows clambered onto the longship. They were introduced as Arif and Satia. As a gesture of goodwill (and understanding) each carried a skin bag of water. It was too little to go around the whole crew, but it sent a potent message.

Agung leaned over the side and shouted again. His vacant space in the two-man boat was taken by another man who jumped from one of the bigger boats. After a brief conversation between the three brown sailors, Arif pointed east-southeast, jabbing his finger emphatically.

When the small boats raised their sails and set off in that direction, Sigurd was more than willing to follow their example. *Serpent-fang* glided alongside the little fleet of praus, as they quickly learned the narrow boats were called, like a mother swan alongside a cluster of cygnets.

Over the ensuing hours the three men identified themselves as Macassan, indicating that their home, a place called Macassar on an island named Sulawesi, lay some way to the north. They, like the Norse, were traders. Much like the Norse in their home seas, the Macassans had a network of regular sailing routes to familiar trading centres and reliable merchants and providers of particular goods. Sigurd and Hrolf were impressed by the parallels.

This particular voyage was one of their longest. Their destination was a great landmass to the southeast. Over several generations, they had built up a good trading relationship with the people who lived there. Their spices and some decorative items were exchanged for a variety of unique goods.

Despite his weariness, Sigurd couldn't help but be interested. New markets, new products, new opportunities, these were why he'd set out on this journey, however long ago it was.

Picking up on his reaction, Arif explained that after they'd finished in the great southern land, they would return directly home. The Norse were welcome to accompany them – Macassar welcomed traders from many places, including great empires to their north and west.

West? Did the name 'Baghdad' mean anything to them, Sigurd asked as casually as he could?

Oh yes, they'd heard of it. Some of the wealthier merchants who passed through their markets were travelling to or from there.

"The Macassar of the west," laughed Agung.

As their conversation skills improved, curiosity prompted Sigurd, with Katrine's help, to attempt to explore the question of a possible Madagasikara connection. Agung at first looked at them blankly. No, his people came from the north of where they now were, not west. Nor did they travel much in that direction, beyond the points where they would routinely meet traders from the great kingdoms of what would later be called the Indian sub-continent.

Then, as the Macassan came to more fully understand the detail of what the Norseman asked, he laughed. That seemed to be his response to most things, the fair skinned captain thought to himself. No, his people didn't sail to settle. They went to sea to trade. Their home was perfectly adequate, and had been for many generations. Upon saying that though, the Macassan began to reflect. He was a deeper thinker than his jovial character at first suggested.

The sun wasn't far above the horizon when they reached their destination. By now the current was doing much of the propulsion work, a fact the Macassans knew well and were often grateful for. It was another coral outcrop. Up from a substantial reef rose three small islets – bare outcrops of sand and bleached coral covered with low shrubs and grasses. Even coconuts hadn't made it here!

They aimed for the western-most of the islets, bringing their vessels on a sweeping westerly arc that brought them into something like a lagoon. They pulled most of the boats up onto a white beach, startling a large flock of birds of various types. These took off noisily, circled once or twice, and flew en masse eastwards to the next islet squawking and shrieking in apparent irritation. The Macassans called the place Pulau Pasir, which Katrine was able to translate as 'sand island'. Unimaginative, but accurate.

The two small boats that didn't pull in both had four-man crews. They did a circuit of the reef. Pairs of men from each took turns at intervals jumping overboard, clutching nets. There were plenty of sea snakes in the water, but the reptiles were of no interest to the fishermen, and although highly venomous weren't aggressive at all. By the time they'd travelled the circumference of the reef and come in to join the rest, they'd caught a good quantity of small turtles – no more than a hand span or two long.

It was a deliberate choice of catch. There were plenty of larger turtles available, but the hunters knew that the bigger specimens were of breeding age, and were best left alone to continue providing new generations of what was more tender meat anyway.

As the Norse watched, the brown men set about a flurry of activities it quickly became clear that Pulau Pasir was a familiar resource. A few strode around the fringe of the islet gathering driftwood. Some dived into the sheltered water, pulling up clams. Others went scavenging amongst the sand dunes, where they found a quantity of eggs of some of the various birds they'd disturbed.

Most valuably of all for the Northerners, three groups set out for three natural freshwater wells known to be on the island. Their destination having been explained, they were accompanied by fair-haired men and women carrying casks that had been terribly close to empty.

By the time the light was fading and a fire had been lit from the plentiful driftwood, a substantial meal had been prepared from the shellfish, eggs and turtles, with sticky rice cakes made from the store of the grains the Macassans habitually carried, and a spicy stew the brown men called coto, made from some of the dried beef that had survived from Madagasikara.

As they sat and ate, Agung sought out some of the older and perhaps wiser men of the little fleet, and they talked about the question of a settlement of their people far to the west. Eventually he called Sigurd and Katrine over to relate what he'd been told. He explained that there were old stories, indeed the oldest of their stories, bare fragments whose telling was scarcely remembered, that told of a time when the world was very different. Then the people travelled not by sea but by land, on foot across vast distances.

A great migration, it had been, with no clue from where or why. His own people – *the* people he emphasised, had settled in the place they now called home, but there were said to be others who had journeyed on, following the setting sun. Perhaps the white men had met those people?

For all that he appreciated his new acquaintance's attempt to offer a solution, it was beyond Sigurd to accept it. Thousands of miles of water could not be walked across. The concepts of continental drift, tectonic shifts, land bridges and the inexorable slow change of geography were utterly unknown.

Suddenly, one of the Macassans stood up, clutching his stomach, and ran out of the circle of light cast by the fire. It was the other occupant of Agung's small boat. Agung cast a puzzled look in the direction he'd gone in.

"Cempluk? You alright?" he called.

There was no reply. Instead, there was the sound of retching from the darkness. Then it was echoed, by one of the Norse sailors.

Over the next hour the sickness spread. It afflicted the stomachs of a third or more of the group, Norse and Macassan alike. Vomiting, and a pale diarrhoea that looked like watery milk. It continued through the night and into the morning.

The northerners suffered worse. Their bodies had been wracked by sickness and dehydration from the long voyage already – the fluid loss was too much. Within hours of dawn, several were dead. The scourge of cholera would stay with this little island for a very long time to come.

Why some and not others? Hrolf had been telling the story of their adventure in Zawaia, and had taken one of the mosaic tiles from the city out of the leather purse in his shield boss as he'd spoken. Now he turned it over in his hands as he watched his friends sweat, tremble and die. A pattern. There must be a pattern. He said as much to his captain, but neither of them could see it. As far as they knew, everyone had eaten much the same variety of food.

There was no question of sailing on across open sea while so many were so unwell. The small fleet stayed on, to try to nurse the sick. The Macassans had seen this before, and knew that sometimes, if they could get a sick man to take in water and some food before he'd purged himself completely, he might recover quickly.

Agung explained this as he mopped the forehead of another trader. Heeding the advice, Sigurd was about to pour water into the mouth of Anna Sjelsdottir. As the first trickle splashed her lips he stopped. Water. He suddenly realised that all of these who were sick had drunk from the same well – the well that Agung's crewmate Cempluk had led the way to. The water he was about to give her – where had it come from?

Immediately the captain voiced his suspicions. Arif and Agung exchanged thoughtful looks. The seemingly permanent grin had gone from the latter's face when Cempluk had died an hour or two earlier.

"You right, I think," said Arif, who hadn't the linguistic skills of Agung.

He stood and spoke in his own language. The Macassans didn't have a leader as such, but if they were ever to choose one it would probably be Arif. The contents of any water skin known to have been filled from what he called 'Cempluk's well' were poured out into a sand dune some distance away, and the skin thrown onto the embers of the fire. The same was done with any container that could not be positively identified as being filled from either of the other wells.

Saemundsson gave a similar order, wincing as he saw precious water casks thrown onto the fire that was starting to blaze up with its new kindling. There was no option though – if that water was tainted the toxin would be in the wood now, and anything new added to the cask would surely pick up the same poison.

Before they left the islet, he would ensure that the remaining casks, and anything else that could hold water, were topped up to capacity from the 'safe' wells.

It was a long day, leading into a long night. By the time the sun rose again over the scrubby island, several more of the *Serpentfang* crew, including Anna and Sindjely, had died. So had another three of the Macassans. The rest, though, were already showing signs of recovery.

Bare as the islet was, it had to be home for several more days until there were enough people physically capable of facing more time at sea. There was a plentiful supply of turtles, eggs and birds to keep them fed, and there was a good supply of water available from the 'safe' wells. That the other one had been the source of the malady seemed to be confirmed by the fact that nobody else fell sick after the first onslaught of the disease.

Arif had conveyed a small party to the other islets in one of the larger praus. They'd caught a few birds to supplement the meals, and gathered driftwood and anything else that looked likely to burn. There was one stunted tree that the Macassans indicated was good for this use, even when green (hence its much later name of kerosene wood). It also bore some palatable egg-sized fruit. No more water, though.

The two groups each had their own way of dealing with their dead. The Norse constructed a single pyre with some of the driftwood and dry scrub scoured from the three islets. The bodies were laid on it side by side. Anna Sjelsdottir and her N'Dar lover lay with their arms together one last time. It was a poor send-off for honoured friends and companions, many of the survivors reflected, but they all recognised that it was all that could be done in the circumstances.

"They have been given the very best ceremony possible in the place where they died," said Fafhrd consolingly, after the fire had been lit. "That's more than can be said for many worthy souls."

The captain could only nod in sad agreement. He'd had to do this far too often on the journey. It was essential that a man be durable in his position, but he truly did feel sick at heart. Feeling Katrine's discreet gentle touch on his arm was perhaps all that stopped his spirit from breaking as he watched the embers spiral up into the night sky.

Respectfully the Macassans watched the Norse ritual, just as the northerners had, earlier in the day, formed a sombre circle around the pits in which the brown sailors had interred their lost companions. Sigurd himself had been among those who'd bent their backs to aid in the digging of those pits.

There had been one macabre element before the burial of Cempluk, when one of the luckless man's legs had been hacked off at the knee and placed in the shallow seawater under a securing weight. On the morning after the Norse cremation ceremony, Agung and an elder Macassan named Gusti took themselves to a discreet distance away from the others to carry out the unpleasant task of stripping the brine-softened flesh from the leg.

It turned out that there was no religious purpose behind this gruesome exercise. The two long bones were taken to the poison well. A post of sturdy wood was driven into the ground by the well, and the two bones, crossed, were lashed to the post with a length of walrus hide rope that *Serpentfang*'s captain had willingly provided.

Other boats would visit here. The atoll and its islets were an important stop for Macassans on their long voyages north and south, and it was hoped that this warning might prevent others meeting the same fate as Cempluk and the rest.

By the time they were ready to set off for the Macassans' southernmost trading centre, each group had learned quite a bit about each other, including how to communicate effectively, if not fluently. They'd had a good look at each other's trade goods. The men from Macassar loved a deal and traded individually, not collectively. There had been some hard bargaining as they competed for items from the longship.

Arif had spent considerable time examining *Serpentfang*. To his eye she had a great deal to recommend her as a trading vessel. Much of her construction was beyond him – the prau was a fairly simple boat – but the *deck* had him interested. One of those on a large prau would provide a lot more room for stock. Something to look at when he got back to Macassar.

There were inevitable cultural differences. Many of the sailors from the south could not understand why there were women on board the northerners' longship, far less why they were evidently treated as equals. Strange set of gods some of them worshipped, too.

Differences notwithstanding, traders were traders, wherever their origins. Experience taught that there was business to be done at a place some days' sail away. So that was where they were all headed.

.ooo.

16

AUSTRALIA – THE GOING DOWN OF THE SUN

The Macassans knew the local currents well, and so the little fleet made good time in reaching their destination. It was a matter of days until they skimmed their boats onto a beach in a broad bay.

The beach led onto a low area of grass and a pink flowering creeper, much of which was flattened by footprints. It was impossible to tell if the spot was a natural occurrence, or had been deliberately cleared from the dense jungle that surrounded it.

Sigurd looked around warily. The place appeared deserted, and he said as much to his Macassan companions.

Agung laughed and said, "Just because you can't see them, doesn't mean they haven't seen us. Someone in that jungle will have spotted us, and the rest of them will be here soon."

So it proved. Within minutes, a dozen or so very black-skinned men emerged from the trees. Some made gestures of greeting to the Macassans, but all of them hung back warily from the fair-skinned traders.

Arif put an arm around Sigurd's shoulders and walked towards a small group of the black men. Agung walked beside them – he had a much better command of the local language. The Macassan grinned broadly at the darker men and introduced their unfamiliar companion.

A peculiar conversation ensued, carried out in a mix of two languages. While Agung spoke the local tongue, two of the black men had some command of the Macassans' language and addressed them in it. Sigurd caught some of what was said, and occasionally contributed a few words of Macassan when he could.

Eventually, the men who'd come out of the jungle nodded and even smiled at the Icelander. The eldest of them was introduced as Walan. He extended a confident arm towards Saemundsson in a gesture he'd learned from the Macassan traders. The captain clasped the proffered arm. Not quite the action that Walan had expected, but he was alert enough to reciprocate it.

Then Walan walked away and gathered the rest of his men together to address them, gesturing over his shoulder towards the newcomers.

Meanwhile Agung explained the situation to the Norseman.

"These people are called the Kuthant. We like them! They bring a good timber that doesn't grow up our way, and sometimes got good dried meat from these big fat birds they call wonga. Different tribes, they trade different stuff. I mean, they all bring more than one kind of thing, but they've got... what's the word...?"

"Specialties?" suggested the Norseman.

"Yes! One make really good fishing spears, from better wood than we got. Others have learned how to prepare taripan for us – saves us a lot of work. There's another..." Agung looked and sounded like he was about to launch into an enthusiastic catalogue.

Sigurd quickly interrupted. "What's this taripan you mentioned?"

"Ah – good food! They gather them up from the shallow water on another part of the coast, then boil them, dry them out and smoke them over a fire of just the right wood. Done like that, taripan lasts a real long time, and tastes *mmm!*"

To be honest, dried and smoked sea cucumber was an acquired taste that many of the tribesmen never really acquired, but they knew good business when the opportunity arose.

"It must be good if you travel all this way for it!" exclaimed Katrine.

Agung laughed. "Oh it is! But it's not all we come for. We stay here for days, different tribes come and go, and we trade with them in turn. Get a good supply of stuff then go home."

Saemundsson stroked his moustache. "You trade with one tribe at a time? Why not all at once?"

The Macassan shrugged. "It's how it's always been. You'd have to ask *them* why."

As he spoke he indicated over Sigurd's shoulder. The Kuthant men were approaching as a group. There was no trace of hostility though. Some caution and puzzlement perhaps, but no strong sense of distrust.

In broken but passable Macassan, Walan introduced some of the senior members of his tribe. Saemundsson returned the courtesy, calling Hrolf, Fafhrd and Katrine to his side.

If the Kuthant shared the Macassans' bemusement at the status of Norse women they gave no indication of it, something Katrine noted for further enquiry.

Before trade was to commence, the shrewd Walan wanted to know the newcomers better. What goods did they have? How could the Kuthant be sure of their quality? What did they want in return? Would they be back, and if so, when?

That question almost provoked a wry laugh from Sigurd, who barely restrained his reaction. How should he, or could he, explain their journey? Could he or anyone else ever contemplate repeating it? It was Hrolf who most successfully dealt with the question. He wove fragments of their story into an expression of how unlikely it would be that they would return, and in so doing held the elders enthralled.

"You are the holder of your tribe's history," observed Walan. "We have Karumbari who does that for us."

A slender, surprisingly young man gave a gesture of acknowledgement. He had inherited the role, the latest in a long line of keepers of knowledge that stretched back countless generations. Karumbari and some of his companions were sufficiently intrigued to ask to spend time that evening hearing the fair-haired people's stories, and sharing some of their own.

Others demurred. They had to be gone by morning. It was to be the Yanuwas' turn then, and it wasn't good to cross the Yanuwa. They were jealous of their long-agreed place in the trading order.

Sigurd was starting to glean some idea of the locals' system of trading. Each group had their own 'products', and their own place in some sort of schedule. It was expected, demanded even, that each vacate the common trading centre before the other arrived. The alternative was to fight for the place – an approach some tribes pursued aggressively.

The captain of *Serpentfang* probed a little further, and learned that 'local' was quite the wrong term. Some tribes, like the Marrgu who were the taripan specialists, lived a fairly sedentary existence in a place not too far from the spot they were in. Others though, like the Kuthant themselves, were travellers. In a way they were like the Norse, making long journeys along a regular route, gathering goods and supplies as they went. The Kuthant travelled great distances on foot – as challenging in its way as the Icelanders' customary sea voyages.

Having established what seemed to be a good rapport, Sigurd and most of his crew got down to the business of business. Based on the advice of some of the Macassans familiar with this bay, a few of the Norse were detailed to do some fishing. There was an unspoken thought that this may prove to be the most productive activity of the day. In truth, there was little of great appeal among the Kuthants' offerings.

The dried wonga – an oversized pigeon, it seemed, was more palatable than the big slow birds of the long-past western island had proved when boiled and dried. But that wasn't difficult. The Macassans were very happy with it though, and traded enthusiastically for some of the rice they carried.

The wood that was their other 'specialty' was a considerable surprise to the northerners. It was very like one of the common timbers of their home region. Iceland's forests were mostly birch, but the cypress pines that the Kuthant cut sturdy branches of were close relatives to the pine trees common in Norway. Some good pieces were acquired with a view to future damage repair. Its flexibility would be better suited for the purpose than the hard black wood they'd relied on earlier. But with only one of their original vessels left, there seemed little need for a great quantity of it.

The brown men knew it as a reliable wood for construction, and a few individual traders with building projects underway back in Macassar obtained some, in exchange for axes that would be of use to the Kuthant in obtaining more timber for their future meetings. It was a sensible cycle of trade.

Of some appeal to Sigurd himself were the skins that the Kuthant travelled with. These weren't intended as trade goods, but when the captain saw the shape of a few spread out on the ground he was intrigued. The Kuthant explained that the animals were called kangaroo. Good eating, with hardy skins for keeping out the cold. Saemundsson rightly suspected that the black man's perception of 'cold' was very different to his own. The kangaroo skin seemed durable but not especially warm.

Some of the items among the Norse inventory were simply too unfamiliar to appeal to the Kuthant. There was interest in some light clothing, but most of it was far too generously sized for the wiry black men. Metal axes and knives were popular, as long as they weren't too heavy to be easily carried for long distances. The tribesmen were also keen to obtain some of the tough rope made from the skins of the incomprehensible 'red whales'.

Meanwhile, Katrine had a quiet word with Karumbari. Unlike the Macassans, the Kuthant traded as a collective rather than individuals, and it wasn't his role to be a negotiator. She felt that there was something about the young man that inspired a level of trust. She asked, quite simply, where were the Kuthant women and children? If they travelled the great distances that had been mentioned, surely they all walked together and didn't just meet up in passing?

Smiling at that thought, Karumbari confirmed that yes, the tribe walked together, except when a particular ritual or ceremony was to be conducted only for the men, or women of the group. At present though, the women and children were a little distance away, camped in a clearing. With diplomatic caution he revealed that some of the Kuthant did not entirely trust all of the Macassan traders. Not necessarily these fellows here now, he stressed tactfully, but there had been trouble in the past.

The trade negotiations among the Kuthant, Macassans and Norse gradually resolved themselves. Some of the longship crew set about building a fire and busied themselves preparing a meal. A few of the brown-skinned traders who'd finished conducting their own business started to assist.

Two different substantial stews were prepared. One was a Macassan coto, using a mix of wonga, dried beef, and some kangaroo meat. Bubbling away in another pot was plokkfiskur – an Icelandic fish stew being made from the day's satisfactory catch.

The aromas drifting up the beach added to the temptation of the Kuthant. When the trading was complete a few headed back to where the women and children were camped, but many more elected to stay, accepting the invitation to eat and talk.

As appealing as the food, was the prospect of satisfying their natural curiosity about a people whose type they'd never encountered before.

It turned into a long night. Karumbari, Hrolf and Fafhrd, and the old Macassan Gusti, took turns relating stories from the history of their people. None of them had any sense of talking about mythology – these were the explanations of things that had happened, even if in some cases they were from before the time of men as they were now. As simple as the storytellers tried to make their words, Katrine and Agung were kept busy translating the narratives for those whose language skills weren't up to following what was being said.

Other conversations ebbed and flowed around the assemblage. Walan was interested in the weaponry of the northerners, both the metal swords and axes (mostly too heavy and unwieldy for his men) and the small stock of clubs made from the hard black wood. The Macassans had a similar timber, but less intricately worked than those pieces the Norse had traded for. His people were not aggressive, they would more usually seek flight than fight, but he was also pragmatic.

He showed Sigurd examples of their armoury, such as it was. Spears mostly, some clubs, and what looked to Saemundsson to be heavy crooked sticks, carved almost flat. They were called boomerang, Walan said, painstakingly trying to explain that they were a type of flying club used in hunting. If the hunter missed the target the weapon would return to him, if he'd thrown it correctly.

This seemed far-fetched to Sigurd, although he did recall that one of the legends of Thor was that his mystical hammer Mjolnir would always return to him if thrown. If a hammer could do so, why not a club? Although these didn't look very mystical – but Fafhrd would probably point out that the best magic didn't have to be obvious to be effective.

The time passed quickly, and the slender moon had travelled much of its journey across the sky before the last of the conversations wound up. From long habit, the Macassans had retired to their praus to sleep, as had a few of the Norse, back to *Serpentfang*. The Kuthant and the other fair-skinned sailors had stretched out on the sands to get at least some sleep.

It was a mistake. Carelessness perhaps, on the part of the Kuthant. Ignorance on the part of the Norse. And a large amount of bad luck.

The eastern horizon was barely colouring when the Yanuwa were approaching the seaward fringe of the jungle – far earlier than would normally be anticipated. They'd been harried by an encounter to the south with an aggressive tribe of nomads who had a taste for the flesh of the young of other tribes. Such people were rare, but much feared. Their flight had been successful, but stressful.

Then had come the painful discovery that the spot where they'd tried to settle for the night had turned out to be shared with some large, vicious ants. The creek bank that they'd then moved to was damp and uncomfortable, so they'd set out long before they ordinarily would have. Early, and in a foul temper both collectively and individually.

When they pushed out of the jungle they expected to find the Macassan fleet bobbing in the water off shore. The narrow sailboats were in the right place, but there was another, bigger boat of strange construction resting on the beach. And around the remains of a fire lay a number of the Kuthant. They should *not* still be here! Who were the strange figures with them? Pale of skin, fair of hair? No matter – *they* should not be here either! Several of the leading Yanuwa shouted angrily as they advanced.

The shouts woke Kuthant and Norse alike, but no one from either group immediately grasped what was happening.

Unfortunately, one of the first Kuthant to react did so in exactly the wrong manner. He instinctively grabbed a boomerang and hurled it in the direction of the shouting new arrivals. To make matters worse, one of the Norse crew followed his example by throwing his knife.

Both boomerang and knife struck glancing blows. Not enough to do real damage, but enough to inflame the Yanuwas' already belligerent temper. The 'rightful occupiers' of the trading place swept from the jungle in a wave of ferocity.

Most of the Norse barely had time to register any of the circumstances before they were caught up in the fighting. Those on board *Serpentfang* had been woken by the screaming, and all rushed to aid their crewmates. But they at least had some moments to observe the situation.

The Yanuwa seemed to be a different race to the Kuthant. They were taller and more brown skinned than black, although they had similar hair and facial features.

There were more of the newly arrived warriors than the Kuthant. The Norse weren't quite outnumbered, but the newcomers had three significant advantages: they had the element of surprise, they were actually prepared for a fight, and they were a great deal healthier than the exhausted northerners, many of whom were still suffering the after-effects of sickness.

The Macassans kept their boats safely off shore, wide eyes watching a frenetic scene of bloodshed. Some of the fair-skinned sailors had by now grasped their weapons and were fighting back, but many had been overwhelmed in the initial onslaught. The Yanuwa fought with clubs and spears and boomerangs. Some picked up the weapons of fallen foes, although the heavy axes and swords were just as quickly discarded as too awkward. Others grabbed lengths of still burning wood from the fire, trying to set ablaze their beleaguered foes – their hides, their clothes, anything that would catch alight.

Sigurd was engaged in striking down a warrior who'd tried to attack him with a long club. With his sword arm raised, his side was exposed to a brawny Yanuwa who ran to impale him on a heavy spear. Suddenly, Katrine sprang between them, her sword cleaving deep into the tribesman's neck.

Death didn't stop his momentum, though. The spear rammed clean through the translator's body, and into the captain's ribs. Even as the Yanuwa man fell, Katrine av Ord was pinned to Saemundsson.

With her weaponless hand she gripped his shoulder, as they both gasped in shock and pain. She was just able to sigh, "My dear captain..." before her legs crumpled, the weight of her falling body pulling the weapon from his side.

Sigurd stood, swaying for a moment, oblivious to the blood streaming down his shirt as he looked down at the beloved figure at his feet. Yes, beloved. Neither of them had ever said as much, but it was undeniably true. That was the moment he knew it was truly all over. It was as though he'd felt his heart stop.

Looking about slowly, it was like a dream in which time moved at a crawl. Sigurd could see the end now. The last of his crew lay dead or dying. Hrolf, with his skull caved in by one of the strange flying clubs. Bjarni and Fafhrd both speared. But the final fall of fortune, the ship was aflame.

Poor old *Serpentfang*. No other ship, surely, had travelled so far, seen and suffered so much. Now she would sail no further, perishing here on this distant, too-hot shore. It was certain now, she would never return to the icy harbour of Hofn. Nor would he. There would never be a *Saga of Sigurd the World-Farer*, for there would be none to tell it.

Fleetingly he remembered the young priest Erp declaring he'd not be welcomed back home. He hoped Thordja had put the churchman in his place. He'd never know, and truly, didn't care. As he thought of his wife, a fond smile crossed his face. Good times in younger days came to mind.

Almost casually, he felled a black warrior with a backhanded sweep of his sword as he walked towards the waterline. He left the weapon embedded deep in the man's torso, releasing his hilt and trudging across the sand. The spear wound in his side may or may not be mortal, but the wound to his soul most certainly was.

Wading out to *Serpentfang*, he severed the mooring rope with his axe, and then climbed aboard as she started to drift. Ignoring the flames that were spreading rapidly across the weathered timber, he pulled the folded woollen sail and the o'api skin of the Khoikhoi to a point at the head of the prow furthest from the fire.

With a deep sigh he lay down on the hide, his head resting on the sail. He held his axe to his breast and closed his eyes. He felt the blood from between his ribs soaking the fur of the wonderful pelt – yes, it was getting harder to breathe, he realised. The smoke of *Serpentfang's* demise wasn't helping that, of course.

He thought of Valhalla, and the crew already waiting there. Hild and the others who'd fallen fighting the Berbers of Zawaia. Poor Bardi Goosefoot, whose loyal heart had more responsibility for his falling under the Ba'tu's rockslide than his clumsy gait. Lars Magnusson, who died in battle with the storm off N'Dar, surely as terrible a foe as any faced over steel. Corri, perhaps, if he too had been claimed by the storm – he'd know the answer to that soon enough. And old Sverrir Bent-knee. For his sake, Sigurd hoped that the Hall of the Dead opened onto a sea.

He wondered whether, when he reached Valhalla, he would meet the bravest of the warriors from other lands he'd met. Anders el Espada, as ready with his wit as his fine steel blade. K'pah, the great-shouldered black who'd died at his side in the slaughter of the Ba'tu.

Even Walan, the shrewd trader who he'd seen be one of the first to fall under the Yanuwa spears. Surely the hall of heroes could not be exclusively the domain of the Norsemen, not when he knew first-hand that honour and bravery were not confined to his own race.

The last image in his mind was a pair of eyes, the blue of a midsummer sky.

Sigurd had lost consciousness before the flames reached him. On shore, the fighting stopped as the tribesmen became aware of the spectacle of the blazing longship drifting out to sea. The concept of a funeral pyre was unknown to them, but there was an unmistakable grandeur to the sight.

The Macassan traders, sailors themselves, gave their own signs of respect as the dying longship limped by. They kept their small boats at a safe distance, still waiting for the fight between the locals to resolve itself. They would trade with whoever remained, as they had ever done.

The lull in fighting gave the Kuthant the opportunity to slip away. They truly had no stomach for battle. Their extended stay at the trading place had been inadvertent, due to the unexpected encounter with the strange fair-haired men, their extraordinary wares and their even more extraordinary stories.

The Yanuwa accepted their opponents' acquiescence and let them gather their dead and wounded, and some of the things they'd legitimately traded for – they weren't interested in wiping out the Kuthant, only in establishing their long-standing rights to trade.

The fleeting encounter with the fair-headed people was a story that survived among the Kuthant for only a few generations, although that was longer than the walrus-hide ropes and steel tools they'd obtained.

As an old man, Karumbari told the story to the grandchildren of the tribe, sitting in the shade of the rocks of Kata Tjuta on the south-ernmost part of their cyclic wanderings. The knife he'd received from Sigurd had long since lost its edge, but with its tough point he was able to chip and scratch at the red rock.

"Here," he said to the young ones, pointing to the small picture he'd carved. "Here is the vessel of the fair-haired men. It burned that day, and the leader of those men with it. They came, they said, from a place far far away, but there is nothing left to mark their passing."

The Kuthant moved on again, as they always did. The passing of time was seen in the rise and fall of the sun, and measured only by the phases of the moon, when it was measured at all.

The memory of Sigurd Saemundsson – Sigurd the World-Farer, is gone. Karumbari's carving remains.

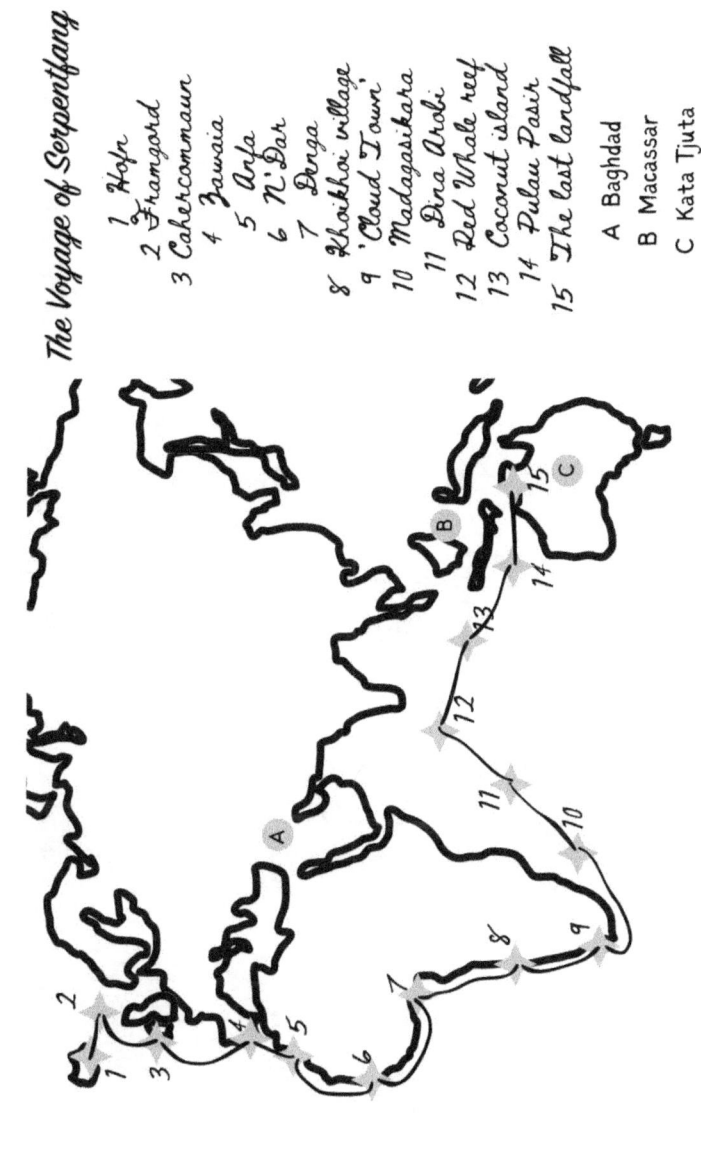

The Voyage of Serpentfang

1 Hofn
2 Framgard
3 Cahercommaun
4 Jawaia
5 Arfa
6 N'Dar
7 Denga
8 Khokhoi village
9 'Cloud Town'
10 Madagasikara
11 Dina Arobi
12 Red Whale reef
13 Coconut island
14 Pulau Pasir
15 The last landfall

A Baghdad
B Macassar
C Kata Tjuta

AUTHOR'S NOTE

On an undistinguished rock, near what Westerners once called the Olgas in Central Australia, is a carving. I was shown it by a local man one afternoon, under an open cloudless sky.

Stone carving is unusual among the art and artefacts of Indigenous Australia. Without metal, in time past they lacked the tools to work hard surfaces. A hard rock might scrape a design or picture in softer one – basalt on sandstone perhaps – but it doesn't seem to have been a common practice.

This was a hard stone. The lines had taken some real effort to be dug into the rock, so it wasn't casual graffiti. The location was innocuous enough – quite a gentle stony slope at the foot of a rock formation. Nothing to suggest anything sacred about the site, and my guide said there was no known tradition that the area had special significance.

The rock formation ahead of us had stories of course, and its own special place in the Dreaming. All of the land does. But this carving didn't. It was known by his people to have been there for a long time, but its origin was a mystery. Where we stood was a path much travelled by many nomadic tribes and families for many generations. The guide's own people weren't wanderers, but their place was a little way distant from this well-beaten track.

The carving was small, about the size of the palm of my hand. It was a boat. A tall prow was shaped into something recognisably an animal head, but without detail to identify a species. A single mast held a roughly rectangular sail. There was no identification or explanation.

"Unusual, eh?" said my guide. "Bloody long way to the sea!"

I've carried the memory of that moment in my head for decades. Over the years my imagination has spun several explanations, some more plausible than others.

In recent years, I've visited Norway, the Orkneys and the Shetlands, developing a serious interest in Viking history and culture. I've also spent time along the coast of New England in the US, reading and hearing stories suggesting Viking contact there that's been lost in the mists of time.

They were extraordinary sailors, these Norse. There are faint impressions of their footprints across the world – trade items from long ago in unexpected places, odd words in old tribal languages.

This story has been shaped by my imagination and a lot of research, but maybe they're not all that's been at play. Racial memory perhaps? Or perhaps the shadow of a real Sigurd the World-Farer reached out and laid a hand on my shoulder. If so, I trust that I've done him justice.

RENOIR

2023

ABOUT THE AUTHOR

Over the years, Renoir has had more jobs than you can poke a good-sized stick at. Or even a decent spear.

After travelling around Australia and around the world, he's settled, for now, behind a keyboard in the Northern Rivers district of New South Wales, in Australia with his patient family and two impatient cats.

His brain seems constantly crammed with stories, so he writes to prevent his head from exploding.

It also means he often lives in his own little world, especially when engrossed in one of his DUBIOUS MAGIC urban fantasy novels. He seems to like it there, mostly.

ALSO BY RENOIR

Find us at *www.meredian.com.au*

The DUBIOUS MAGIC series:

- The Wizard of Waramanga
- The Carvings of Cobbemarmoo
- The Mad Machines of Mundara
- The Warriors of Wiwo'ole
- The Spirits of Sron Dubh
- The Sailors of Svalgsay
- The Treasure of Tepatamwa
- The Masks of Manovalo

ALSO:

- He Was Beeb When I Knew Him
- Mixed Blood
- These Old Bastards...
- After 40 Years It Gets A Bit Vague
- For The Young And Old Souls
- The Rivers Run Deep *(editor & contributor)*

The MEN'S HEALTH - A QUIET WORD books:

- Mid-Life Crisis MANagement - Surviving Middle Age and Male Menopause
- Move It Like You Mean It - A Quiet Word About Parkinsons Disease In Men

www.ingramcontent.com/pod-product-compliance
Lightning Source LLC
Chambersburg PA
CBHW070017120726
47909CB00003B/969